FEAR

The Reapers

CONTENTS

PLAYLIST

Daddy Issues by The Neighborhood
Angels & Demons by jxdn
Devil Eyes by Hippie Sabotage
The Reaper by The Chainsmokers
I Want To by Rosenfeld
Way Down We Go by KALEO
Twisted by Two Feet
Love is Madness by Thirty Seconds To Mars
E-GIRLS ARE RUINING MY LIFE! By CORPSE
Like That by Be a Miller
Smoke (Son Lux Remix) by BOBI ANDONOV
Wrong by MAX & Lil Uzi Vert
Killer by Valerie Broussard
Talk to My Skin by Stalgia
Slave by Ramsey

TRIGGER WARNING

The Reapers are not good men. They have no moral code and they certainly have no limits. If you're looking for a story where the heroine turns the bad boys good, well then this story isn't for you. This is the world of The Reapers and the only way to survive is to play by their rules.

The Reapers of Caspian Hills is a Dark Romance and features content that some readers may find disturbing. Visit author's website for a detailed list of potential triggers.

This one's for you my beautiful reader who understands that you can be a kick-ass feminist & still love yourself some toxic book boyfriends.

PROLOGUE

Stevie

I STILL REMEMBER THE SOUND OF HIS LAUGHTER. THE DEEP timbre of a chuckle that was unmistakably his. I remember his scent too. Fresh air and earthy moss tinged with a little sweat from a long day on the construction site. I remember the feeling of jumping into his powerful arms as soon as he got home and the unease I felt in my belly every time I didn't see his truck pull into the driveway at 5:35 PM.

"How's my little bunny?" My father would ask, with a gigantic smile gracing his face.

I remember watching my chubby little toddler hands reach up towards his face, trying so hard to rub away the strange lines around his eyes. The ones that marred my dad's otherwise youthful face. I hated those lines. I think even back then, I knew they were mocking me. Serving as a constant reminder that our time together was fleeting. That one day he would leave and I'd be alone… with her.

From an early age, I knew that my mother hated me. At first, I didn't want to believe it. I mean, everything I saw about mothers told me that their job was to love their children unconditionally. To be the ones to kiss their wounds and make everything feel better. But making me feel loved was never my mother's priority.

Carla Alexander hated me with every fiber of her being. Everything I did would set her off, but she especially hated when I drew attention to myself. Under her care, I quickly learned what wasn't acceptable in her household. Every time I cried, she'd slap me. Every time I whined, she'd pinch me or pull my hair. Every time I expressed any emotion at all, there were consequences awaiting me. At just four years old, I learned to live in constant fear of the ticking time bomb that was my mother.

After a while, my self-image became skewed. I saw myself as weak and defective. After all, I was the one letting my feelings spill out. I was the one that was "acting out" against my mother's wishes. There was something wrong with me.

I thought that if I could just do what she wanted and keep my feelings at bay, she would have no other choice but to love me. So I did just that. Day by day, hour by hour, I taught myself to feel less. I'd sit by myself for hours practicing how to bottle up my emotions until the day came where I stopped feeling them at all.

My father loved my mother, but he loved me too. It terrified him to see his lively and energetic four-year-old dwindle down to nothing more than a shell of a person. He'd beg me to tell him what was going on, beg me to talk to him, but I couldn't bring myself to tell him the truth. My father didn't know my mother was hurting me. Carla left no lasting marks.

I knew that if I told my father, I'd be forcing him to choose. So I suffered in silence.

Despite the secrecy of it all, her hatred towards me still had a way of seeping into their relationship. Their relationship turned rocky and by my fifth birthday, they were fighting nearly every night. The fights would start out over something unrelated, but eventually, they'd find their way back to the most polarizing issue in their relationship, me.

My mother wanted to send me to boarding school in the fall. Her family came from money and she passed it off to my father as a family tradition she wanted to uphold. But my father grew up in a tight-knit working class family. He didn't want strangers raising his daughter.

One night, during an exceptionally explosive fight, my mother finally acknowledged the elephant in the room. Her rage had reached a boiling point, and she confessed what my father and I had always feared.

"You stole everything from me, you vile leech." She screamed, pointing an accusing finger at me. "My looks. My life. My husband. You are the reason I'm miserable. Giving birth to you was the biggest fucking mistake I've ever made."

Her words shattered my tiny heart. I hoped that if I just behaved enough or if I just stayed quiet enough that she would learn to love me.

People in fairytales fell in love all the time. My five-year-old mind figured that if I tried hard enough, my mother could learn to love me. But there was no mistaking the conviction in her voice. She hated me. Earning her love was just a little girl's naïve pipe dream.

My father never wanted to have to choose, but her brutal words left him with no other option. We left the house that night. He contacted a lawyer to start the divorce proceedings the next morning, and he never spoke to her again.

My father adorned me with the love and affection of two parents. He did everything he could to repair Carla's damage, and though I could never quite show it, I loved the hell out of my father.

Before his untimely death three years later, my father made me make him a promise. One that I etched into my heart and carried with me.

"Bunny, I need you to listen to me carefully." My father said as he wrapped his large hand around mine.

His skin was icy to the touch, so much colder than I remembered. I let out a ragged breath as I stared at our intertwined hands. I could do this, I could be strong for the man who stayed strong for me.

"The next words I say will not mean much to you now, but one day, when you're older, you'll understand."

I nodded as I looked into the brown eyes that looked just like mine and took in a shaky breath.

He smelled different too. Still clean, but gone was the earthy muskiness I'd always associated with him. His scent

4

carried remnants of the sterile hospital room they had banished him to for the last two weeks.

God, I was going to miss him.

"I need you to promise me that no matter what happens, you move on and you live." He said, drawing out the last word with agony in his eyes.

Pain sliced through me as I replayed the words over in my head. He wanted me to move on without him. Live forever without him. Gnawing on my lower lip, I shook my head. I couldn't promise him that.

"I don't want to move on and I don't want to forget you. If I live forever, we'll never see each other again." I mumbled, casting my eyes to the dull linoleum tiles beneath him.

"I want you to live, Bunny." He said, squeezing my hand as hard as his weak body would allow. "It's okay to die when it's your time, but you have to live."

"I don't understand..." I said, searching his tear-filled chestnut eyes.

My head hurt. I didn't understand his words, and I didn't want to say goodbye. I wasn't ready. I still needed him.

I escaped the wicked witch, and I had my happily ever after. It wasn't fair that the universe was taking it away from me. Taking him away from me...

"I know, sweetheart." He said, pulling me in for a tight hug. "And I'm sorry I won't be here to explain it when it does make sense. But I need you to promise me. Can you do that, Bun?"

I gave him a soft nod. His words were confusing, but I could see the resolve in his eyes. I knew he needed to hear me promise, even if I hated doing it.

"I promise." I said as I blinked back the tears stinging my eyes.

"I love you, Bunny." He mumbled as he eased back into his hospital bed and closed his eyes.

"I love you too, dad." I whispered, uttering the words he longed to hear for the last four years.

There were so many other thoughts going through my mind that I couldn't bring myself to say. Things like...

I've always loved you, dad...

I'm sorry I'm so messed up...

Thank you for loving me, anyway...

He smiled as he pulled my hand to his heart and the crinkles were back, his pale, thin skin making them even more pronounced. I hated cancer. It was stealing the one person in the world who cared about me.

I held his heart in my hand until my legs went numb. Past his last heartbeat and past the moment my tears finally shed.

After my dad's untimely passing, I had no choice but to go back to the monster I thought I'd escaped. Carla was the only family I had left and with no record of her abuse, the courts granted her custody.

It didn't take long for Carla to move on. In the three years without us, she found herself a brand new life, complete with a new husband and a new daughter.

The rules in her house were the same, only this time, my father wasn't there to protect me. I hoped that her new husband would deter her, but he didn't seem to care what she did as long as her trust fund kept the cash flowing.

I always assumed my mother's hate resulted from who I was as a person, but when I noticed the same signs of abuse happening to my three-year-old little sister, I knew it was a problem ingrained into Carla. I couldn't let the cycle repeat itself with another innocent child, so I stepped in.

Our mother's bitterness towards me was always stronger. It was easy to shift her rage my way. Whenever my sister, Alex, would make a 'mistake', I'd make a bigger one. Whenever she'd cry, I'd cry louder. Whenever she did anything that would trigger Carla's rage, I did everything in my power to bring her attention back to me.

The day Carla overdosed on meth was the day I could breathe again. When I got the text in the middle of my ninth grade history class, I couldn't even bring myself to cry. The reality of it was, even if I could, they would've been tears of joy. I didn't mourn my mother's death, I only wished it would've happened sooner.

With the loss of his wife and her family's wealth, my stepfather jumped headfirst into the drugs that killed her. He and Carla had been hiding their addiction from my sister and I for years, and with Carla and her money gone, my stepfather had nothing left to lose.

Malcolm was the polar opposite of my father in every way that mattered. He never gave a shit about me or his daughter. He played the part of the dutiful husband when Carla was around, but once she died, so did his incentive to care.

At fifteen, life threw me into adulthood. Shackled with not only the responsibility of taking care of myself, but taking care of my nine-year-old half sister. I was in over my head and without loving parents to guide me into adolescence; I clung to my father's last words and used them as my guiding principle.

I did what I needed to do to survive. Maybe that's why when life threw me yet another curveball, I didn't even bat an eyelash.

The choice I made kept us alive, even if it was the most reckless, idiotic, and senseless thing I've ever done...

ONE

MY BODY JOLTED AT THE SOUND OF A HUSHED WHISPER filling my ear.

"Stevie."

Disoriented from sleep, I rubbed my eyes and waited for the hazy figure standing next to me to come into focus. Recognition clicked and relief seeped into me. It was just Alex.

Fuck. It was *Alex.*

"Shit. What time is it?" I asked, swiping the drool from

the corner of my mouth and almost spilling the bowl of cereal I had fallen asleep next to.

"It's 4:37. I waited for you, but got worried when you didn't show. I got a ride over here." She said with a grimace.

"Fuck. We have to go. Now." I said, shooting up from the kitchen table as I stuffed my feet back into my beat-up white sneakers.

Sleep evaded me again last night, making a quick power nap at the kitchen table turn into almost six hours of sleep.

"I'm sorry." Alex grimaced, pacing back and forth, "I didn't know what to do. I mean, I couldn't just leave you here alone."

Her heart was in the right place, but she knew better than to come home alone. Especially during one of Malcolm's benders. Malcolm had a routine. We may not count on him as a parent, but my dear stepdad was always consistent. He was a barely functioning drug addict. He held a job, albeit a pretty shitty one. Every Friday, he'd get off of work at 4:00 PM on the dot, pick up his drugs, shoot up, and lock himself up in the house for the weekend.

Fridays, Saturdays, and Sundays were the days we made ourselves as scarce as possible. We had a system, and I had just royally fucked it up by falling asleep. Naps during the day seemed to be the only thing that worked for the nightmares, but I should've known better. I just prayed we both wouldn't have to pay for my stupid mistake.

Slinging my bag over my shoulder, I grabbed Alex's hand and pulled her towards the front door. Passing through the hallway as quietly as possible, every step we took made my stomach drop a notch further.

Maybe he wasn't home yet. Maybe if he was, he wouldn't

notice us. Maybe he'd already smoked and would be too high out of his mind to pay us any mind. Maybe.

We were a few feet from the door, when out of nowhere, the door flung open and in walked Malcolm.

"Where the fuck do you think you're going?" He spat, catching us mid escape.

Still in his uniform of a navy blue jumpsuit, he spread out his arms and acted as a blockade between us and the door. Leaning forward, he inched his face towards mine and the bitter stench of sweat and stale cologne hit my nose.

Anytime Malcolm would shoot up, he would douse himself in cheap cologne, trying to mask the foul scent only desperation and days of not showering could give him. The fresh wounds and dilated pupils on his gaunt face were also dead giveaways that he was already high as a fucking kite. *Fuck.*

"We were just leaving." I mumbled, pushing Alex behind me.

"No. You know the fucking drill. Hand over the cash." He ordered with a smug smirk.

"What? No!" Alex asserted as her eyes darted between the two of us. "I saw her leave you an envelope full of cash two nights ago. We pay you rent once a month."

"She hasn't told you." He said with a smirk as his dull eyes flashed towards mine.

"Told me what?" She hissed, keeping her eyes trained on the man she refused to acknowledge as her father.

"She pays when I tell her to. Period. If she doesn't, she knows exactly what the fuck will happen." He didn't need to say anything further for Alex to understand the threat in his tone.

I fixed my gaze on the floor as shame licked across my skin. Everything Malcolm said was true. I wanted to tell Alex. To talk about the abuse I encountered daily at the hands of her father. But how could I reveal such an awful secret without destroying the trust between us?

"You are an asshole!" She screamed, trying to claw her way towards Malcolm's face. "God, what the fuck was Carla thinking having a child with a lowlife like you!"

The mention of our mother's name wiped the smirk off of Malcolm's face. His lip twitched, and he cocked his head to the side. I knew the warning signs of Malcolm's violence like the back of my hand. I could see what was coming and with only seconds to act, I shoved Alex as fast as I could and jumped into her place in time to receive the full force of his punishing blow.

His fist collided with my cheekbone and the impact of his swing sent my body careening for the ground. The room went quiet as my back hit the hard linoleum floor with a crack and both of their eyes followed my descent. I watched the contents of my bag spill out and scatter across the floor, and my heart sunk to the pit of my stomach. Laid out for all of us to see was the forty dollars I had set aside for groceries that week.

I glanced at Malcolm and could see the hunger in his eyes. Money fed his addiction, and he didn't care who he harmed to get his fix. Without hesitation, he reached down, grabbed for the cash, and tucked it into his pocket as if it had always belonged to him.

I wanted to kill him. To kick and scream and claw for my money back. But fighting him was pointless. He would only get more aggressive if I tried to stop him and with Alex here, I couldn't risk it. I could deal with his violence, but she shouldn't have to.

Malcolm disappeared before we even had time to process what happened. That was the one redeeming quality about my stepfather. Once he got what he wanted, he left us the hell alone. At least until the next time he needed something.

"Why didn't you tell me?" Alex whispered as she helped me pick up the contents of my bag.

My words lodged in my throat. What was I supposed to say? I lied because it was easier. I lied because I didn't think she could handle the truth and it was the only way I could protect her. I lied because it was what I always did.

Alex was still in her last week of high school and whether she liked it or not, my job as her big sister was to keep her safe. I was the one who could afford the bruise already forming on my cheek. She couldn't. Her teachers would ask questions, and CPS might try to take her away. Alex was Malcolm's biological daughter. Because of our mother's passing, he had full custody of her until she was eighteen.

We tried to run away before, but once Malcolm realized that the money disappeared, he reported her missing. The cops found my car and shit hit the fan. Alex almost had to repeat ninth grade, and I barely escaped criminal charges.

In two weeks, she'd be eighteen and we could be free of Malcolm and this fucking town for good. But until then, we needed to keep a low profile and avoid him as much as possible. June 16th couldn't come soon enough.

TWO

Tristan

"To what do we owe the pleasure?" Atlas asked, leaning into the blue crushed velvet seat.

His dark eyes meticulously grazed the man standing before us as his thumb mindlessly twirled the ring on his middle finger. It was mental manipulation at its finest and At was doing a hell of a job of fucking with the man.

To the untrained eye, his casual posture came off relaxed, bored even. But simmering below the surface was an insurmountable amount of pressure. I could see it in the slight tick of his jaw and the tension radiating off his shoulders. He sat poised and ready to strike at the idiot requesting our audience.

"I... I have something to offer the four of you," the dick mumbled, "as payment for my debt."

"Interesting." Cyrus noted, his eyes trained on the twitching junkie that stood before us. "We don't know you. You don't know us. So how is it you owe *us* something?"

How he emphasized the word "us" had the man nearly shitting himself. At this point they were toying with him, like children playing with their food. Everyone in this town knew that if you so much as spoke ill of The Reapers, you were as good as dead. This motherfucker had to have a death wish for showing up at our club unannounced.

"I, uh... know Johnny. Your dealer on the west side of town? I've come into a little debt with him and he... uh... one time when he was high off his ass, he told me where I could find you."

Johnny was a dead man for two reasons. One, he sent this asshole to Hell's Tavern to find us, and two, he sampled the product. Our club was our sanctuary, and we hired our employees under one condition; they stayed clean. Johnny fucked up, and by the murderous look in Ezra's eyes, Johnny-boy's hours were dwindling.

"And the canary finally sings." Atlas mocked, standing up from his seat. The man eyed his every move and I could almost taste the fear that oozed out of him. Atlas' hands moved to smooth the wrinkles in his jacket before reaching into his pocket and pulling out his phone.

"Ez," he said, grabbing my older brother's attention, "he's all yours. The rest of us need to make a few *arrangements*."

By arrangements, he meant tracking down Johnny's ass.

Drug distribution was just one of the many businesses our syndicate ran, and to put it bluntly, keeping track of a dealer was beneath our pay grade. But Johnny made himself our problem. If he was talking freely to this asshole, who knows who else he was talking to. We needed to send a message and nothing compared to the personalized ones we hand-delivered.

At the mention of his name, Ezra leaped to his feet and stalked towards his new prey, cracking his neck as a smile brimming with malice spread across his face.

"Ple... Please! Wait!" The man cried, waving his arms around frantically. "It's an excellent offer, take it and I'll leave town and never say a word of this to anyone."

His pleas fell on deaf ears as Ezra's movements didn't falter. Ezra enjoyed the hunt almost as much as he enjoyed the kill, and this man looked like he'd be stupid enough to put up a fight. Poor fuck had no clue fighting back would only intensify Ez's torture.

"I... man... please." The man pleaded, his blown-out eyes frantically darting between the four of us.

Maybe it was the smell of desperation that wafted towards us the moment he entered the club. Maybe it was just my morbid curiosity. But I wanted to see what he offered.

Cuing them all in on my thoughts, I cleared my throat and nodded towards the man. I wasn't one for words, especially around strangers, but my brothers understood. The subtle message was all they needed to figure out where my head was at. It was the dynamic we'd always had, even before the stutter.

The one thing you can rely on in life is family. It was the reason we kept our leadership small, with each of the four of us heading different aspects of the business. We had a chain of command for whatever remedial tasks we needed, but we only truly trusted each other. That small circle of trust was the key to sustaining our power over Caspian Hills for the last six years.

"It's not every day that a meth-head comes looking for us." Ezra hissed as he approached the man cowering beneath him. "This offer of yours better be worth your life. I was looking forward to watching your pathetic body bleed out."

The man's face inadvertently ticked when the word "meth-head" tumbled into his ears. The term clearly bothered him and I smirked to myself at the irony. He was high off his ass, not giving a fuck about jeopardizing his own life by being here, but still cared about what complete strangers thought of him. The fragility in his eyes was almost humanizing. Almost.

The world is full of sinners, some are just better at keeping their sins hidden from view. While men like Malcolm were desperate to conceal their flaws, my brothers and I took on a more unapologetic approach.

We were brutal business men and when the time called for it, lethal killers. Did we deny it? Of course not. We embraced our demons, bathed in the blood we spilled, and lived up to our fucking reputation. That's how my brothers and I earned the name The Reapers. People knew that when we came for you, death was calling and your time was up.

Caspian Hills was ours, and no one was stupid enough to fuck with what was ours. The men who tried didn't live long enough to gloat about it.

The man standing before us had willingly walked into a lion's den. He was either incredibly brave or remarkably stupid. Based on the interaction so far, I was betting on the latter, with or without the meth that was probably coursing through his system.

"I have someone for you. A girl." The man stammered, smiling eagerly.

I had no clue why this man thought offering a girl to us would change his fate. In our world, women were a dime a dozen. People either wanted to be us or they wanted to fuck us. We emanated power and even if they didn't know who we were or what we did for a living, they could sense that shit from a mile away.

"We don't deal in flesh." Atlas glowered, giving the man a look of utter disgust. The sheer force of his words wiped the man's stupid smirk off his face.

"She's worth it." He pleaded, his body trembling. "Blonde bombshell. She'll do anything you tell her. She'll earn her keep. Th..th-think of her as an investment that keeps on giving. I ran it by Johnny and he wanted her for himself, but I knew you were the ones with the actual power here."

Fuck. We now had a dilemma on our hands. If we didn't take what he offered, Johnny would run his stupid mouth, if he hadn't already, and word would spread across town that The Reapers had gone soft. We didn't want that kind of publicity. Not when The Diaz Cartel was hungry for ammo to use against us. Tired of slumming it in Caspian Valley, they were looking for any cracks in our foundation.

We could kill the bastard here and now. I could practically see Ez's demon begging for the bloodshed, but then we'd have a bigger mess to clean up and frankly, the asshole wasn't worth the hassle.

Taking the girl would send a message and help cement the fact that we always collected our debts. She'd stay with us until we grew bored with her and as long as she did nothing stupid to get herself killed, we'd let her go once the dust settled. We'd solidify our reputation and our men wouldn't have another body to bury. No harm, no foul. Looking towards my brothers, I could see that they were all slowly drawing the same conclusion.

"Okay, asshole." Atlas boomed, tossing a business card on to the coffee table. "Send the girl to this address at midnight tonight and disappear. If we see your face again, we will kill you. If you try to escape without fulfilling your end of the deal, we will kill you. Understand?"

The man nodded his head rapidly as he grabbed the card, stuffed it into his pocket, and scrambled for the exit.

"Not so fast." Cyrus ordered, halting the man's jerky movements.

"Ez, he's all yours." Atlas mumbled without sparing the man another glance.

"Wha- wait, I thought we had a deal?" The man cried, getting hysterical.

"Oh, we do and you better deliver." Cyrus interjected, tilting his head slightly. "You didn't honestly think you could come here uninvited and leave unharmed, did you? I know you're a meth-head, but you can't be that fucking stupid."

The man's eyes grew wide as terror raked through his entire body. Ez relished in his fear, flashing a wicked smile as he stalked towards the man. We all stood up and moved to get a closer look.

The unmistakable smell of piss filled the room as the trembling man backed himself up against a wall. *I felt for whoever had to clean that shit up.*

Blow after blow, Ezra pounded into the man's clammy

flesh until his own scarred knuckles bursted from the force. The man's brow had split open and I could see the bruises already forming on his sickly pale skin. The man's legs had given out on him and he crumpled to the floor in a heap of bones and bloodied flesh as he desperately tried to block Ez's savage blows.

"Let this be a reminder, you piece of shit." Ezra spat, wiping the sticky mixture of blood and sweat from his brow. "Never fuck with The Reapers."

He gave him one last punishing kick to the gut before walking away with a little skip. Ezra looked elated as he made his way back towards us. It would've seemed shocking to those that didn't know him, but there was nothing Ezra enjoyed more than pure, unfiltered violence.

"Hell," Ezra quipped, looking at the blood splatter all over his black oxfords, "that's my third ruined pair this month."

"Maybe you need to switch up your finishing move?" Cyrus joked, nudging me with his elbow.

"Nah, you boys love a good splash show." Ez said with a wink. "I can't disappoint the fans."

"You're a s… sick fuck." I mused, shaking my head.

Ez blew us a kiss as he headed back to the lounge, making me and Cyrus chuckle. The fucker was the craziest one out of all of us, and that was really saying something.

"Alright, dickheads." Atlas spoke up, garnering all of our attention, "That's enough action for the evening. Let's get back to business, shall we?"

As security dragged the man's unconscious body away, we all retook our seats in the back of our low lit VIP area as if nothing happened.

It was just after 5:00 PM and the club didn't open for

another few hours. That gave us plenty of time to get the floors cleaned and have the guards prepare our house for our newest asset.

Poor thing had no clue that her piece of shit pimp had just sold her freedom. No idea that her mind, body, and soul no longer belonged to her.

If we were better men, we'd let her go. Unfortunately for her, my brothers and I were never raised to be good men.

THREE

Stevie

I COULD FEEL ALEX'S EYES ON ME AS I WIPED DOWN THE tables for the fifth time in a row. I'd been avoiding her for most of my shift, but I could only dodge her attention for so long. It was getting close to closing time, and I'd already finished most of the pre-closing duties. Soon we'd be driving back home, and I'd have to face the questions brimming behind her eyes.

Even though Alex was six years younger than me, in a lot of ways, she and I were equals. We had gone through the same hardships together and were both thrown into adulthood sooner than we expected. The one major difference between me and her was I didn't allow myself to feel anything while she, ironically, felt everything.

Alex was the epitome of an Empath and sometimes, my need to shield her from the cruelties of the world outweighed my instinct to treat her as an equal. I lied to my little sister about what went on when she wasn't around. Though my intentions were pure, it didn't stop her from feeling betrayed.

What she witnessed wasn't anything new. Malcolm always resorted to violence when he didn't get his way. But after years of hiding it from her, everything was hitting her all at once.

"Everything okay?" Alex asked, pulling me out of my thoughts.

I was so stuck in my head; I didn't even realize I was wiping down her table.

"Yeah, sorry." I said, taking a seat across from her, "Just a little tired. How's the homework going?"

"Good, I guess." She paused, tapping her pencil against her notebook. "You think you'll get out early tonight?"

Her emerald eyes glanced around the barren coffee shop.

"We close in ten minutes," I said, giving her a small smile as I pulled a cookie from my apron pocket, "hopefully no one else comes through."

I stuffed half of the cookie into my mouth, swallowing the lie I told right along with it. That night, there was someone I hoped to see. The same person who, for the past two years, was my last customer almost every night.

He and I met by chance nearly two years ago. One of the

other baristas called out for her closing shift, forcing me to stay and work opening to closing. I could use the extra overtime, so I took it in stride. Little did I know what that night had in store.

It was a rainy Tuesday night in the middle of October, and Cafe Au Lait was vacant. Tapping my fingers against the reclaimed wood countertop, I sliced my eyes at the clock that refused to budge. The caffeine high of the morning rush disappeared, leaving me feeling jittery, yet exhausted. By 8:30 PM, I gave up waiting for customers and started the closing process. The streets were vacant, and I doubted anyone would come in that late.

Just as I began mopping the floors, in walked Mr. Tall, Dark, and Delectable at 8:59 PM on the dot. It took a special asshole to come into a place one minute before they closed without so much as an apologetic smile. His shiny and most likely designer shoes tracked in mud-soaked leaves from the sidewalk and I cursed underneath my breath, knowing I'd have to sweep again.

"8 ounce doppio cappuccino. Dry. Extra hot." He barked with his ear pressed to his cell phone. There was nothing that irritated me more than bad manners, and this guy was exhibiting all of them. He didn't even bother to look at me when he barked his order into the air.

"Name." I chirped back, out of sheer habit.

The moment my mind realized what I said, blood came rushing to my face. There was no one else in the cafe. Why did I ask for his stupid name?

"You need my name?" He asked, glaring at me as he broke off the call.

Fighting a smile, he looked around the empty cafe as if to

make his point even more obvious. I know there's no one else here, asshole.

"I'll have it right out for you, sir." I responded sweetly, ignoring his question and attitude completely.

I had mastered the art of telling people what they wanted to hear, and this guy looked like the type to get a hard-on from people kissing the ground he walked on. His entire demeanor screamed power. The pristine suit, the wide stance, his perfectly quaffed dark hair, even the formal tone in which he spoke told me everything I needed to know. He and I were nothing alike.

I plastered on my fakest smile and turned towards the espresso machine, trying to bust out his stupid cappuccino as quickly as possible. Of course he had to pick one of the hardest drinks to make. God, he would be a 'dry cappuccino' kind of guy.

"Just for future reference, dickface," I hissed under the sound of the steaming milk, "we close at nine and just because you're sexy as fuck doesn't mean that you get to be an inconsiderate asshole."

"Dry Cap." I called out, sliding the cup forward on the handoff plane and not even bothering to look up. He wanted to be rude? Well, two could play that game.

For a split second, warm fingertips grazed mine. The alien feeling created this delicious sensation that blanketed my entire body. Warmth. Comfort. Safety. No man's touch had ever made me feel that way and for a few beats, I stood there dumbstruck, staring at my fingers like they were malfunctioning. Before I could process what happened, he slipped out of the shop and back into the dark night.

What the hell was that?

Shaking the thoughts of the stranger out of my mind, I went back to cleaning and cursed at myself for being so eager to leave to begin with. I should've waited until 9, like I was supposed to, and I would've avoided creating double the work for myself.

Thirty minutes later, I stepped out into the chilly autumn night and tugged my flannel across my chest. A grey t-shirt dress and light flannel was cute during the morning, but was practically masochistic at night. The wind's frigid bite sent Goosebumps spreading across my bare legs. I cursed as I grit my teeth. If I didn't die from freezing my ass off, I was going to kill Marie for calling out sick.

It was eerily quiet out and something in the air felt off. I couldn't pinpoint what it was, but my body felt the presence of danger. I spent a few seconds staring out into the darkness and looking for any signs of a threat, but all I saw were a bunch of vacant cars and empty streets. It wasn't exactly safe to be in downtown Caspian alone this late at night, and had I known I'd be closing, I would've gone for a closer parking spot.

Seeing no immediate signs of a threat, I turned around to lock the door behind me. The second I turned my back, a throat cleared and my body froze. On reflex, I whipped my body towards the sound and nearly fell over when I saw who it was.

"Hey." He said, barely containing the smile he was trying to fight.

"Jesus Christ! Dry Cap? You scared the hell out of me." I exclaimed, pressing my hand against my racing heart. "What the hell are you still doing here?"

"Sorry, I wanted to make sure you got to your car okay. It

isn't safe in this part of town, and I couldn't leave you by yourself in good conscience. Since you closed at 9," he said, flashing me a knowing grin, "I figured I wouldn't have to wait long."

Had he heard me? I wanted to die. Like, have a higher power remove me and any traces of my big, stupid mouth from this earth. *Nice one, Stevie.*

"It's fine." He offered, seeing my discomfort. "I was an asshole. Hearing that my face resembled a cock was brutal, but I definitely earned the verbal lashing."

It didn't. At all. It was a stupid handsome face on what looked like a stupid perfect body. He had a sharp, chiseled jawline peppered with the perfect amount of scruff. Dark, full brows that framed his sultry brown eyes and thick lashes that most women would kill for. The most alluring part of his face was his mouth. He had the most perfect smile I'd ever seen, and his lips looked like they could make even the filthiest words sound beautiful.

Before I could think of a clever or witty comeback, he had already turned on his heel and began walking. And after a moment of shock, I quickly caught up with him.

"Which one's yours?" He asked, nodding his head to the row of cars lining the street.

"The uh... the Focus." I chirped, still in disbelief at how this night had turned out.

"You shouldn't park so far." He noted, keeping his eyes on the sidewalk ahead. "A girl like you could get in a lot of trouble this late at night."

A girl like me... I didn't know whether to be flattered or annoyed. DC had already made an assumption about me, and we'd known each other for all of thirty minutes. Then again, I made my own quick assumptions about him and he was already proving them wrong.

By the time we arrived at my car, I realized we walked the rest of the trek in silence.

"Well, we're here." He said, gesturing to my car.

I nodded and gave him a small smirk. I didn't know what to say. 'Thank you' seemed lame and 'see you later' seemed presumptuous. But he didn't miss a beat.

"See you around..." He paused, letting his eyes roam my breasts unabashedly. "Stevie."

My heart slammed in my chest as my body rebelled against the calm composure I tried to cling on to. The name tag, Stevie. He was only reading the name tag. *Get a hold of yourself and pussy, don't you dare quiver right now.*

In that moment, as his golden brown eyes roamed my body, I felt exposed and objectified and strangely excited. No one had ever looked at me like that, let alone caused my body to react so strongly to a damn look. The rush was addictive. I wanted more.

From that day forward, I requested to close on every shift I worked. It was stupid, but I secretly hoped we would meet again and I'd have more chances to feel that rush.

Two years later, our meetups had sort of become our unspoken rule. Almost every closing shift Dry Cap or DC as I liked to call him, would show up, order his drink, and hang out to make sure I made it safely to my car.

For nearly a year, I refused other guys' advances. I waited for DC to make a move that never came. I could never be in an actual relationship. I learned the hard way that there are too many emotional expectations that I just couldn't deliver on. But sex was fun and uncomplicated, and well, my body wanted him. But every night, he'd walk to his car, I'd walk to mine, and we'd go back to our lives as if nothing happened. As if the spark crackling between us was a hoax.

Alex usually stayed at a friend's house while I worked, but after that close call earlier, I wanted to keep my eye on her. Maybe it was a good thing that he hadn't shown tonight. I hadn't spoken a word about him to Alex. I told myself it was because we'd be leaving eventually and it didn't matter anyway, but that was a lie.

The truth of the matter was, I cared about him. Probably more than I should've. When his piercing eyes looked at me, it was like he was looking deep within my soul, seeing each fucked up layer. But instead of being repulsed by what he saw, he embraced it.

I rarely laughed at his jokes, but it didn't seem to bother him. Other guys I'd dated in the past couldn't handle the blow to their ego, but DC didn't seem to care. He had this quiet confidence about him that made me feel at ease. I didn't have to worry about my reactions offending him. Carla's conditioning was still so deeply ingrained into me that my body still feared expressing emotions, even eight years after her death.

Overtime, I grew to be more comfortable with this formidable stranger than I was with my own flesh and blood. Alex was my sister, and I loved her to death, but we couldn't have been more different. She was warm and trusting, while I was cold and suspicious. She was tan, svelte, and cool blonde, while I was pale, curvy, and deep brunette. She was spunky and outgoing, while I was quiet and closed-off.

But in him I found a kindred spirit. I enjoyed pretending that in a different life, he and I could be something more.

Something beyond this pseudo security guard/confidante relationship that we had fell into/ so easily.

I debated asking him for help with Malcolm once, when one of Malcolm's fits of rage resulted in a cracked rib, but I didn't want whatever the dynamic between us was to shift. He viewed me as a normal person, not some girl with a fucked up life. The last thing I wanted was for him to take pity on me. I couldn't stand seeing that look in his eyes.

Almost as if thinking of him had brought him into fruition, the sound of the fan over the door kicked on, showing that someone had walked through the door.

"Be done soon." I mouthed as Alex popped her headphones back in with a nod.

Butterflies swirled through my stomach the moment my eyes caught sight of his familiar 6'3 frame. As usual, DC came in dressed impeccably. He probably worked in law or finance because after two years, I had yet to see him without a sharp suit on.

Tonight was no different. He walked in the cafe wearing a perfectly tailored navy suit with a crisp white button-up shirt that made the healthy glow of his skin stand out.

"Hey DC, the usual?" I called out as I breezed by him.

I purposely kept things platonic with us after realizing that nothing more was coming from this. He didn't need to know that my stomach did flips every time he walked into the room. Or that my traitorous pussy pulsed every time his seductive scent of smoky sandalwood and soft amber surrounded me.

Without warning, his large hand encased my arm in a gentle, yet solid hold, halting my movements. I whipped my head to face him. He had never grabbed me before and it was so unlike the polished man I knew. The look on his face was cold, dangerous, and lethal.

"Who did it?" He hissed as his sharp jaw ticked and his large body trembled with what looked a lot like rage.

"What the hell are you talking about?" I asked, brows furrowed in confusion.

I had never seen this side of him before.

"The bruise that's blooming on your face, Stevie." He said, his fingers gently grazing the tender flesh. "Who did it?"

My hand involuntarily floated towards his. It had probably gotten worse over the last couple of hours. *Shit.* I had been in such a rush to get the hell out of there, I completely forgot to cover it up.

"It's nothing." I lied, faking a smile as I chewed the inside of my cheek. "I clumsily tripped right into a door knob this morning."

It disgusted me how easily the lie spilled from my lips. I never wanted to lie to DC, but he had backed me into a corner. Omitting was one thing, but this was a flat out lie and it made me feel awful. But his pity would have felt worse.

"You tripped." He deadpanned as his sharp brown eyes pierced right through me.

"Yes, so… the usual?"

I didn't wait for a response. Moving towards the espresso bar, I could feel his eyes probing and assessing me as I made his drink. The force of his gaze made me want to shrivel up into a little ball and confess all of my sins, but involving DC would only lead to more trouble. I was leaving in less than two weeks. I could keep our secrets until then, even if he ended up hating me for it. *He'll end up hating me anyway for leaving without saying goodbye.*

DC left the shop without saying another word to me. I hoped that he'd be outside waiting, but after I locked up the shop, there was no sign of him. I told myself that it was better this way. I was only prolonging the inevitable. Maybe seeing the mark on my face gave him an insight into how messy and imperfect my life truly was. He had no room in his perfectly tailored life for the chaos that consumed mine.

FOUR

Ezra

PERCEPTION WAS EVERYTHING IN OUR WORLD. IT WAS THE reason this entire town feared us. It was what drove my brothers to deal out brutal punishments, and it was what kept them from teetering over the edge of their sanity. My brothers relished in our reputation and fought with everything they had to keep what was ours.

A different beast drove me. Perception meant little to me, and truthfully, I didn't give a fuck about what anyone else thought. Dealing punishment wasn't a necessary evil. It was a means of releasing the darkness within. Inflicting pain was the one thing in the world that made me feel alive.

The basement below Hell's Tavern was my domain. It was the one space where I could unleash without ramifications or judgement. The heavily insulated grey concrete walls surrounding me ensured no one could hear what went on. It went without saying that if they dragged you down to the basement of Hell's Tavern, chances were, you weren't ever coming back up.

Imagine Johnny Santos' surprise when his own boys dragged his ass down here and left him at my mercy. He should've known their allegiance was with us. People rarely exhibit loyalty when up against a wall, and poor Johnny was the poster child for what happens when you trust the wrong people.

Wiping the sweat off my brow, I unplugged the power sander and tossed it aside. Slowly strolling back towards my tray of implements, I smiled to myself as I weighed my options.

"So many choices," I taunted, grazing my fingertips against the various blades, "so little skin left."

Grabbing the six-inch filet knife, I tossed it from hand to hand as I slowly made my way back towards Johnny's hanging body. He winced when saw what I selected and gave him a broad smile in return. I made the right selection.

Everything I did had purpose, from the calculatedly slow stride of my oxfords to the uncomfortably warm, dimly lit room encapsulating us. Every move I made was to elicit fear from people like Johnny.

Genuine fear could make a three hundred pound grown man grovel on his knees. It could make an atheist pray to a

God they never believed in. And in the tragic case of Johnny Santos, the fear of losing even more skin pulled gut-wrenching screams from his body.

He thought it would stop me, but his screams only egged me on further. I lived for fear and relished in the pain of others. Hurting a man who deserved it, only made his pain taste sweeter.

I sliced into his skin with expert precision, letting my blade glide through his flesh like a hot knife through butter. Starting with his forehead and working my way down, I sliced his flesh over and over again until there was nothing left to slice. It wasn't until I'd run out of skin on his chest that I realized his screaming had stopped.

He was still breathing, but his eyes and mouth had stretched unnaturally wide, almost as if the fear had frozen him in place. When I inched closer to him, I could just make out the tiny rasps of breath that would've been his screams, had his vocal cords still been intact. Johnny was alive alright, but the fight in his eyes was no longer there.

As I stared at the man bleeding out before me, a small part of me felt for him. Not because of the wounds coating his raw flesh, but because he knew this was only the beginning.

Johnny had seen what my wrath looked like. All of our employees had. It was an initiation of sorts. It was hard for people to fear the unknown, so my brothers and I made it a point to show everyone who worked for us exactly what happens to those who betray The Reapers.

After another hour of slicing, his body had finally given up on him. Too weak to hold himself up, he allowed the chains around his wrist to carry the brunt of his weight as his body rotated in the center of the room. His resemblance to a slab of meat hanging in a butcher's shop window was uncanny.

As I watched the last bits of Johnny's life leave his swollen eyes, I placed a blank canvas beneath his swaying body and stared as his blood splatter bloomed across the canvas. Art had always fascinated me, but abstract expressionism was where my true passion lied.

There was something so enamoring about deciphering the story behind each stroke and splash of paint. Each piece told a story, if you searched hard enough. While I collected pieces from Pollock and Rothko, my own creations were my most prized possessions. Nothing could come close to watching someone's sins literally bleed out on the canvas. It was my way of giving them one last chance to leave their mark on this earth.

With Johnny taken care of, the pressure in my skull eased and my steps felt lighter. Sure, killing Johnny was necessary, he had mis-stepped and his death was inevitable, but I needed the pain and violence for my sanity. It was my way of satiating the demons burrowed within me.

My brothers never fully understood it. Then again, they didn't grow up in the same hell I did. The need to unleash myself was primal, and without it, I may end up hurting people who don't deserve my wrath. People that I care about. People like my brothers.

I especially needed that release before our new pet came home. She would be a walking temptation, and the last thing I wanted to do was kill her before we had a chance to play.

The girl had been weighing on my mind ever since that pathetic imbecile offered her up. Whenever I unleashed on anyone, I always knew what they did and why they were in my domain. But with her, it would be different. I didn't know a thing about her, only that she was ours and she once belonged to the meth head.

Logic would dictate that she had to be a user herself. Why else would she agree to be ours? It mattered little either way. My demons would welcome hers with open arms.

I had no idea what she looked like and already my cock was hard just thinking about her agony. Would pain make her scream? Or was she more of a silent crier? Would she let me fuck her while I licked up her tears? Would she try to fight me off?

Fuck, I thought, readjusting my cock. I needed to calm down. After all, she was ours now and wouldn't be going anywhere. I could take my time with her and enjoy every second. Real art was a labor of love, and her downfall was going to be my greatest fucking masterpiece.

FIVE

Stevie

THE SOUND OF A HIGH-PITCHED SCREAM JOLTED MY BODY awake. Still groggy with sleep, it took a few moments for my eyes to adjust to the scene happening before me. It was like something out of a movie.

On the floor below me laid Alex trembling with fear. Her eyes were welling with tears and her body convulsed as she pressed her hand against her flushed cheek. Looming above her stood Malcolm, red-faced with bulging eyes.

The cash he got this morning should've made it so

Malcolm wouldn't be bothering us for at least a few days. *What the hell was he doing here?*

"Get up and let's go!" He spat, grabbing for Alex and causing the fresh cuts on his face to rip open.

"What's going on?" I asked, scrambling up from the bed and stepping between the two of them.

"That little bitch is going to pay back a debt for me." He hissed, pointing a finger at her.

"The hell I am!" Alex spat back, crawling away from his reach.

I bent down to help her up. Malcolm had caught us off guard, but if we both attacked him we had a good chance of holding him off. At the very least, it'd give us time to make a run for it.

After making sure Alex was okay, I turned back around to face the asshole that had just crossed several lines. My eyes refocused on him just in time to see the barrel of a .45 aiming for the center of my forehead. On the other end of it stood Malcolm, trying to still his quivering hands.

"What did you do?" I whispered, feeling the icy tip of his gun press into my skin.

He had never been this desperate before and by the state of his battered face; he was in some serious trouble.

"I owe The Reapers a little money. Alexandra here is going to work for them to pay it off. Now move the fuck out of the way. I don't want to have to kill you, but I will."

I should've moved, but it was as if my mind couldn't wrap around the words he was saying. He had sold my sister. *My baby sister.* "Paying off a debt" meant different things to different people, but messing with The Reapers was begging for trouble.

God, why did it have to be the *fucking* Reapers? No one in town would speak of them out loud, but their reputation preceded them. Those cold assholes could do whatever they wanted to her, and there would be no one to stop them. They had all the Caspian Hills cops and judges in their filthy pockets. I knew that whatever "work" they had in mind for her wouldn't be good. No way in hell was I ever going to let them get their hands on her.

"Okay." I said, pushing Alex behind me and slowly backing away. "We'll do whatever you say. Please, just put the gun down and let me help her pack her things and say goodbye." I asked, trying my best to show the signs of defeat that the sick fuck wanted to see.

"Stevie, what the hell? I'm not going-" Her words died at the sight of my icy glare.

"Yes, you are." I hissed, staring deeply into her emerald eyes. "It's the only way, Al. Don't be stupid. Your dad is right. No one needs to die tonight."

I needed her to trust me, and I prayed that referring to Malcolm as her dad would cue her in on what I was doing. No way in hell would I ever call him that. A plan was forming, she just needed to play along.

"Finally, you little whores start doing as I ask." He gloated, lifting his dirty shirt to holster his gun. As the material slid up, it revealed a pristine white card hanging out of his pant pocket. The item looked so out of place on Malcolm's dirty and disheveled body that it had to have been a recent acquisition. Maybe it could give us some clues as to what the fuck was happening. I needed to get my hands on it.

"Malcolm?" I asked, calling for his attention while offering him my fakest smile, "thank you for letting me say goodbye to Alex." I said, pulling him in for an unexpected hug.

If the man had any brain cells left at all, he would've questioned why I, the girl that showed no emotion, would hug his repulsive ass. But his brain cells were long gone, and I used his ignorance to my advantage.

Swiping the card from his pocket with ease, I quickly slipped it into my own without him noticing. All of that practice pick-pocketing to survive in my teens had come in handy.

"Sure, whatever." He replied, pushing me off of him. "I'll be outside. We leave in ten. Don't try nothing stupid. If she doesn't show, they'll kill us all."

He was right. They'd stop at nothing until they found us. Everyone knew The Reapers always collected on their debts. I just never imagined that my baby sister would become one of them.

I knew what I needed to do. It was stupid and reckless, but it was our only chance. Even if what I was planning on doing meant I lost everything, Alex's safety was worth it.

"TELL me you have a plan and aren't actually going to send me to those assholes." Alex glared at me with her hands firmly planted on her hips.

"I do; well, sort of. Right now we need to pack as much as possible and get the hell out of here." I replied, tossing her a duffle bag before grabbing for my own.

Without another word, we got to work. We gathered the

little belongings we had in complete silence and crept towards our bedroom window. I grabbed the emergency rope ladder we had bought years ago and tossed it over the window's edge. Thank god living with an erratic addict had taught us it was always smart to have alternate escape routes.

My heart slammed in my chest as we descended the flimsy ladder. Escaping on the side of the house left us exposed for anyone to see. Malcolm could catch us running at any moment.

He was desperate and in trouble, and for the first time, I truly didn't know what he was capable of. He had never threatened us with a gun before, but he also had never been beaten so savagely. The Reapers were dangerous, and Malcolm's fear of their wrath outweighed any logic he may have had.

Landing on the grass with a soft thud, we snuck towards the driveway. My white Ford Focus stood less than thirty feet away from us, shining in the soft moonlight like a beacon of hope. We just needed to get there before Malcolm spotted us.

"Hey!" Malcolm screamed into the night air, "get the fuck back here!"

The sound of his hoarse voice echoing across the lawn cut terrified me. Dread inched its way up my throat. *He caught us. He fucking caught us.* I glanced up at my sister, who was already a few steps ahead of me.

"Alex… run."

That was all she needed to hear before bolting for the driver's side. I did the same, letting my legs carry my body as fast as they could go. Malcolm was still upstairs. If we could just get to the car, we'd be in the clear.

A loud pop sounded in the distance, but I ignored it,

focusing all my attention on that passenger door. My arms pumped as my feet pounded against the dirt road. We were so close to freedom, I could almost taste it.

Another pop went off, and a powerful force propelled the right side of my body forward. I ignored the sharp pain in my arm, and kept moving as adrenaline poured into me.

It was clear Malcolm was trying to kill me, and I knew that if he caught us, he wouldn't hesitate to finish what he started. I picked up speed I didn't know I had, bolted for the car. My fingers grasped the door handle as I threw myself into the passenger seat and screamed at Alex to floor it.

Alex threw the car into drive and slammed on the gas. The violent movement combined with the sudden sprint caused a wave of nausea to hit me. My body tried to empty my stomach's contents, but I forced it back down, and tried to breath through it.

"Are you okay?" Alex asked, her hands trembling as we barreled down the road.

"Yeah. I'm fine." I replied. And I was, for now.

Luckily, the bullet barely grazed my skin. My nerve endings were on fire and I could already feel the warm blood pooling. But I was familiar with injuries and knew it wasn't life threatening. I needed to get it cleaned up, but that could wait.

"What are we going to do now?" She asked, glancing over at me.

"Head north on I-5. I have a plan."

SIX

Stevie

We checked into a desolate motel on the outskirts of town. We were on a time crunch, so I washed up, dressed my wound as best as I could, and filled Alex in on the plan I haphazardly slapped together.

"You're seriously out of your mind!" Alex screamed, pacing outside of our motel room's bathroom. "We don't even know how long they'll keep you."

She was probably right, maybe I was out of my mind, but living in fear for the rest of our lives wasn't an option. If we tried to escape, all we would do is run. The Reapers were powerful men and would stop at nothing until they found us. We needed freedom and if it meant working off this debt to be free, then so be it. I could handle working for The Reapers for however long it took to get us out of their grasp for good.

"Do you have a death wish or something?" She griped, staring at my reflection in the bathroom mirror. "Seriously, you don't even know where to go."

I flashed her the thick card I swiped from Malcolm as I layered on some red lipstick. It was a business card for Alessandro's, some fancy ass Italian place uptown, with the word "midnight" scribbled in Malcolm's chicken scratch writing. No way in hell would Malcolm ever be able to afford to eat at a place like that, not-to-mention they wouldn't be open at that hour. Whatever was happening at midnight was business.

"This has to be the drop-off location." I said, sliding her the card and giving myself a once over in the mirror. "It isn't up for debate, I have to do this."

My tight black jeans left little to the imagination. Combined with my heeled leather booties and I looked like a total badass. The flimsy black corset top I wore once on Halloween may have been over-the-top, but I threw it on under my thin leather jacket, anyway. I needed to make sure I looked like someone they wouldn't refuse.

"I'm not letting you go." She insisted, shaking her head as tears welled in her eyes. "You can't leave me, I can't-" Her words choked on a sob as tears streamed down her quivering chin. "We stay together. That's the rule."

"I know," I said, stoning my own features and being strong for her, "but it'll only be temporary. I'll check in with you when I can and it'll be over before we know it. This could be our chance at freedom."

"Yeah... but at what cost?" She whispered.

I didn't want to think about what was going to happen to me. All I would focus on was keeping her as far away from this shit as possible. I couldn't let her know how terrified I truly was, because the thought of what they'd do to her scared me more.

I gave her all the cash I had saved up over the last couple of years and made her promise to finish out school and avoid running into Malcolm at all costs. As far as he knew, we had run away for good. We would be okay as long as we stuck to the plan.

Hopefully.

SEVEN

Stevie

"I'M HERE TO REPAY MALCOLM WARNER'S DEBT."

As they slipped past my lips, the foul words left a bitter taste on my tongue. It was one thing to repeat the words over and over again in my head and another thing entirely to say them out loud.

The cryptic message didn't faze the stone-faced guard, who greeted me at the guard post. He offered nothing more than silence and an averted stare as he ushered me towards the main gate.

It shouldn't have surprised me. The men at Alessandro's treated me with the same indifference. Speaking once, before blindfolding me, throwing me into their car, and leaving me here. I wasn't expecting a warm welcome, but the indifference of it all was unsettling.

Once we reached the main gate, Stone-faced handed me over before rushing back to the empty post at the bottom of the hill. The three guards he left me with were the ones tasked with allowing me entry into the property. They looked exactly like what you'd expect seedy security guards to look like. Muscled, filthy, and dangerous.

The short, stocky one was the first to step forward. He was all business as he motioned for me to hand over my duffle bag and rifled through my belongings. His movements were quick and efficient, and I could tell by his cool disregard and composure that he'd been doing this job for a while.

The lanky blonde one was the next to make a move. His face looked bored as he gestured for me to pass him my hand-bag. I placed the bag in his hands and tried not to watch as he rummaged through my most prized possessions. Within a few seconds, Lanky Blonde found the cell phone I tried to hide in the lining and snatched it away with no explanation. My heart sunk, but I maintained my composure. I knew it could happen, but that didn't make it any easier to watch.

Then there was guard number three, the average-looking meathead. He differed from the other two. The moment he caught sight of me, he puffed out his chest, rested his hand on his gun holster, and gave me a smug smirk. I'd bet my life savings that he was the newest of the three and therefore, had the most to prove.

He glued his dull eyes to my form as he informed me of

the full body search he would be conducting. The outfit I had on left little to the imagination. He and I both knew there was no way I could hide anything. Meathead just wanted to put on a show of dominance for his buddies and unfortunately for me, I was at his mercy.

Gritting my teeth, I followed Meathead's orders and stood wide, raising my arms to help expedite the process. I could feel his hot breath cascading down my neck and without looking, I already knew he was standing too close to conduct a normal search.

His clammy hands roamed my body, pressing harder than necessary and forming a knot in my stomach and a lump in my throat. I closed my eyes and focused on my breathing.

I let myself relax a little once Meathead had made it down to my ankles. *He's almost done, just keep breathing...* But when his hands went for another round of grazing my ass, the unease in my chest skyrocketed.

I looked to the other guards for help, but they saw nothing, too caught up in their own tasks. My mouth wanted to call out for help, but I worried that bringing attention to it may only end up making it worse for me. I didn't know any of these men; who's to say they wouldn't just join in on the action.

Meathead took full advantage of our 'privacy' and began painfully squeezing and rubbing my denim-clad flesh. A wave of nausea hit me and my mouth pooled, preparing for the vomit that was threatening to surface. I tried to stop it, but the sensation of his hands violating me had consumed me. I tried to squirm out of his reach but only exceeded in egging him on even further.

Meathead's idiotic self took my wiggling as a sign of my body reacting positively to him and stepped in even closer.

The second I felt his vile erection press against my ass cheeks, I fractured. My pulse thundered in my veins and a gleam of sticky sweat coated my skin. I tried to regain my composure, to focus on my breathing again, but all I could see was red. All I could feel was disgust.

Eyeing the foot he stupidly planted beside mine, I stomped down on his cheap black loafer with full force, relishing in the crunch of bones underneath my heel. The yelp that escaped his lips felt like a healing balm, washing away most of the nausea in my gut.

"You stupid bitch!" He reeled, gripping my bicep to swing me around like a rag doll.

I kept my face expressionless. Meathead seemed like the type of guy that enjoyed people's fear, and I refused to feed into his ego by cowering beneath him. He was just a tiny blip on the mountain of shit I was in, and I had much bigger things to be afraid of.

"I'm sorry, it was an accident." I deadpanned, staring off into space.

"Let her go, Nate." Short and Stocky ordered, grabbing Meathead by his beefy arm.

"Fuck that." He spat, shaking out of his hold. "She needs to learn respect."

"She isn't yours to touch, you idiot." Lanky Blonde mumbled, not even bothering to look up from the purse he was still searching through.

"I don't give a fuck who she belongs to!" Meathead yelled, sending spit flying in every direction. "She ain't going to disrespect me and get away with it."

I made a show of wiping his spit off my cheek before staring off into space again. He wanted a reaction, but he was barking up the wrong tree. My emotions were like Fort Knox, and the bastard would get nothing from me.

"You should give a fuck," Short and Stocky warned, "for all our sakes."

Meathead had gone off the deep end and refused to let go. Minutes ticked by and I could already feel the bruise forming under the pads of his dirty fingers as he increased the pressure. He wanted me to cower, but I refused to. My mother's conditioning ensured that I now had complete control over my emotions. The dumb asshole was fighting a losing battle.

"I hope she's worth dying for." Short and Stocky mumbled, "If you don't let go, we call the bosses, otherwise they'll kill us too."

That threat finally struck a chord, and I felt his grip lessen. No matter how big and bad meathead thought he was, he knew The Reapers were much worse.

"Forget it." He said, flinging my arm away from him like discarded trash. "The bitch is obviously fucking crazy. She didn't even try to fight me off."

"Of course I am." I said gesturing towards the gate behind them. "Why else would anyone agree to come here willingly?"

No one said another word. They knew what being here meant and based on the looks in Short and Stocky and Lanky Blonde's eyes; it was a fate they wouldn't wish on their worst enemy.

My eyes drifted to the monstrous gate as the two guards resumed their searches and Meathead trekked back into the guard station he crawled out of. With the threat of Meathead now far in the back of my mind, I refocused on the task at hand; getting through the gate.

The gate itself was gigantic, standing tall at least twelve feet of ornate metal. The thick metal bars were slippery; slick with dewdrops of the evening's mist. My eyes clung to the beads of precipitation as they slowly rolled down, softly gliding and building momentum only to plummet to their unceremonious death. It was a morbid distraction from the feeling of dread trying to creep its way into my thoughts.

If I lingered too long on what was happening and what was most likely going to happen once I entered that gate, I'd either run away or crumple in on myself and neither of those were real options.

The two guards finally handed back my belongings and stood to the side as the heavy metal gate slowly crept open. My heart rate kicked up a notch as my eyes flicked up, searching for what was next.

So much in this world was kept under wraps, and no one bothered to fill me in on the details. From the moment I arrived at Alessandro's, no one said a thing. I didn't know where I was going or who I would encounter. When I tried to ask questions, I'd get ignored. It was as if my thoughts and opinions no longer mattered, and I had no say in anything that happened to me from here on out.

That's why when my eyes spotted a literal mansion in the distance, I audibly gasped. I prepared myself for a lot of things, but I did not prepare myself for that.

The colossal home was strangely disarming, and its over-whelming elegance almost made me forget it should terrify me. Large tinted floor to ceiling windows encompassed the entire first floor, illuminating the front of the house in a soft inviting light. The wide modern moat that surrounded the property was bottomless and if I wasn't studying every detail,

I would've missed the discrete slate slabs that rose from its inky depths at my arrival.

It was a dream home in every sense of the word and a far cry from where I expected The Reapers to live. But I was quickly learning that in this world, it was better to expect the unexpected.

Stepping over the slabs, I quickly made my way towards the front door and tried to calm my nerves. I couldn't swim; having to walk over thirty feet of seemingly bottomless water wasn't helping the situation.

The moment I stepped off the last slab, I heard the *whoosh* of water moving. Looking back at the path I'd taken, I watched as the slate slabs descended back into the water, leaving me with no escape.

I felt the fear bubble up again, but I stuffed it right back down. I refused to show them my fear. Villains love to prey on helpless victims. I was many things, but I wasn't a victim. *Not anymore.*

Taking a deep breath, I shook off the last bit of nerves and raised my fist to knock on the door. I watched the heavy door slide open and a man's scrutinizing eyes peered out. Hidden by the door's shadow, it was impossible for me to see much more than the vivid green eyes staring back at me. The silence hung heavy in the air as he continued to stare without speaking a word.

After a few tense moments, I couldn't stand the silence anymore, so I repeated the only proper words that had left my lips since I entered their world.

"I'm here to repay Malcolm Warner's debt."

I fought the instinct to run as he pulled himself out from behind the door. His stride was graceful for such a large man, and as he moved to stand before me, the difference in stature was almost comical. I stood at around 5'5 on a good day and he had to be nearly a foot taller than me. His soft emerald eyes scanned the vacant air around us before looking down to settle on me again. His gaze was penetrating, and I was at a loss for words.

I didn't expect him to look like *that*. He was painfully handsome. His silky brushed back dark hair and bold, striking brows combined with his full lips, sharp jawline, and high cheekbones made him arguably the most attractive man I'd ever seen. He had the height and striking facial structure of a male model and the physique of a Greek god. If his body wasn't covered from the neck down in ornate tattoos, I would've assumed I had the wrong house.

His enormous frame slowly circled mine, like a beast sizing up his prey. I ignored his bout of machismo and the delicious wisps of crisp citrus and spice his movements created, focusing instead on the carvings of the massive door he had closed behind him.

Much like the house itself, the door was intricate and polished. It was beautiful. Hell, everything about this place was beautiful. And if I didn't know what kind of sadistic deals went on behind that door, I probably would've fallen for the illusion.

After years of living in a world full of lies and deceit, I knew better. Before her passing, all my mother cared about was her image and what other well-off people thought of her. She spent her entire life pretending to be someone she wasn't. Even married men she didn't love because they looked good on her arm. But like most webs of lies, you can get tangled in them if you aren't careful. Eventually the false narrative she created grew to be too much for her to manage and the skeletons in her closet made their escape.

The house, much like the man standing before me, was just a beautiful facade masking the ugliness hidden within. It was imperative I remembered that beyond all the fancy cars loaded in the driveway and the glitzy bullshit, this was hell and the men that lived here were the gatekeepers.

"You aren't who we were expecting." He mused in a cold, lifeless tone.

All the moisture on my tongue dissipated. I didn't think they would know *who* to expect.

"I'm better." I purred, trying to sound seductive. "She's weak. She'll break easily. I won't." I finished, offering him a playful wink.

My attempt at seduction reeked of desperation, and if I was in my right mind, I would've winced at how pathetic the attempt was. But frankly, I didn't give a fuck. Desperation became my friend long before this man came into my life and I'd do whatever I could to make The Reapers forget all about her. As far as they knew, she never existed.

"Sorry princess, tell Malcolm a deal is a deal." He hissed, glaring at me. "Now get out of here before you do something you're going to regret." He said, roughly turning my body back towards the gates.

I instantly deflated. *This can't be happening.* I needed to do something. *Anything.* I couldn't let them get their hands on her.

"She died." I lied, keeping my expression blank as I turned back to face him. "Malcolm didn't want to disappoint, so he sent me instead."

A frown formed across his face, but vanished almost as

quickly as it arrived. He flashed me a smile that was anything but friendly as he gave me another once over and turned to leave.

"You have no idea what you're doing." He shot over his shoulder as he walked back inside, leaving the door open in his wake.

I ignored his words; nothing he could say would stop me.

Steeling my nerves and shaking off the last bits of hesitation, I gave the doorway one last hard look. I knew that the moment my feet crossed the threshold, my life would no longer belong to me and everything that happened from then on out would be because of my own choices.

I dug my grave with The Reapers of Caspian Hills, and tonight; it was time to lie in it.

EIGHT

I COULDN'T DECIDE WHAT I LOOKED FORWARD TO MORE, MY brothers' reaction to the girl at our doorstep or the commotion that her presence in our home would create. She wasn't what we were expecting in the slightest. In fact, I was so surprised by her appearance that I stupidly offered her an easy out.

The delicious porcelain skin, long raven hair, and full pouty crimson lips proved too much for my pussy-motivated brain to handle. The moment I laid eyes on her, I froze and transformed into Mr. Fucking Gentlemen. As I circled around her curvy form, I had to restrain myself from reacting to her intoxicating scent of creamy vanilla and freshly cut pears. She was temptation, personified.

My fingers wanted to touch her soft skin, my hands itched to wrap her long tresses around them, and my teeth wanted to sink into her juicy bottom lip. Dressed in all black, her doe-like chestnut eyes made her look like a good girl you couldn't help but want to taint.

No wonder Malcolm tried to pawn off his other girl first. This one had to have been his prized possession. If she was a drug user, she hadn't been using long. The drugs had yet to wear her body down. She still had a youthful radiance to her skin, a luscious ass, and a set of full tits to match. But if she was working for him, she had to be a user. No other reason a girl like that would go anywhere near the pathetic piece of trash.

As I watched her through our mirrored windows, I could see the indecision weighing on her features. I had given her an out. I may be a murderous asshole, but I was a man of my word. She'd be free to go if she walked away now. I'd smooth things over with my brothers if I had to.

If she had some common sense in her, she would. The only people dumb enough to enter our world did so out of desperation. Caspian Hills was a dirty city beneath all the shine. She could get drugs anywhere in town, so what was making her want to stay?

Walk away, Princess.

Stay far away from me and my brothers.

Her features morphed into a scowl. She mumbled something under her breath and winced as her arm inexplicably twitched. *How disappointing.* That subtle twitch told me everything I needed to know. S*he was a user.*

I hoped she would differ from the other woman that tried to crawl into our laps, but I should've known to never trust such a beautiful face. She may be after something different from the gold diggers that usually came our way, but desperation was desperation.

She was coming down from something. Crystal meth, more than likely. It was a shame too, because with those looks and that soft, curvy body she would've been an excellent fuck. At least now we knew who we were really dealing with.

Sorry Princess, but if you think we're going to be your sugar daddies, you're sadly mistaken. We aren't the heroes in your story, we're the villains.

NINE

Stevie

THE SOUND OF MY HEELED BOOTS CLICKING AGAINST THE pristine marble was the only noise echoing across the grand foyer. If I hadn't just seen the man that entered before me, I would have assumed that no one lived here and hadn't for quite some time. The place was cold and empty. The floor was almost too clean, and its grandeur made it feel more like an art museum than someone's home.

The entire place smelled of wood and leather, and the interior was surprisingly bright. Clean white walls with dark wood accents and sparkling marble floors filled the space. The foyer led me towards two sets of glass stairs that framed the open living space beyond it. The place was absolutely stunning.

They revered The Reapers in this town, but I had no idea they had *this* kind of wealth. The art pieces that hung on the walls alone had to have been worth more money than I could even fathom.

I expected them to be savage criminals. Ones I could easily outsmart given the right opportunity. But the more I explored their domain, the more my assumptions were off. The entire place oozed sophistication, and I was out of my element.

As I continued my exploration, a canvas hanging on the right side of the room caught my eye. The piece was a stark contrast to the more minimalistic pieces hung on the walls. While those felt flat, dull even, this one seemed full of life. It was dark, nearly black, and I could almost feel the emotions radiating off of the canvas. Rage. Sorrow. Power.

Gravitating towards it, my eyes studied each splatter and stroke meticulously. My fingers inched closer of their own volition, drawn to the chaotic texture.

An oversized palm slashed across my vision and wrapped itself around my wrist in a firm hold. Like striking a match, the sensation stirred phantom memories that should've stayed buried.

In an instant, I wasn't in the house anymore; I was pinned to the dirt. With them. The distinct tinge of blood, sweat, dirt coated my senses, encapsulating me in the nightmare and making it feel real. I couldn't breathe. I gasped for air, desperately trying to ground myself. *This isn't real. This isn't real.*

I took another deep inhale and an unfamiliar scent dominated my senses. Citrus, wood, and spices. Like wrapping myself in a warm blanket by a crackling fire. Where was it coming from?

I blinked.

The flashback vanished. No cold sweat, no lump in my throat, nothing. I opened my eyes to find that the man from the door had released his grip and was staring at me like I had sprouted another head. I stared daggers back at him. *How the hell did he pull me out?*

"Hands off, princess." He ordered, not missing a beat and pretending that he didn't just witness my psychotic break. "Trust me, Ezra is the last person you want to piss off."

I scoffed at his warning. *Trust him?* Just because my delusional mind somehow trusted him didn't mean that I would. I was smarter than that. *Then again, I did just sacrifice myself to a group of savage drug dealers, so how smart could I really be?*

The thought made me smile.

"Something amusing?" He asked, probably not expecting an answer.

My mouth had always gotten me into trouble, and this situation proved to be no different.

"My apologies, Master," I bit out, "it isn't my place to express myself so frivolously. Will you ever forgive me?" I asked, driving the point home by fluttering my lashes.

I should've feared him. Hell, I should've feared this entire situation, but I refused to live my life in fear anymore. I volunteered to be here, but that didn't mean I had to just shut up and take the intimidation tactics.

"It's not Master, it's Cyrus." He offered with a crooked

grin. "Though with that ass, you can call me anything you want." He paused, gesturing towards the stairs. "After you."

I hated the way he made my body react, like my brain and my body were from two different planets and an all-out war was exploding in my head. My brain knew he was dangerous and wanted nothing to do with him, while my body craved his attention and my pussy pulsed at every word uttered from his gorgeous mouth.

A blush crept across my cheeks as I stiffly moved in front of him. I tried tilting my hips forward as I ascended the stairs, doing my best to make my ass look as unappealing as possible. I'm sure I looked like a zombie fresh out of Thriller climbing up the steps, but I didn't care. It was worth it if it made him rethink his new fascination with me. I didn't like the way my body felt around him.

"Where are we going?" I asked, mindlessly staring at the industrial looking light fixtures that adorned the wide hallway.

"To your room." He mumbled, sounding distracted.

At least I knew this wasn't a march to my death or some awful dungeon. They were giving me an actual room.

"Where exactly is my room?" I asked, feeling like we were walking in circles.

"About four doors ago." He mumbled, stifling a laugh.

I spun on my heel and cut my eyes at his silently shaking form.

"What?" I asked, dumbfounded.

"My mistake, I must've gotten… distracted." He offered, biting into his lower lip with a lazy smirk.

"Please take me to my room." I growled out, trying to reign in the confusing anger that wanted to jump out.

It took everything I had not to explode on him, which

wasn't normal for me. How in the hell could one man get so deeply under my skin in such a short time?

I needed to reign myself in. I could walk on the edge of pissing him off, but I couldn't allow myself to cross that line. Despite how easily it was to be near him, he was still a Reaper and I needed to remember that The Reapers were capable of anything and wouldn't hesitate to put me in my place.

⎯⎯⎯

AFTER LEADING me to my room, Cyrus left me to my own devices and gave me strict orders to *"unpack my shit and drag my sweet ass back to the living room"* when I finished. If he made one more comment about my ass, I was going to find a way to murder him in his sleep. Reaper or not, the asshole had it coming.

Upon entering the room, the first thing I noticed was the enormous floor to ceiling windows that completely made up the far wall. *For being notoriously private, The Reapers sure liked their big ass windows.* Vivid moonlight cascaded through them, blanketing the room in a soft ethereal glow. I've lived nowhere near the hills before, and from this elevation, the moon looked enormous.

As I placed my duffel bag on the bed's black silk sheets, the flickering of a long natural gas fireplace caught my attention. Directly in front of the fireplace stood two cozy cream armchairs and a small coffee table adorned with a stack of weathered books. By anyone's standards, the room was beautiful. But I couldn't help but wonder, *why the hell did they give it to me?*

I was nothing to them.

A means of repayment.

Nothing more.

As I unpacked the little belongings I had, the pulsing of my forearm kicked up again, sending pain radiating outward. I needed to check on the wound I haphazardly dressed at the motel.

Sneaking out of my room, I carefully crept towards the bathroom we passed down the hall. I wasn't even sure if I was allowed to use it, so I made it a point to get in and get out as fast as I could.

Tucking myself inside, I locked the door behind me, stripped off my jacket, and got a good look at my arm in the mirror. The wound had already leaked through bandages, but that wasn't the worst part. The surrounding flesh was red and painful to the touch. It needed to be cleaned and dressed properly, otherwise I'd get an infection.

I tossed the soiled bandage in the toilet, flushed it, and ransacked their cabinets, looking for some kind of first aid kit. The rich assholes had to have some kind of medical kit considering their line of work. When I reached the bottom drawer, I hit the jackpot and found a fully stocked drawer full of medical supplies.

I grabbed a bottle of rubbing alcohol and without thinking, raised my arm over the sink and drenched my entire forearm in it. The wound burned like a motherfucker, and my teeth bit hard into my lower lip to stifle the scream that tried to claw its way out.

Grabbing the gauze, I redressed the wound in seconds and

tossed some ibuprofen back for the pain before putting every-thing back as I found it. I still didn't know how volatile The Reapers were and it was in my best interest to avoid doing anything that might piss them off. After living with a volatile man for nearly over half of my life, I understood the impor-tance of being cautious in a dangerous environment.

Sneaking out of the bathroom, I blindly rushed towards my room, looking over my shoulder to make sure that no one saw me. I made it about ten feet before my body slammed into a solid wall of muscle. The force of the impact sent my body crashing towards the ground. It was almost as if the universe was serving out karmic retribution and it wanted to remind me of my place in this world, just in case I forgot after seeing my new living space.

"Fuck." I stammered, laid out on the hardwood as my eyes tried to refocus.

A rugged hand covered in tattoos slashed into my line of sight. I reluctantly accepted the help. It was bad enough that I had stupidly crashed into him, I wouldn't let my embarrass-ment stop me from being polite.

As soon as my eyes looked up at the man in front of me, all common sense left the building. I stared at him. *Hard.* It was almost impossible not to.

His tall frame stunted mine and from his sharp jawline down, intricate tattoos covered his porcelain skin. The slightly unbuttoned white shirt he wore gave my mind just enough ammo to run with, and I stupidly wondered what other parts of his body had tattoos.

My heart slammed in my chest as his dark grey eyes skimmed my body and took on an almost primal look as he peered at me through his disheveled black hair. He wasn't big or bulky, but there was something about his presence that had my nerves on edge. My mind and my body were on opposing ends. I couldn't shake the overwhelming need to run, yet something about him made my traitorous body long to get closer to him.

Thank god my survival instincts kept my ass firmly planted where it was. Even they knew better than to trigger the dangerous man standing in front of me.

It was then that I noticed the stains littered across his body. It looked to be the same deep crimson on the artwork I spotted downstairs, but as the sharp, coppery aroma filled my senses; I realized my terrible mistake.

The man I just slammed into was Ezra, *The Artist*, and the deep red liquid splattered all over him wasn't paint, like I naively thought. It was blood. Ezra wasn't an artist at all; He was a goddamn killer.

"A fallen angel." Ezra murmured softly as a sinister smile crept onto his face.

His thumb reached out to graze my lower lip. The sensation of his touch sent delicious shivers down my spine. My mind urged me to get out of there, but my stupid legs refused to budge.

As I watched his hand pull away, my eyes locked on the bright ruby streak now staining his thumb. My brows furrowed in confusion. *Is that my blood? Did I bite my lip that hard?*

Acting on instinct, my tongue swiped out to lick the spot that his thumb just brushed and sure enough, my taste buds picked up the distinct coppery flavor.

I watched with a mix of fascination and horror as he slowly brought his thumb towards his mouth and licked off the stain. The alarm bells that were once chiming softly in the distance were now blaring in my head. *Bitch, get out of there!*

"Mmm," he growled, licking his lips, "just like I thought. Delicious."

Before I could even utter a response, a blur of a body came lunging towards me. One second, I'm paralyzed in front of Ezra, seconds away from being devoured and the next I'm being tossed into the air like a beach ball.

The velocity of my stomach landing on a hard shoulder knocked the wind out of me and as I felt an arm curl tightly underneath my ass, I knew exactly who the culprit was. *Cyrus.* He had just secured his position on my shit list.

I lifted my head in time to catch a smirking Ezra enter the bathroom I had just walked out of. An icy chill crept up my spine. If I had gone into that bathroom five seconds later, he could've trapped me in there and no one would've been able to stop him.

"Stay out of trouble, Angel." Ezra taunted, flashing me a devilish grin.

I couldn't help the maniacal laugh that bubbled out of my lips. His warning was absolutely ludicrous. *Stay out of trouble? How the hell was I supposed to stay out of trouble when I was now living with it?*

As Cyrus stomped his way down the stairs, my face banged against the rigid muscles of his back. I fought the urge to kick him in the balls as my sense of self preservation only slightly outweighed my irritation at his barbarian act. I didn't enjoy being hauled away like fucking property, but he saved me from whatever the hell that interaction with Ezra was, and I'd be lying if I said it didn't feel good to have his god-gifted body so close to mine.

Once we reached the bottom of the stairs, his movements halted. Strong hands gripped around the back of my thighs and he pulled my body down. He paused as our eyes met and his hands gripped onto my waist, suspending me in the air like I weighed nothing.

The size and strength of this man alone could put my pussy in a frenzy. I wasn't a tiny girl by anyone's standards, yet he carried me with just his hands and showed no signs of a struggle. He gave me a look that said he wanted to defile me in the most depraved ways possible and for just a moment, my pussy took control of my brain and screamed that she was all in. His little hero act had sent my hormones into overdrive and I was too caught up in the moment to stop it.

My legs tightened around his waist of their own accord and I pressed my body against his ferverously. I buried my face into the crook of his neck and breathed in his alluring scent of freshly cut grass and leather. His skin was hot to the touch and deliciously smooth. I rubbed my cheek against the softness as my body grinded against his waist. I felt him hardening beneath me as his breathing grew just as ragged as mine.

A tiny whimper escaped my lips. The sound broke through the dense fog, muddying both of our minds. He yanked me away from his body and stared at me, baffled. Whatever spell I had cast over him quickly broke, and he dropped me to the floor like a sack of potatoes.

Fuck you pussy, you backstabbing hoe. We had an agreement. Just because he can toss us around like we weigh nothing doesn't automatically mean we try to fuck him.

Surprise momentarily flashed across his features before his scowl returned as if it had never left. Now avoiding touching me all together, he carefully picked me up by the nape of my leather jacket and set me on my feet.

"Never grab me like that again!" I hissed, pulling away from his hold. "God, what are you, a fucking brute? What is wrong with you?"

I didn't actually want an answer. My stupid mouth just kept digging the humiliation grave deeper. His blatant rejection hurt. He was all about it when I first arrived, but now he wouldn't even look at me.

"Cyrus!" I fumed, finally garnering his attention.

His angry eyes flashed in my direction as his sharp jaw ticked, but he still said nothing. His silence was worse than any cutting remark he had made earlier, and I could see the pure hatred for me all over his face. That's when I noticed a discrepancy that I would've seen earlier had I not been so *dickstracted*.

"Did you do something different with your hair? Because I could've sworn it was shorter only a few moments ago."

"Damn, Princess, I'm touched that you noticed." Called out a familiar voice from behind me.

I swung my head back and had to do a double take. Behind me stood Cyrus, looking as full of himself as ever with a smug smile plastered on his face. The man who carried me down the stairs wasn't Cyrus at all, and based on the splitting image I was seeing, he had to have been his twin.

As I gaped at the two men, it was obvious they were identical, but the way they carried themselves couldn't have been more different. Where Cyrus's stance exuded confidence and charisma, this man's presence seemed standoffish and brutal. They both had the same sexy emerald eyes and were exactly the same height and build. They even both had black and white tattoos all over their body. The only physical discrepancy between the two was their hair. While they both had dark brown locks, Cyrus' twin's hair was an inch or two longer, giving him a more wild and animalistic look.

"Tristan, meet... Princess."

"Stevie." I bit out, scowling at Cyrus and offering Tristan a small smile. "Stevie Alexander."

It wasn't his fault that his twin was an ass. *Maybe he was the good twin?*

His eyes stared at my smile for a brief second before flashing back to Cyrus and looking at him pointedly. After a few beats of silence, he left the foyer and headed towards the living room without another word.

Okay, definitely the evil twin.

TEN

Ezra

THE FALLEN ANGEL TASTED LIKE HEAVEN. WHEN SHE CRASHED into me, I had no intention of interacting with her. My body was still buzzing from my session with Johnny, and I wanted to avoid her until I was ready. The release was so much sweeter when I had a few days to heighten the need for pain. But something about seeing the sticky scarlet substance drip down her flawless creamy skin changed my mind.

When my thumb swiped that blood from her lip, a few things happened I didn't expect. Her delicate tongue swiped at the last remnants of blood on her lip and revealed tiny silvery scars. It was a minute detail that most who have never dealt with pain would never notice. The scar tissue there told me she had been biting into that same spot for years, a clear sign she was used to hiding her pain.

I bet if I examined her palms, she'd have four crescent-shaped scars in each one, from years of her nails digging into the flesh. I recognized the scars that only years of pain and frustration can bring. She was a fighter.

My eyes locked in on her, seeing her in a new light. The look should have intimidated the fuck out of her, but it only seemed to make her hold her head higher and jut her chin out further. She eyed me hard with a mixture of fear and excitement as she took in the blood splattered across my body, but instead of pulling away like I had expected, her body leaned towards me. It appears darkness enticed the little thing.

It was an interesting twist when Tristan came in and broke up all the fun. I didn't want to hurt her. Not right away, at least. No, she was strong. So much stronger than what I had expected. I would need more time. Luckily for her, all we had these days was time.

After washing up, I headed downstairs to find her frustrated, staring at Cyrus and Tristan as they held a private conversation. Tristan only spoke openly around us. It was the reason my brothers and I were the only ones who lived in our home, and the staff stayed in separate quarters on the property.

Initially, we thought of keeping the girl with the staff, but we didn't exactly employ the most virtuous men. We don't allow anyone to touch what is ours, but having her live with them would be like throwing her to the fucking wolves.

Frustration marred her features as she scowled at the two of them and strained her neck trying to listen in on their conversation. She wouldn't hear anything. Tristan was always careful with strangers.

I descended the last few stairs and made my way towards the three of them. The sound of my incoming steps had the entire room on edge. She couldn't see it, but I recognized the look in my twin little brothers' eyes. Me coming near her made them nervous.

They assumed I was going to attack her and because of my track record, I couldn't blame them. Before my interaction with her upstairs, I probably would've done exactly that. But she was different. *Special*. She deserved much more than that.

"Where the fuck is Atlas?" Cyrus asked, crossing his arms over his chest.

Out of the corner of my eye, I caught Tristan's subtle movement as he stared me down and mimicked his twin's pose. Subconsciously the two were more connected than anyone else would ever understand.

"He's taking care of some business. Don't worry about it." I said, silencing their worries with a lie.

Truthfully, Atlas wasn't answering any of my calls either. I had no clue what he was doing. I checked in with security and they reported he took a drive a few hours ago.

It was clear Atlas wanted to stay off the grid. If he were in any real danger, he would've called. Out of the four of us, he was the most responsible, so if he needed a little time away, I'd cover his ass.

"Should we wait?" Cyrus asked, nodding his head towards the girl.

"No, let's just get this over with." I said, advancing towards her eerily still body.

The girl had some sense of survival in her, after all.

"Don't you fucking touch me." She hissed, her eyes morphing into rounded orbs as she shot up from her seat and backed up against the wall.

"Relax, Stevie," chastised Cyrus with a smile, "we aren't going to hurt you... yet."

The name Stevie didn't match the woman standing in front of us. It was masculine and rough when this woman exuded femininity and softness. Long, midnight hair, pristine creamy skin and delectable curves that begged to be bit into. She was a fallen angel, if I ever saw one.

"What are you guys planning to do with me?" She asked, her chest heaving despite the calm tone in her voice.

She was good at hiding it, but I could see the panic sinking in and the sick sadist in me loved watching her squirm. I stepped forward, ready to play with my meal just a little. Atlas had already given us strict orders on what we could and could not do to the girl, but that didn't mean we couldn't have a little fun at her expense.

Tristan recognized the look of mischief in my eyes and stormed out of the room without another word. He hated the beast that dwelled within me because it reminded him so much of the one he had to face almost every night as a child. I couldn't take that pain away, but at least my beast would ensure that no one ever fucked with any of my brothers again.

"Turn around." I ordered, my features completely void of emotion.

To my surprise, she did what I asked without a word of protest. I could see the fire in her eyes the moment the order left my lips. The tightening of her fists and the slight tremble of her body told me exactly how she felt about following my orders. So, I didn't understand why she was following them so easily. *Just how far would she allow me to push her?*

"Take off the jacket." Cy ordered, smiling smugly to himself.

"No." She countered, focusing her eyes on one of the few blank walls in our home.

"Do as he says." I hissed, letting all the playfulness leave my voice.

After a few beats of silence and to both of our surprise, she moved. Slowly, she pulled off her jacket before crushing it into a ball and flinging it at the couch. *Such a little fighter, even when she's giving in to our demands.*

She moved to wrap her arms across her chest in an act of silent protest, and it was then that I noticed the white bandage wrapped around her forearm.

"Who did that to you?" I growled as rage licked across my skin.

Based on the blood pooling on the bandage, the wound was fresh. My brothers and I were the only ones allowed to fucking touch her. Whoever he was, he was a dead man.

She met my question with silence, but she knew what the fuck I was talking about. The moment her fingers grazed the bandage, her entire body froze. Neither of my brothers would have harmed her so soon. That narrowed the suspects down to the assholes we employed.

"Answer him." Cyrus bit out, both of our eyes locked on her now trembling form.

"No one." She mumbled, her back still to us.

Gritting my teeth, I charged towards her. I'd had enough

of her fucking games and she was going to speak up whether she liked it or not. Tris could easily check the footage to find out who did it, but this was a game of wills and our new pet needed to be house-broken.

Cyrus, seeing my approach, moved to block her from my wrath, but I shoved him out of the way. Strength-wise we're evenly matched, but he knows my cruelty knew no bounds, even with my own flesh and blood. I gave him one last warning glare. *Stay out of this.*

Once he recognized the look of death in my eyes, he knew that there was no point in trying to fight. Our girl had sealed her fate.

He stepped aside, the look of defeat written all over his face. Without him in my way, my thoughts centered on one thing and one thing only. Making her break.

I told myself that the anger rolling through me had everything to do with her defiance and nothing to do with the fact that somebody hurt her. She was nothing to me, nothing to any of us, just a toy and a symbol of our ruthlessness.

Standing mere inches behind her, I offered her one last chance to change her destiny.

"Give me a name." I hissed, my furious breath cascading across the nape of her neck.

"No." She responded, jutting her chin out further.

My hand tightly wrapped around her throat, as if it had a mind of its own. Not enough to cut off her air supply, but enough to give her the fucking message. We were dangerous men, and this little defiance act of hers wouldn't get her anywhere.

"Sure about that, Angel?" I taunted as I pressed my body

against hers. "It would be a shame to lose your life over such a tiny request."

I could feel the muscles in her throat struggling to pull in gasps of air and hear the steady thrum of her pulse as fear crept into her thoughts. *Good, be fucking terrified.*

From my vantage point, I could see her milky breasts rising and falling with each labored breath she took. The feel of her trembling body writhing against mine went straight to my cock and before I knew it, its rigid length had pressed firmly against her soft ass.

I expected her to cower. To break into tears and beg for forgiveness. What I got instead was anything but. Her head lolled back to rest against my chest and instead of squirming away from my cock, she pressed her ass into it even harder. Almost painfully so.

She grabbed my free hand and placed it on the zipper of her black corset top, and guided it down, letting the fabric fall to the floor in a heap.

Too thrown off by her behavior to continue, I released her throat and attempted to pull away, but she wasn't done yet. She grabbed my hand and placed it on one of her firm tits, encouraging me to squeeze and massage her heavy breast. Not one to resist temptation, I flicked my thumb against her pebbling nipple and grinned, feeling her body convulse against me. My other hand reached up to grab her jaw and force her to face me. I wanted to see that angelic face of hers react to what I was doing. But before I could latch onto it, she turned her head and slipped my index finger into her soft mouth. She moaned, sucking on it as she deliciously swirled her tongue up and down its length.

I forgot we had an audience. Forgot where we were and

how this started. I relished in the feeling of her. Of her soft, delectable body pressing so close to mine. Of the way her tongue lapped my finger with so much enthusiasm, you'd swear she was expecting it to come.

She may have looked like an angel, but this girl was a sinner at her core and I couldn't wait to defile her. I wanted her to look as wicked on the outside as she was on the inside. I-

Clarity hit me the second I heard Cyrus clear his throat.

"Fuck." I grunted, roughly shoving her away from me.

What the fuck was I doing? I didn't give a fuck about seeing her naked or taking her to my bed. This was about breaking her will. Not an audition for how well she could suck my cock.

She turned to face me; her face contorted with anger.

"Oh, come on, why'd you stop? We knew where this was going. I was just making it easier." She said in a mocking tone as a bitter smile formed on her lips.

My eyes roamed her bare upper body unabashedly. Lingering on the creamy skin of her breasts before traveling towards her smooth navel. It was then that I noticed what she was really trying to show us. There, just below her navel, was a word etched in angry silvery scars. *Whore.*

My jaw ticked.

"This is what you wanted, right?" She asked, pulling my attention away from the jagged scars. "Well, take what you want. As you can see, others have. But just know, you can't break me."

She gave me an icy glare as she jutted her chin out further and waited for my response. I had to give it to her. The girl was good. She had almost won my cock over with her little stunt back there, but if sympathy was what she was after, she would never find it in me. I was the Reaper that had no conscience and no soul, and while her naivety was almost endearing, it was time I showed her how cruel our world really was.

"What?" I asked, raising a thick brow with a blank expression. "Were you expecting me to feel sorry for you?"

She said nothing as her hollow eyes stared into space. I continued.

"Did somebody do bad things to the poor pretty girl?" I mocked, slowly circling around her stiff body.

I was pushing her, but I wanted a reaction. Wanted to see the pain marring her beautiful face. Then I spotted it. The slight tremble of her lower lip that was so small, I would've missed it had I not been scrutinizing her every move. My words were affecting her after all, and the sadistic bastard in me wanted to see more.

"I'll bet it was mommy's boyfriend." I said with a dark laugh. "Is that it, Angel? Did mommy slice you because you fucked step daddy?"

"Fuck you." She spat, finally showing some spark behind her haunted eyes.

"No, thanks." I retorted, looking at her with disdain. "I prefer my pussy pristine."

Energy crackled between the two of us. Hers, angry and venomous. Mine, lethal and cruel. But if I dug deep down, beneath the emotions I was letting her see, there was something else filling the depths of my chest too. Something unexpected. Something that felt a lot like respect.

She refused to back away, as did I. It was as if our egos

had tethered to each other in a game of tug of war with neither side able to gain an inch.

"I bet you still like shouting Daddy when you get fucked." I taunted, inching my face towards hers.

She closed her eyes as a single tear trickled down her cheek. I stared at it and paused, baffled by my reaction. *I'd won.* I'd pushed her beyond her breaking point. I succeeded. I should feel satisfied, but all I felt was disappointment.

"Enough." Cyrus bellowed, pushing me away from her. "Stevie, grab your shit and go back to your room."

Keeping her eyes firmly locked on the ground, she grabbed her clothes and left. She refused to look at me again, but I could almost see the hate seething off of her shoulders. She hated me. *Good.* She should hate me. It meant she knew exactly what kind of man she was dealing with. The problem was, after that show, I had no idea who I was dealing with.

ELEVEN

Stevie

THE MOMENT I WOKE UP AND TOOK IN MY SURROUNDINGS, reality hit me. I was still in their home, which meant everything that occurred the day before was real.

I crawled out of bed and slipped in and out of the restroom with little incident. It was a blessing if there ever was one. I couldn't handle another awkward encounter with the men of this house. Not after what happened the night before.

As I pulled on my usual wardrobe of black denim, a cut-off band tee and leather ankle boots, I thought about what life would be like working for The Reapers. I still didn't know what kind of work they wanted me to do and it was nerve-wracking to have everything so up in the air.

I could be a maid and spend my days cleaning up after them. The house was spotless as it was, but I could cook or do laundry. I could deal drugs. It wouldn't be my first choice, of course, but anything was better than the bullshit they pulled last night.

Ezra and Cyrus tried to treat me like I was their personal lapdog. Like they could say 'jump' and the only response I was allowed to have was 'how high'. But I was not their fucking pet. That is where I drew the line, and last night was my attempt at making that clear.

I knew they were trying to test me. Trying to see how far they could push me before I broke. But they failed to realize that for me, being pushed around was nothing new. Someone had been pushing me around my entire life. Last night was my breaking point.

The thing between Ezra and I went a little further than I planned. I wanted to scare him off, to show him I wasn't afraid. I didn't expect him to like my aggression and to take things even further. How he touched my body and the electric current between us was unlike anything I had ever experienced. If he didn't push me off, I don't know if I would've stopped him and that terrified me.

Ezra was bad news and even my body could feel it. Whenever he came near me, my heart would thunder in my chest and my adrenaline would surge. But the rush he created was addictive. He was unpredictable and intriguing and completely off limits. All of them were dangerous, but Ezra was fucking suicide.

IT HAD REACHED 6pm before I heard the garage door opening. I had spent the larger part of the day just sitting and waiting for someone to check in on me. *What the hell were they thinking leaving a stranger alone in their home?*

I tried to be patient, but after raiding their fridge and a few hours of complete silence, my idle hands had enough, and I went to explore the rest of the house.

Based on the contents of the bedrooms, there were four men that lived here. I had already met three, which left only one man unaccounted for, the illusive Atlas.

A part of me hoped the car pulling into the garage was him. After listening to their conversation last night, it was clear he was their leader. If I could get into his good graces, maybe he'd keep the other psychos away from me. At the very least, he could be the one to make sure my clothing stayed on for the duration of my stay.

"I SEE you've made yourself at home." Cyrus called out, as I heard footsteps approach the living room.

I was curled up on their smoky grey couch in the middle of a reality T.V. binge on their gigantic flat screen.

"Yeah, well, it wasn't like I had much of a choice." I countered, twisting on the couch to face him.

"We had business to take care of." Ezra spoke up as he and Tristan walked up to flank Cyrus on either side.

After last night, Ezra was the last person I wanted to see. He was an asshole and an egotistical asshole at that. He may have hit the nail on the head with my mommy issues, but he was way off about my scars. I wouldn't touch Malcolm with a fucking ten-foot pole. Luckily for Alex and I, his vile ass didn't have a fascination for touching little girls, just beating them. Regardless, my past was none of his fucking business and I refused to let him get under my skin again.

"That's fine," I responded coolly, "though I'd like to start work soon, I can't imagine leaving me to sit here all day is helping to pay off Malcolm's debt."

"Work?" Cyrus answered with a single brow raised. "No offense, darling, but you aren't cut out for our kind of business. Why the fuck would we make you work?"

"But how else would I pay off the debt?"

"You are the debt," Ezra spoke up, tilting his head with a smirk, "paid in full."

What? In a split-second all the air rushed out of my lungs and the living room that once felt ostentatious became suffocating. His words shook me to my core and left me dumbfounded in the aftermath. That wasn't what I agreed to. *At all.*

Fucking Malcolm. It had to be his doing. The Reapers had no incentive to lie. With their power, if they wanted to keep me, they would.

Seeing the confusion on my face, Cyrus continued.

"In exchange for his life, Malcolm offered yours. This contract doesn't have an end date, Princess. You are ours, indefinitely."

Cyrus went into further detail, but my ears stopped listening. My expression was blank as a war of emotions rushed through me. *I was theirs...* I wasn't going back to Alex, not now and possibly not ever. I wasn't just repaying a debt; I was the goddamn debt.

Nausea bloomed in my gut. *This wasn't possible.* This had to be some kind of mistake. I never agreed to any of this.

I needed to leave, but even I wasn't foolish enough to think that they'd just let me walk out of here unharmed. I knew too much. Had scoped out their living quarters and had clearance with their security teams. I knew each of their faces so intimately that I could describe them from memory, and their anonymity outside of their inner circle was sacred.

I was upset, though mostly with myself, for being so fucking naïve. *This explained so much.* Why I couldn't leave the property of my own free will. Why the guards went through such great lengths to ensure that I couldn't see where we were going and why they had taken my only means of contacting Alex before I had even arrived. I was in deep shit and the reality of it was I had no one to blame but myself.

Slowly rising from my seat, I excused myself and made my way out of the room. Once I was out of their line of sight, my feet ran towards the nearest restroom. The moment my knees landed on the cool ceramic tile, my stomach began heaving its contents into the toilet. Silent tears streamed down my face as my body curled in on itself.

What have I done?

TWELVE

Tristan

SHE'S HIDING SOMETHING.

As I watched Stevie walk back into the living room, the nagging thought reared its ugly head again. Since her arrival, I've had my people meticulously research everything there is to know about Stephanie Alexander.

According to the sealed records I called in favors for, she had a pretty tumultuous childhood. Her father died when she was eight years old. Child protective services called on her behalf at least a dozen times before age thirteen. Orphaned at fifteen. From ages sixteen to eighteen she was in and out of juvie for a slew of charges, including petty theft and more than a few cases of physical assault. At nineteen there were a few medical bills from a lengthy hospital stay, but no record of what took place. Since then, her record has been virtually spotless. She's laid low and even held a job for the last few years at a local coffee shop. Still, something didn't add up.

As I scrolled through her court documents on my phone, the other phone in my pocket vibrated with a new notification. I ignored the disruption and went back to scrolling. I'd had her phone for less than twenty-four hours and there hasn't been a single hour that has gone by without a fucking text or call. Worst of all, every single notification was from some dude named Alex. *Who the fuck was this guy?*

I heard about the crazy shit she pulled with Ez, so Alex being her boyfriend was pretty unlikely. He was probably just some pussy-whipped ex-client distraught over the fact that he'd never get to touch her again.

It crossed my mind to peek at the messages, but I ignored them instead. Snooping through her phone was beneath me and my people already hand-delivered all the pertinent information. Something about her just felt... off.

Chancing another glance at her while Ez and Cyrus bickered, my eyes latched onto the purplish bruise marring the side of her face. I hadn't noticed it before, but it didn't come as a surprise. Cyrus told me about the scars on her body and the fresh wound on her arm. I checked our cameras and while one guard, who we would deal with personally, got too fucking touchy with her; all evidence showed that she arrived with the wound. Someone from her old life was hurting her and probably had been for some time.

The need for vengeance burrowed under my skin. No amount of violence or retribution would ever change what happened to her, but that didn't stop me from wanting to find the person responsible and deliver the fuck's head on a platter.

I almost asked her for a name. The words danced on the tip of my tongue. But before I could get them out, my dark thoughts got in the way.

Just what the fuck was I expecting to happen?

Even if, by some miracle, she gave me a name, and I found the fucker who gave her those scars. *Then what?* Would I profess my need to kill him because he hurt her? Would I tell her that since she walked through that fucking door, I haven't been able to stop obsessing over her?

No. I'd keep my mouth shut, just like I always did. And she'd think I was just a psychopath with a thirst for blood. I was better off staying out of whatever the hell was going on with her. She didn't give a fuck about me, and her problems weren't mine to handle.

"Ready?" Cyrus asked, pulling me out of my thoughts.

I waited for Stevie's inevitable rebuttal but when nothing came from her mouth and she continued to stare at the blank wall, three sets of eyes glared at her. In the little time we had gotten to know her, silence was not one of her strong suits. *Something was wrong.*

"Is there a problem?" She asked, her voice lifeless.

"No," Ez offered, piercing his eyes at her, "but you're coming with us."

Cyrus and I both looked at him like he was the stupidest motherfucker on the planet. We agreed to stop by to check on her. That was it. We never agreed to bring her with us.

"Okay." She said, moving towards the door, as her haunted eyes focused on anything but the three of us.

Ez loved playing with his toys, but even he had to know that bringing her to Hell's Tavern wasn't a fucking game. It would be like throwing her to the lions.

I wanted to stop him, but when the crazy fuck sets his mind on something, there was no talking him out of it. I just hoped that for her sake, she could still fight like she did when she was sixteen.

THIRTEEN

When we loaded up into Ezra's grey G-wagon, they didn't blindfold me, which was surprising. Ezra sat me in the passenger seat while Cyrus and Tristan stuffed their large bodies into the back. Every few seconds, I'd glance in the rearview mirror and notice one of their eyes on me. I was in a car full of men that looked like and probably were deranged killers, but that wasn't what scared me.

On the drive into town, I realized The Reapers had to seriously value their privacy. Their home was so deep in the forest that it would be impossible for someone to stumble upon it by accident. We drove for miles at a steep decline down windy roads surrounded by dark, lush forest. It wasn't until we leveled out that I started to see signs of civilization. I now knew that if I tried to make a run for it, it would take hours for me to make it down the hill on foot.

After another ten minutes of driving through downtown Caspian, the car finally stopped and pulled up behind a large brick building.

Ezra seemed relaxed as we made our way towards the building's back entrance, but Cyrus and Tristan were on edge. They walked behind us and though I couldn't see their expressions under the dark night sky, I could feel the tension radiating off of them. Neither of them seemed to like whatever was about to happen.

Ezra slipped his hand into his pocket for his access card. It was the same card the guys used to enter and exit the house, and as the light turned green on the card reader, I could see that it also worked to access whatever this building housed.

Ezra's arm reached out to push the heavy wooden door open, allowing me room to enter before him. The pitch black hallway vibrated with the steady hum of house music playing in the distance. I hesitated for a few beats in the darkness until I felt Cyrus' arm slide across my back. His hand was gentle yet firm as he guided me forward, and his distinct scent of warm citrus and spice put my mind at ease. I had no idea why my body zinged every time I felt his touch, but I lavished in the assurance he gave me.

As we made our way down the hallway, a small beam of light radiated from the end of the hallway. I moved to follow that light and prayed that whatever was about to happen wouldn't make things worse than they already were.

After a few feet, my eyes made out a small figure standing in the distance. It was a woman, and she was stunning. She had warm olive skin, a dark wavy bob, and bright emerald eyes that reflected the club's hypnotic lights. She was wearing a ruby spaghetti strapped, floor length silk dress that hugged every curve and paired it with a dazzling pair strappy and probably designer heels.

"Who do we have here?" She asked with a smile as her eyes carefully assessed me.

"Jessie, meet Stevie. Stevie, this is Jessie, the manager of this fine establishment." Cyrus said with a wink.

"Welcome to Hell's Tavern." She said, giving me a toothy smile.

"Thank you." I responded, relieved that there was at least one kind person in their world.

"Hey Jess, can you do something about Stevie's attire?" Cyrus asked, giving me a once over, "She doesn't quite fit the dress code."

I hated the embarrassment that flamed my cheeks. Out of the five of us, I was the only person in the room not dripped head to toe in expensive designer clothes and for the first time in my life; I gave a fuck about what that said about me.

"Of course." She nodded, slipping her hand into mine. "Come with me, Love."

I glanced at the guys, unsure if I should go. Then immediately cursed myself for looking to those assholes for permission. They may have bartered to have me in their home, but they didn't own my thoughts or my body.

"THAT LOOKS GREAT." Jessie said encouragingly as she squeezed my shoulders and looked at my reflection in the mirror.

As I stared into the reflective glass, I barely recognized the girl staring back at me. The dress was a short, silky number in all black. It hugged every curve of my body, accentuating my hourglass figure and thick thighs. When the light reflected on the material, it almost looked like a dark pool of water rippling across my body. The outfit was sex incarnate, and it made the Halloween corset I tried to pass off as sexy, look cheap and comical.

The shoes she gave me were just as beautiful. Strappy black heels encrusted with little silver spikes on the straps. The ensemble was definitely different from my usual wardrobe, but I somehow still felt like myself.

"Jessie, I don't know how I'm ever going to pay you back for these things."

"Girl, don't worry about it. Your guys are taking care of everything." She said with a wink.

"They aren't my guys." I said, shaking my head.

"It doesn't seem that way." She said, giving me a pointed look. "They've never brought a woman here before."

I didn't respond as I eyed myself in the mirror one last time and let the weight of her words sink in. I didn't have the heart to tell her that the only reason they were so protective over me was because, for all intents and purposes, they owned me.

I didn't give a fuck about their reputation, but I didn't want Jessie to feel sorry for me. After getting to know each other, Jessie felt like a friend. She grew up in Caspian Valley, like me, and she understood how out of my element I was.

"Come on, you look fab. They're literally going to be eating out of the palm of your hand."

That made a small smile appear. Maybe I could find a way out of this. A man's greatest weakness was his cock. If I could get The Reapers to think with theirs, I might stand a chance of getting out of here in one piece.

After finishing up my makeup, Jessie led me straight to the bar for a drink. I leaned against the cool granite countertop and fought the urge to search for the guys in the crowd. Something about her words struck a nerve with me. I wanted to see what kind of reaction my new wardrobe would elicit from them.

As Jessie began collecting the ingredients to make me one of her signature Hellhound cocktails, my eyes wandered around the crowded room in search of The Reapers.

Scanning the crowd of people swaying to the music, my eyes caught on a light streaming in from the front entrance. A figure appeared in the light, and I had to do a double take to make sure my eyes weren't deceiving me. *What the hell was DC doing here?*

I don't know why it surprised me. This place with its classy suede furniture and extravagant cocktails seemed like a place someone like DC would love. I just never expected to see someone from my old life in this new world.

If he knew what happened to me, knew what kind of

danger I was in, surely he'd step in and save me from these assholes. We never spoke about what he did for a living, but he seemed like a guy that had connections in high places.

I broke away from the bar and pushed into the crowd, trying to move towards him. Body after body banged into me, but I couldn't stop now. The asshole Reapers had probably seen me leave Jessie's side, and if I turned back now, they'd be waiting for me and I'd miss my one shot at escaping.

DC looked as stoic as ever as his eyes searched through the crowd. He hadn't seen me, that much was obvious because he made no move to step towards me. As I pushed my way through the crowd, a window opened, finally giving me a better look at him.

Relief swelled in my chest. I would tell him everything and maybe he could help me get out of here and get back to Alex. I'd run forever if I had to, but I couldn't risk being stuck with them for good. DC was my way out.

The moment a slim blonde woman stopped in front of him and wrapped her slender arms around his torso, my heart sunk. DC pulled her in for a kiss on the cheek and whispered something in her ear before grabbing her hand and rushing her to the other side of the room. I stood there in shock, unable to move or think as dancing body after dancing body bumped into me.

I felt a small hand grip my wrist and physically yank me away from the dance floor. I knew I should have moved my legs and helped whoever it was get me out of there, but all I could focus on was the feeling of my heart shattering. *He had a fucking girlfriend.*

"Are you okay?" Jessie asked, a look of concern furrowing her brows.

"I'm fine." I responded, trying to hold back the tears welling in my eyes.

"What happened? Why were you staring at him like that?"

"Nothing." I said, shaking my head. "It's stupid."

"It's okay babe," she said, squeezing my hand, "don't take it personally. Out of all of them, Atlas is the one who cares the most about appearances. He may want to fuck a girl that comes from our side of town, but he'll never love someone without status."

"A-Atlas?"

"Yeah, I saw you staring at him and Melanie Diaz."

I stared at her, unmoving. *Atlas. DC was Atlas.*

"The engagement news is all anyone can talk about. Let me guess, you guys were fucking around?"

"Something like that." I bit out, my eyes looking everywhere but at hers as deep shame flamed my cheeks.

"You're better off without him. Don't waste your heart on him or any of his brothers. I don't know how your paths ended up crossing but trust me, they may be a good fuck, but none of them would ever settle down with a girl like us."

"Thanks." I said, faking a smile I didn't feel for the new friend that just ripped my heart apart.

The need to cry barreled through me, but I fought against it and followed Jessie back towards the bar. This was all too much to handle. DC was Atlas. Not only was Atlas the fucking leader of The Reapers and therefore the man that negotiated buying my sister, but he had been visiting me almost every night with a fucking girlfriend, I'm sorry a *fiancée* .

I hated him. Hated everything about him and all the lies he

let me believe for the last two years. He wasn't a hero; he was a villain, and he was going to regret ever playing with my life.

He and his brothers wanted to own me? Well, I would make sure that they would regret the day they ever agreed to Malcolm's arrangement. No one could ever own me, and The Reapers were about to find out just how broken their little toy was.

FOURTEEN

Fuck.

I didn't want to come tonight, but when I got the text from Ezra, I knew an appearance was well overdue. I hadn't been to Hell's Tavern in over a week and no matter how loyal our men seemed, deep down every single one of them was waiting for an opportunity to overthrow their kings. Hell's Tavern was their playground and the one place our most 'trusted' men could rub elbows with me and my brothers.

But power is volatile. One minute you can have a surplus

of it and a split second later, it can get swiped out from underneath you. My job was to make sure we sustained ours, by any means necessary. Unfortunately for me, my latest 'means' popped up at the worst possible time.

"What the fuck are you doing here?" I hissed, pulling Melanie away from the watchful eyes surrounding us.

"Oh come on baby, don't be like that." She cooed, pressing her body against mine. "We have to keep up appearances of being a happy, newly engaged couple."

"Enough with this shit." I said, backing away from her. "You and I both know what we agreed to."

Her face twitched at my words. Mel hated being told no, only slightly more than she hated being embarrassed. Why she continued to throw herself at me was still a mystery. I shut down her advancements every chance I got and made it a point to avoid touching her, never wanting to confuse her about what our situation was.

"You'll learn to love me." She said, trying to grab for my cock through my trousers. "Just stop fucking fighting it."

"Let's get some things straight." I hissed, grasping her jaw as I pushed her away from me. "We will have a loveless marriage. You will keep your fucking hands off of me and in exchange I will turn a blind eye to the lovers you bring into your bed, in your own home, that will be far the fuck away from mine. You will fuck the pool guy, or your tennis instructor, or whoever the fuck else tickles your fancy, Mel. This isn't a test or a ploy to win your heart. Trust me, I don't want it. We have an arrangement, nothing more. You show up here again, uninvited, and the truce between our families is off, do I make myself clear?"

"Yes." She said, visibly swallowing with a stiff nod.

"Great." I snapped, offering her a toothy grin. "Now get the fuck out of my club before I have security escort you out."

She turned around on her stiletto heels with a huff and clicked her way back towards the girlfriend she left dancing in the crowd.

Pressing my thumb into my temple, I tried to massage away the headache her high-pitched voice induced. How was I supposed to get married to this woman, when I couldn't even stand to be around her for more than a few seconds?

Making my way towards our VIP lounge in the back of the club, my mood instantly perked up when I saw my brothers. They were the only reason I was doing this shit with Melanie to begin with. Agreeing to marry her meant that The Diaz Cartel would never touch them or any of our men. If the price for their safety was my fucking sanity, so be it.

"Hey asshole, where've you been?" Cyrus asked, moving over to make room for me on the blue velvet couch.

"Out." I responded, relaxing into the plush seat.

They didn't need to know that I'd spent the last twenty fours digging up everything I could on a girl they knew nothing about.

For the last couple of years, Stevie has been my forbidden fruit. Something I could look at, talk to, hell, even occasionally fantasize about, but something I could never have. She was a good girl, pure and innocent, and I was already in talks to marry a woman I hated.

I should've walked out of that coffee shop and never looked back. If I was thinking with my head instead of my dick, I probably would have. But just being around Stevie was intoxicating. She was why I came back to Cafe Au Lait almost every night. It definitely wasn't for the twenty-minute drive or the shit coffee they served.

The careful veneer I always wore around her shattered the minute I saw the bruise on her face the other night. I kept her far away from my world for a reason and it pissed me off that even in her own world, someone was hurting her. My world was dangerous, and if people had the slightest cue that she was important to me, her life would be in jeopardy.

Everyone, including my little brothers, assumed Melanie was important to me, but our relationship was all an act. Mel knew I didn't care for her in that way. I'd told her from the beginning what this was, she just refused to accept it. The problem with Mel was that she wasn't used to hearing the word no. Her daddy got her everything she ever wanted and for whatever reason, what she wanted most these days, was me.

As Robert Diaz's only baby girl left, she's had a target on her back pretty much since birth. Most people avoided her like the plague. Everyone knew that if you even so much as misplaced a hair on Melanie's head, The Diaz Cartel would start an all out war to avenge her. She was Robert's weakness and after two sleepless nights, apparently Stevie was mine.

She had infiltrated my thoughts so much that I'd swore I'd seen her in the crowd of people dancing earlier. I needed to crash, badly. But staying for an hour or two to appease my little brothers wouldn't kill me. Keeping up appearances in front of our crews was a non-negotiable. Besides, Stevie was closing at Cafe Au lait tonight and staying longer would give me an excuse to swing by and check in on her later.

As I leaned into my seat, I looked up at my brothers and noticed that their eyes were all pointed in the same direction.

"What are you dickheads looking at?" I asked, my curiosity perking up my senses.

"Our new pet." Ezra mumbled, with his eyes staring daggers towards the bar.

Shit, I had been so caught up with thoughts of Stevie and finding out what happened; I had completely forgotten about the girl. I wanted nothing to do with her, but who was I to stop my baby brothers from having a little fun and reaping some benefits of our business.

Following their gaze, my eyes froze on the familiar silhouette I dreamt about almost every night. *Was I hallucinating again?* She was leaning against the bar, looking very fucking real, and pounding back a Hellhound, Jessie's signature cocktail of vodka, grapefruit juice, and grenadine. By the looks of it, she'd already thrown back at least four and her movements were becoming a little sloppy.

Shooting out of my seat, I reached the bar within five long strides and latched onto her arm without thinking.

"Ouch! What the fuck?" She screamed, pulling her arm away and causing every eye in the room to stare at us.

I gave her a blank stare, hyper aware of the audience surrounding us. My expression was completely void of the emotions that were warring inside of my head. It wasn't safe for her to be here. But before I could do anything about it, I needed to get the curious eyes off of us.

"My apologies," I said, loud enough for everyone to hear, "I thought you were someone else. Here, let me buy you a drink."

She gave me an icy glare as I took the empty seat next to her.

"What are you doing here?" I hissed, slowly losing the little control I had left.

I kept my eyes locked on the bartenders as I waited for an answer. We didn't need anymore attention directed our way.

"Wow." She mumbled, turning her body back towards the new bartender that still hadn't made himself scarce.

Jessie obviously hadn't given him the rundown of who his new bosses were. If she had, he'd know to stay far the fuck away from my conversations. Yet there he stood, like an overeager puppy dying for attention.

Anger boiled beneath my skin as I watched him hand her a fresh cocktail that she didn't fucking need. Stevie placed her hand on his, thanking him for the drink, and the stupid blonde pretty-boy motherfucker actually smiled at her.

"Are you going to answer me?" I asked, painfully gritting my teeth. I needed to get her out of here. The lack of sleep was affecting my control, and I was one wrong move from blowing the fuck up and putting her in even more danger.

"Atlas," she said cooly, "you can stop pretending. I've heard everything there is to know about you and your brothers."

She used my actual name and the realization of what she must have heard hit me. *Fuck.* I should have corrected her two years ago when she started calling me DC, but a part of me enjoyed the anonymity of it and I liked our inside joke.

"Let's go." I said, readying myself to pull out her chair.

"No," she hissed under her breath, "I still have my freewill."

What the fuck was she talking about?

"Jacob," she called out after downing the rest of her drink

126

in one gulp, "another one pretty please." She said, flashing him an obnoxious grin.

He was obviously not the smartest tool in the shed. The pretty boy began making her another drink, completely oblivious to the tension mounting between her and I. At least we'd never have to worry about the poor fuck eavesdropping. He was dumber than dirt.

"Jason," I called out, waving him towards us. "If you serve her another drink," I hissed, "I will cut off your balls and serve them as olives in your fucking martini. Understand?"

"It's Jacob." He mumbled under his breath before finally finding some fucking common sense and moving towards the other end of the bar.

"You know, you're being a real ass, DC." Stevie huffed, piercing her eyes at me.

"It's Atlas." I spat through gritted teeth as I pulled her closer. "Now what the hell are you talking about?"

"Please don't act like you're innocent in all of this." She said, shaking her head at me, "Let me guess, your brothers made the deal with Malcolm? You had nothing to do with it, right?" She asked, her tone doused in sarcasm.

Malcolm? Why did the name sound so familiar?

Shit. *The girl.* Malcolm's girl.

"Get up. Now." I ordered, pulling her out of her seat.

This was a mistake. I could fix it and get her ass out of here, but she needed to stop drawing attention to us. The surrounding hyenas would forget about her if she didn't give them anything to remember.

She shook out of my grip and jerked her body away in a flash.

"Where do you think you're going?" I hissed, latching onto her elbow to stop her retreating footsteps.

"Away from you." She spat, just as the song changed, causing every eye in the room to stare.

Fuck.

FIFTEEN

Stevie

Fuck DC.

Fuck Atlas. Fuck whatever he wanted to refer to himself as and fuck his piece of shit brothers who brought me here. I could've stayed blissfully unaware of who DC really was, but now I had to face the cold, hard truth. The DC I knew was dead, and in his place was Atlas, a man that stood for every single thing I hated.

I mean, who the hell did he think he was? Grabbing me

like I belonged to him? Last time I checked, he had a fucking fiancée to worry about. *Asshole.*

And what was his problem with the bartender? Sure, Jacob was a little extra friendly, but who cares? He was falling for my flirty drunken damsel act and I didn't owe DC, err, Atlas, an explanation for my behavior.

For someone so obsessed with what I was doing, he completely missed the reason I flirted with Jacob to begin with. Being a drunk, flirty girl was the easiest way to get someone's guard down. When I held Jacob's arm to thank him for the last drink, my other hand slipped into his back pocket and plucked out his iPhone. Of course Atlas was too preoccupied with trying to control me to notice.

I wasn't stupid enough to steal it. Jacob would eventually put two and two together if the phone stayed missing. My plan was to borrow it and give it back, with everyone none-the-wiser. Of course, Atlas had to come in and ruin everything. Now Jacob was on edge, and he'd probably stay far away from me for his own preservation. It made it harder, but not impossible. I just needed to do it quickly.

Barreling for an empty restroom stall, I slipped Jacob's phone from my pocket and punched in Alex's number, praying she wasn't already asleep.

"Hello?" She answered, the sound of her voice bringing a wave of relief.

Thank god she was okay.

"Hello?" She continued. "Is anyone there?"

Shit. I had been so relieved to hear her talk that I had completely forgotten to say something.

"Hey, Al." I croaked, doing a shit job of reigning in my emotions.

"Stevie! Is that you? Dude, I've been trying to call you and text you for the last two nights. Where are you? Are you okay? What happened?"

"Yes, it's me." I said, laughing while holding back the tears that threatened to fall, "I'm okay. I'm safe. They confiscated my phone, so I had to borrow someone else's to call you."

"Stevie, I-"

"Listen, I don't have a lot of time to talk." I said, cutting her off. "I just wanted to say that I love you and that you need to get out of town."

"Wait, what?" She asked, "What do you mean?"

Fuck. I couldn't tell her about how Malcolm had fucking lied to both of us. She'd probably try something stupid to help me escape and end up getting herself caught up in the mess. I released a shaky breath before continuing, knowing another lie was going to spill from my lips.

"I'll get out of here, but Malcolm's debt is huge and it might take longer than we expected to pay it off. As soon as school is out, I need you to move somewhere far away. I will find you when I get out of here, but Caspian isn't safe for you anymore."

"No, what? I'm not leaving you! I can't! I-"

"You have to." I urged. "I need to know you're safe."

I could hear her breathing change and I knew she was on the precipice of crying. I wanted to comfort her, to tell her that everything would be okay, but impending footsteps sounded at the entrance of the bathroom and I knew my time was up.

"Alex, I have to go." I whispered, hating that I was rushing her. "Just promise you'll leave town."

"Okay." Alex mumbled, finding her voice. "Okay, I promise."

"We'll see each other soon, I swear." I whispered, not wanting to leave the call, yet knowing it was time. "Love you little sis."

"Love you too big sis." She sniffled.

I quickly hung up the phone and choked back the emotions trying to surface. If the guys were the ones barging into the restroom, the last thing I was going to do was let them know that there was someone out there who I truly cared about. I didn't want them to use Alex against me like Malcolm always had.

"God, what is Atlas' problem?" Chirped a feminine voice entering the bathroom.

"Girl, I don't know." Said another woman. "Did you see the girl he was all over at the bar."

"Of course I did," she deadpanned, "what about her?"

"Well, for one, she was fucking gorgeous."

"No. She wasn't." The other woman said, cutting her friend off. "She was just some desperate whore. She'll capture his interest for a few hours, but The Reapers don't fuck with trash."

I tried to hold myself back as I paced back and forth in my bathroom stall. I was fuming. How dare she call me trash? She didn't even know me. My emotions were already at an all-time high after my call with Alex, and these two bitter bitches were about to send me over the edge.

Rage seeped into my bones, and I welcomed him with open arms. It had been years since I'd been in a fight and after my mandated anger management courses; I thought that fighting was beneath me, but suddenly beating both of their asses didn't sound so bad.

Storming out of the stall with my fist clenched and my body trembling, I stomped towards the two women. The minute I saw who it was, my rage dissipated like it was never there. It was Melanie, the woman I saw with Atlas earlier. She was standing in front of the mirror with a red-headed woman I had never seen before.

"Speaking of garbage," Melanie said, staring at my reflection in the mirror as she flashed her friend a wicked grin, "look who it is."

I let her bold insult slide. Melanie had every right to be angry with me. Whether or not she knew it, I'd been flirting with her fiancé for the last two years, thinking it was going to lead somewhere. Maybe letting her take it out on me could be my form of penance.

"Listen," I started, trying to clear the air, "This is all just a big misunderstanding and I-"

"No," she cut me off, "you don't get the privilege of speaking to us. You may entertain him at the moment, but you don't belong in our world and no amount of designer clothing is going to disguise the fact that you are beneath us. If you weren't, we would already know who you were, so trust me sweetie. I'm not threatened."

Anger swelled within me and it took everything I had not to punch her in her smug, filler-injected face. I turned on my heels and headed for the exit, desperate to escape before my temper got the best of me. She wasn't worth it, and neither was he.

"Congratulations, by the way." I bit out, lingering at the door. "You and Atlas really deserve each other."

"We do, don't we?" She said, smiling to herself as she applied more pink lip gloss to her overly plumped lips.

I wanted to come back with another dig, but I felt the sincerity in her words. They were perfect for each other and she may be a bitch, but she was right. I didn't belong in their world.

SIXTEEN

"EVERYTHING GOOD, MAN?" TRISTAN ASKED, HIS EYES shifting towards the restroom.

Everything was not good. Everything could not be further from fucking good if it tried. I wanted to punch a wall and flip every fucking table in my vicinity. *What the hell was this? Some kind of sick joke?*

Waring against my instincts to burn the entire place down, I appeased his concern with a nod. He didn't realize how fucked the entire situation was. None of my brothers did, and

I planned on keeping it that way. It wasn't their fault that my dumb ass got attached to a girl I had no business obsessing over. She'd been off limits from the start, but I defied fate and I couldn't shake the feeling that her being sold to us was my own karmic punishment.

The moment Stevie stepped out of the restroom, every single eye in the building was on her. She was oblivious to the attention, as usual. It was one thing that continued to fascinate me about her. She was striking, absolutely fucking gorgeous, but in the time I'd known her, she never relied on her looks. Never used it as an excuse to be cruel or to get her way.

At the coffee shop, I'd seen a few men crash and burn, trying their best to pick up the sexy barista. She'd always be nice enough and at least pretend to listen as they'd drone on and on, but the minute I'd step through the door, her eyes would light up and she'd quickly excuse herself to greet me.

Maybe I was a selfish asshole, but it made me feel fucking good to know that she was solely focused on me. That I was the man that received her undivided attention and made her eyes light up like that.

I didn't want to let go of that feeling. Maybe that's why I kept her from the truth. But my lies had fucked everything up and suddenly I was the poor fuck, swallowing my pride as I watched her make her way towards pretty-boy Jacob. He looked at her body up and down like she was a glass of water and he hadn't drunk in days. My nostrils flared. *The mother-fucker better enjoy the view while it lasts because that is the last time he's ever going to see Stevie.*

Envy wasn't a palatable emotion. Even if I knew he was harmless, Stevie didn't realize the effect she had on people. The particular getup she had on made her look like a walking advertisement for sin, and every fucker in the vicinity was lining up to join her in hell. Her luscious curves were on full display in the tight black dress she wore, and I had to stop myself from wanting to rip out the eyes of each and every man in the room.

I looked back at my brothers and watched as the three of them stared at her just as hungrily. They saw it too. *The light.* The thing that made her different from anyone we'd ever met before and the one thing sinning motherfuckers like us couldn't resist.

"Tris, get the girl and get her the fuck out of here." I seethed, making my way towards the back entrance. "Who's bright idea was it to bring her here in the first place?"

In unison, the twins tilted their head towards Ezra.

"Of course it fucking was."

SEVENTEEN

Stevie

MELANIE'S WORDS STUNG. IT SHOULDN'T HAVE BOTHERED ME, but as I stepped towards the bar, her words were all I could think about. Sure, I was angry at her for being such an awful bitch, but I couldn't even fault her. There was truth in her words.

I was beneath Atlas and his brothers, and whatever fascination they had with me now was only temporary. It should've made me happy to know that they'd eventually grow tired of me. It meant my freedom was tangible, but all I felt was unease. I didn't want to be a fleeting fascination; I wanted to be worthy.

The emotions I always suppressed were suddenly clawing their way towards the surface and it terrified me. The Reapers made me feel... everything.

"Listen, are you in some kind of trouble?" Jacob asked, pulling me away from my thoughts.

I had been so stuck in my head; I did even see his approach.

When I didn't immediately give him an answer, he stepped out from behind the bar and walked towards me, gently resting his hands on my shoulders.

"If you are, you can tell me." He said, leveling his kind blue eyes with mine.

Jacob was nice. Handsome, too. The kind of guy that should be able to make me feel something. But all my mind could focus on was The Reapers.

"What makes you say that?" I asked with a smile I didn't feel.

"Well, for starters, that guy over there looks like he wants to murder you." He said, glancing behind me.

I followed his gaze and saw Tristan standing a few feet away from us. The flashing lights of the club reflected off of his deep emerald irises as he peered at me through his thick dark lashes.

"He's a friend." I mumbled, never taking my eyes off of Tristan.

"Well, what about the guy from earlier?" Jacob challenged.

Jacob was being awfully inquisitive for someone working

belly deep in a club full of criminals. I could tell from the look on Tristan's face that he didn't like that Jacob still had his hands on me and I was starting not to like it either. He was nice, but in that, "I'm a nice guy so I deserve to fuck you," kind of way.

"He's a friend too." I said dismissively. "Just overly protective."

"Look," he said, painfully jostling my shoulders, "there's an emergency escape in the handicap stall of the women's bathroom. I can get you out-"

"I'm fine." I said, cutting off his words and shaking out of his hold. "Thank you for being cool earlier, but don't worry about me."

I pulled him in for a hug, seizing the opportunity to slip his iPhone back into his pocket. Thankfully, he accepted what I offered with no more protests. He had no clue how close he just came to death. If there was one thing I learned about The Reapers, it was that they didn't take kindly to others touching what was theirs.

"Fucking slut." Melanie coughed, jabbing her bony elbow into my back and sending me stumbling forward.

Jacob helped me regain my balance as I shot Melanie a venomous look. I tried to play nice, but enough was enough. If I continued to let her walk all over me, the harassment wouldn't stop, it would only get worse. It was the same way for me in high school. Girls like her wouldn't stop until they learned their lesson, and Melanie Diaz was overdue for a course on manners.

"How funny," I said, with a smirk on my face, "that's what Atlas growled into my ear last night."

The entire room fell silent as all eyes turned towards

Melanie, waiting to see her reaction. Her toothy smile faded into a grimace as blood rushed to her hollow cheeks.

"He loves his dirty talk." I hissed, never taking my eyes off of her. "But, I'm sure you know that."

Her lip twitched. It was a tiny give, but it let me know I had hit a nerve.

"Don't fuck with me." I whispered, low enough so only she could hear. "Only one of us has a reputation to maintain and I like to fight *very* dirty. Just ask your fiancé."

It was a low blow. Insinuating that I was sleeping with Atlas was fucked-up on so many levels. Truth was, he'd never even laid a hand on me since that first night we met. He always kept himself at a careful distance, almost as if he were afraid to get too close. But I saw a weakness, and I ran with it.

"You fucking bitch!" She hissed, rearing her fist back to hit me.

I closed my eyes and smiled, bracing myself for the pain. I knew what I was getting into the moment I opened my mouth, but feeling her wrath was worth it if it meant she no longer saw me as an easy target. I was done being stepped on.

The air shifted, and the sound of skin against skin echoed in the air. I preemptively winced, but when I felt nothing, I opened my eyes to find broad shoulders blocking my view. Somehow Tristan had stepped in between us with lightning fast reflexes and was acting as my very own human shield.

"D-don't fucking touch her." He hissed, still holding onto her wrist with white knuckles.

"Let go of me." Melanie spat, cursing as she shook out of his hold. "This is between me and that bitch."

Tristan settled into his position, refusing to move an inch.

"You know what, forget it." She laughed, rubbing her

injured hand. "There's no use trying to talk sense in to a stupid fucking fr-fr-freak."

Rage licked across my skin as I watched Tristan bolt and storm out of the club. I didn't realize he had a speech impediment, I just assumed he didn't enjoy talking to me.

I set my eyes on Melanie, who was still nursing her wounded ego. She could fuck with me all she wanted, but I would not let her get away with treating Tristan like that. He was only trying to protect me and he may not want to hit a woman in good conscience, but I sure the fuck would.

"Kenzie!" She spat, waving her little lackey over. "Let's go."

"No. Fuck that." I hissed, getting into her face. "You'll talk shit to a man you know will never hit you. What about me?"

"What about you?" She scoffed, looking down her nose at me.

"You wanted to hit me a few seconds ago." I goaded. "Do it."

"No." She said, her eyes darting around the room at the crowd who was still hungry for action.

"Oh, come on. Should we call Atlas over to help jog your memory?"

"Fuck you!" She spat, chucking a sloppy punch to my mouth.

Melanie Diaz hit like a bitch. I tasted the blood in my mouth before I felt the sting. I wanted to laugh, I'd been hit harder than that most of my life. This fight was about to get very fucking interesting.

I gripped her hair with my left hand and even though she

was bigger than me; I gained leverage as I pulled her to the ground and climbed on top of her.

Fighting Melanie was cathartic. With each punch, all the emotions swirling within me released. Melanie tried to claw and scratch at my face, but she didn't have shit on the moves I had to learn to survive the mean girls at my high school. She was a prissy princess, and it showed.

She tried to push me off of her, kicking and bucking like an angry bull, but her attempts were futile. I wrapped my thighs around her like a vise, and the only way she was escaping is if I decided she could.

It was obvious Melanie was used to having other people fight her battles for her. Her eyes kept searching the crowd for someone to come to her rescue. She acted as if she were the queen of the fucking universe, yet even her loyal subjects weren't coming to her aid; The redhead was missing in action and I smiled at the irony. I was defending a man that I was sure hated me while Melanie's fake friend stood idly by, watching her get her ass beat.

Warm blood trickled from my lips as I hovered above her, smiling like a maniac. Her lashes fluttered as the coppery substance began raining down on her, and she screamed, struggling to escape even more.

I stopped my assault to stare at the crimson drops as they splattered across her face. Watching them fall was hypnotic. I understood why Ezra loved his "art" so much. It was fascinating to see the evidence of your madness and depravity spilled out on a canvas.

A laugh spilled from my lips and once it started, there was no stopping it. I had just gotten into a fight over a man that hadn't said two words to me and I was now finding common

148

ground to the most certifiably insane of them all. *What the fuck was wrong with me?*

Strong hands gripped tightly around my waist and I felt myself being pried off of her. Atlas handed me to Ezra as he moved to help Melanie up. I stared down at my knuckles and saw they were raw with fresh blood seeping out of them. How long had I been on top of her? It felt like seconds, but could've just as easily been a few minutes.

My eyes darted to the devastation I left behind. Melanie's face was coated in blood, though most of it was mine. She had a split lip and I could see a black eye already forming. I winced at my destruction. The violence. The all-consuming rage. It wasn't like me at all. *Who was that back there?*

"You're dead, bitch." Melanie hissed as the redhead moved to grab her, and Atlas carried me away. "Fucking dead."

It was the second time that night I felt her words ring true. A little part of me died the moment I stepped into their world, and it had only been a couple of days. How long would it take before I stopped recognizing myself all together?

EIGHTEEN

Ten minutes into the drive and neither of us had spoken a word. I didn't know what to say to her. I was too fucking enraged to speak.

"Are you going to say anything?" Stevie asked, staring at me from the passenger seat as she iced her swollen lip.

"No." I responded dryly, cracking my neck as I stared at the winding road ahead.

Saying anything would be a mistake. Too many thoughts

were circling in my head. And I was already a ticking time bomb before the stupid fucking catfight.

"Shocking. Atlas Cole, ever the fucking mystery man."

I ignored the jab as silence filled the car.

"She had it coming, you know." She noted, staring out the window.

I clenched my jaw on an exhale. It wasn't a good time to talk, but Stevie wouldn't let the conversation go.

"Really." I deadpanned, glaring at the road ahead that guaranteed at least another ten miles of discussion.

"Did you even hear what she said to Tristan?" She grumbled, crossing her arms over her chest like a bratty child.

No. I hadn't. Seconds before the fight, Cyrus and I had stepped outside for a cigarette while I tried to talk myself down from killing Jessie's new bartender. When I saw Tristan burst out of the back entrance, I knew that whatever went down couldn't have been good. After sending Cyrus to go after his twin, I rushed back inside to find Stevie pummeling Melanie and Ezra watching with sick fascination. But I saw everything I needed to.

"Doesn't matter what she said." I retorted, drumming my thumbs against the steering wheel.

"Why?" She challenged, locking her eyes on me.

"Drop it, Stevie." I snapped. "You don't know shit about this world."

"Yeah, and whose fault is that?" She mumbled, uncrossing her arms as she stared out the passenger window.

She wasn't wrong. I had years to tell her, but I never did. Truth was, I wanted her at a distance as much as I wanted her in my space. I was a selfish bastard, walking the line between two worlds. Karma was a bitch, and she forced my worlds to collide.

"You have impeccable taste by the way," she said, giving me a smile I knew she didn't feel, "congrats on the engagement."

That did it. All of my control shattered in an instant. I slammed on the breaks, pulling the car to a screeching halt and jerked us to the side of the road.

"What I do in my personal life is none of your goddamn business." I yelled, flinging off my seatbelt as I turned to face her.

Her movements stilled as her eyes locked on the road in front of us. The emotions I kept tightly wound were unravelling, and Stevie was witnessing firsthand what that amount of suppression can do to a man.

"I planned to let you disappear from our world," I boomed, my voice filling the small enclosed space, "but you fucked up. You let your emotions fuck with your judgement."

"Sh-she deserved it." She stammered in a voice so small, it barely registered.

"You don't get to fucking decide that!" I yelled, slamming my fist against the dashboard and losing the last bits of composure I had left.

She flinched when I forcibly ran a hand through my hair, disheveling the strands I typically kept in perfect order. My eyes darted towards her and I immediately recognized the tension in her body and the fear brimming in her eyes. *Fuck.* I winced.

Who the fuck hurt you, beautiful girl?

Taking a deep breath, I calmed myself down before continuing.

"There will be consequences for this and we can't protect you in your world." I said, gently grabbing her chin to force her to lock eyes with me. "You fought the princess of The Diaz Cartel, do you have any idea what that means?"

She slowly shook her head in response as her lower lip trembled, the realization of her mistake finally sinking in.

"The only way to protect you now, is to keep you. You can't go back to your old life. Not now. Not ever."

NINETEEN

AFTER WE GOT BACK TO THE HOUSE, I PUSHED ALL THOUGHTS of the stupid fight with Melanie into the back of my mind. I didn't want to think about the ramifications of my actions or the clear warning in Atlas' tone. It was too late to do anything about it, anyway.

I got into my bedroom, kicked off my heels, changed into my oversized cream sweatshirt, and crawled underneath my sheets. Everything was happening so fast and I needed time to process.

I had just closed my eyes when commotion exploded outside of my bedroom door. I ran for my door and opened it just a crack so I could see what was going on.

It was Cyrus and Tristan. They were walking up the stairs with Tristan storming down the hall and Cyrus chasing after him.

"At least let me look at it." Cyrus said, trying to grab for Tristan's bloody and raw hand.

"For the last time," Tristan spat, yanking his hand away, "I d… don't need anyone's fucking pity."

Their voices were so similar that if I wasn't watching them, it would've been nearly impossible to tell them apart. Besides the speech impediment, there was one distinguishing factor I picked up on while they spoke. While Cyrus' voice was velvety smooth, Tristan's voice had a slightly gravelly quality to it, probably from years of being silent.

"You made that fucking clear with the dude you almost killed back there." Cyrus hissed, cutting his eyes at his twin.

I held my breath. *Tristan had almost killed someone?*

"Asshole had it coming." Tristan growled, baring his teeth. "He should've minded his own fucking b… business."

"He was drunk." Cyrus deadpanned, pressing his lips firmly together. "Any other night, you would've ignored him. What the fuck happened to you?"

Tristan met Cyrus' question with silence, and even though he didn't say a word, I knew what the answer was.

I happened. I opened my stupid fucking mouth and picked a fight with someone I shouldn't have. I forced Tristan to step in and I was the reason he was taking out his aggression on some poor drunk asshole. It was all my fault.

"Leave me the f... fuck alone." Tristan snarled, stepping away from Cyrus and towards his bedroom.

"Fine," Cyrus sighed with a sad smile, "I'll drop it. But eventually you're going to have to talk. Otherwise, whatever's going on with you will end up eating you alive."

Seeing Cyrus turn to leave, I quietly shut my door before either of them saw me. Leaning my head back against the door, I let out an exacerbated breath as the guilt gnawed away at my gut.

What the fuck was wrong with me? I shouldn't be feeling guilty over any of this. They were bad people who did bad things. What they did on their own time was none of my business. *Right?*

A loud bang on my door made me nearly jump out of my skin.

"Next time you want to s... spy, Pet," Tristan snarled behind my closed door, "try to be more coy about it."

⁂

No MATTER how hard I tried, my body couldn't fall asleep. I knew what was really bothering me, even if I didn't want to admit it to myself. Throwing off my covers, I shuffled out of bed and headed to the door of the man who had been haunting me all night.

"Tristan?" I murmured, gently knocking as I pressed my ear to his door.

He didn't answer, but I swore I could hear him tossing and turning in his bed. Rest was probably evading him too. I slid

159

my body down to the floor and planted my back against his door.

"It's okay if you don't want to talk." I sighed, chewing my lower lip. "Maybe it'll actually be better this way."

I wanted to apologize to him, but I didn't even know where to start. How could I possibly explain why I did what I did when the violence that erupted out of me had very little to do with Melanie and everything to do with my fucked up life? So, I started from the beginning.

"When I was a little girl," I whispered, looking out into the dark hallway, "I was obsessed with fairy tales, Snow White being my favorite. The whole prince charming thing went completely over my head as a kid. In my mind, he was just there to help break the curse, but it was Snow who had to defeat the evil witch." I paused, taking a shaky breath and trying to find the right words to say next. "I idolized her, Tristan. She was so strong and so brave. She defeated her evil witch, and I was in awe of that. I had a curse too, but it was my mother who ended up being the villain in my story."

I had never shared this story with anyone before, but something in my gut begged me to continue. Maybe it was the fact that for all I knew, Tristan could be fast asleep on the other side of the door. Maybe it was because I knew that after what I did tonight, my days were numbered. Either way, the words didn't want to be contained anymore, and I was finally ready to let them break free. Wringing my hands in my lap, I continued with my story.

"It started before I could even remember. I know that seems far-fetched, but I don't remember a time when I wasn't terrified of her. When my father was still alive, she at least had the decency to hide it, but after he died and I was forced to live with her and her new family, the abuse only got worse."

"She punished me every time I felt anything. Do you know how hard it is to control your emotions as a hormonal thirteen-year-old?" I laughed, bitterly. "Even when I became a shell of a person, it still wasn't good enough to stop the hits and slaps. My mother hated everything about me. When she died..." I stumbled, trailing off. "When she died, I thought the abuse would stop, but Malcolm quickly filled those shoes only he hit harder and as you already know, my dear old step dad was how I ended up here."

"The shit with Melanie was about so much more than a few cheap shots. It was about me finally sticking up for myself after years of being stepped on. I was trying to break my curse." I sighed, blinking back the tears welling in my eyes. "And I'm so sorry you got pulled into it."

TWENTY

Tristan

W͟HY THE FUCK WAS SHE STILL HERE? G͟IVING ME SOME SOB story about her fucked up childhood, to what end? So we can trade horror stories about the shit we went through as kids? So we can be fucking best friends and share our deepest, darkest secrets?

Pulling the door open, I watched her body fall back at the sudden loss of support. I latched onto the collar of her sweat-shirt, inches before her head crashed to the ground, and lifted her to her feet. She quickly wiped the tears from her glossy eyes and looked up at me expectantly. Like I was the one who was supposed to come in and make it all better.

"Go back to your fucking room." I ordered, blocking her from moving any further.

"No." She whispered, jutting her chin out with defiance.

She was as stubborn as a fucking mule. She wanted somebody to lick her wounds and make her feel better. But I would never be that man.

"What do you want, huh?" I asked, looming over her. "S... sympathy?" I hissed, inhaling her intoxicating scent. "I'm a beast in every sense of the word. I can't give you gentle or s... sweet."

"Maybe I don't want you to be sweet." She challenged, pushing her curvy little body against mine to get in my face. "Maybe I don't want anything from you."

The intimidation tactics she was trying were laughable considering her glossy eyes and shaky voice were dead giveaways of her fear.

"Bullshit." I said, sniffing the air for emphasis. "I know a lie when I smell one. You want s... something. You're just too afraid to fucking admit it."

She trembled beneath me and fuck if that didn't bring out my beast.

"I'm not afraid of you." She stammered, her breath leaving her in a rush as loomed over her.

"Is this what you want?" I growled, hiking her sweatshirt up and grabbing a fistful of her curvy ass.

Her body went stiff as I squeezed the soft flesh.

"What about this?" I asked, pushing her out into the hallway and pressing her body roughly against a wall.

She still didn't give me an answer. Poor girl was shocked into silence.

I slipped my hand down her ass, hooking my finger under her white thong, and gently slid it to the side. I took my time, giving her plenty of opportunity to stop what was already starting. We were in the middle of a well-lit main hallway and at any moment one of my brothers could come through and stumble on what was happening, but she didn't make a move to stop me. My fingers explored her folds, circling and gently nudging her sensitive little bud just enough to drive her body mad with lust.

"You're so wet for me." I hissed, biting hard into the nape of her neck.

A throaty moan escaped her lips and her back arched instinctively, pressing her delicious ass against my lap. My cock painfully throbbed in my pants. I could have her. Could strip that ugly fucking sweatshirt off of her, lay her down on this floor, and feast on the fucking offering she was presenting me and she wouldn't utter a single word to stop me.

But I didn't want to take her like this. When I fucked Stevie, I wanted her to beg for it. I wanted her body to writhe against mine and to hear the need in her voice. To see the desperate plea in her eyes.

"Fuck," I chuckled darkly, releasing her from my grip, "you weren't kidding about your mommy issues, Pet."

She looked as if she wanted to cry. Maybe a different man would have felt bad about his words, but the world was cruel and it was about time she realized it. She couldn't live in her fucking fairy tale land forever.

"Get out of here." I said, nodding my head towards the door. "You had no business coming here to begin with."

"I only came to say thank you. No one has ever done that for me before."

"What," I spat with a scowl, "hurt s… someone for you? Get used to it Pet, we'll hurt anyone that crosses us."

She shook her head in response and turned away, stepping back into her room before she spoke again.

"Cared."

IF ANYONE WOULD'VE ASKED me if I thought I'd be pacing outside of some girl's room at one in the morning, I would've laughed in their fucking face. Yet here I was. Feeling like a sack of shit for being cruel to a woman I knew everything and yet nothing about. I was tormenting myself, but the sick masochist in me craved the punishment.

After she left, I laid in bed and shut my eyes. I tried to fall asleep, but no matter what I did, my mind wouldn't stop racing. I just kept thinking about what happened. The feel of her wetness gliding against my hand, her deliciously sweet scent filling my senses. I assumed she was bluffing. She didn't want me; it was just another way for her to prove her strength in a world that would eat her alive if she didn't. But I felt the heat radiating off of her body and the powerful forces flowing between us. She wanted me and I was a stubborn dickhead about it.

I tried to get her off my mind, so I grabbed my phone for an easy distraction. As soon as I unlocked the screen, I saw eight text notifications and three missed calls.

. . .

Ezra (7:47 PM): Where the fuck is everyone? Our kitten isn't playing nice.

Cyrus (7:47 PM): Looking for T. What's up?

Atlas (7:48 PM): Already OMW

Ezra (7:48 PM): Sending a video. Kittens got claws. ;)

The video's audio was shit between all the screaming and music pumping through the speakers, but the visuals were clear as day. The video showed Stevie in a blind rage, straddling Melanie as she punched her in the face over and over again. The camera zoomed in on Stevie's face just in time to catch a menacing smile form across her lips. The entire crowd continued to watch, enamored by the tiny girl with a taste for violence. If I listened hard enough, I could pick up bits and pieces of what the crowd was saying. The overall consensus was that Stevie was now the craziest bitch in Caspian Hills.

Cyrus (7:51 PM): WTF?

Atlas (7:52 PM): Got her. Heading home now. Ez, give the twins a ride.

Ezra (7:54 PM): Np

Cyrus (7:54 PM): We're down the block. T's blowing off some steam.

I'd made assumptions about Stevie that were unfair. The Malcolm shit had blindsided me. We all assumed he was her pimp, not her fucking step dad. Apologizing wasn't something I did freely, but if anyone deserved one, it was her.

"Stevie…" I called out, racking my knuckles against her door.

If she didn't answer, I wouldn't push her. I'd done enough tormenting for the night.

"What do you want, Tristan?" She asked, her voice clear as day. She couldn't sleep either.

My pulse intensified at the sound of her gentle, melodic voice. I didn't think she'd be able to decipher my voice from Cyrus' that easily. Even our own brothers had a hard time telling our voices apart, but it shouldn't have surprised me. In the little time I'd known her, Stevie proved to be observant as hell.

Pressing my forehead against the door, I ransacked my mind for what to say next.

"You fought Melanie." I mused before immediately cursed myself for making such a dumb observation. *No shit, asshole.* I had seen the video and the cuts and scrapes on her face.

"I did." She responded cooly.

"Why?" I breathed.

It was a loaded question. Stevie seemed like a smart girl and every move she made with us thus far was made with extreme caution. When I left them, their petty argument could've ended right then. Something Mel said pushed her into violence, and I needed to know what it was.

"You know why." She hesitated, "you heard what she said. She deserved it after the way she spoke to you."

"I s... see." I said, at a loss for words.

"Did you want to come in? Or..."

"No." I cut her off, more harshly than I intended.

"Oh." She murmured, her voice thick with emotion.

Fuck. I was fucking this up already, and I hadn't even told her why I came.

"My s... stutter." I stammered, grimacing to myself. "It's easier to control when I'm alone."

I could hear the sounds of her settling herself just beyond

the door, and the tightness in my chest eased. She was willing to hear me out.

"I'm s... sorry about earlier."

She'd shared shit about her ugly past and I toyed with her. Treated her like shit because of my own insecurities. Because I didn't want to believe that she actually gave a fuck.

"Okay... " she said, her voice slightly louder than a whisper, "I won't say it's okay, because it wasn't. But I understand that you probably don't trust me."

Stevie perpetually threw me off axis and whenever she was around, I tried to grasp onto the cold disposition I wore like a shield. With every gentle word she uttered, I could feel it wearing thin. She was right. I didn't trust her. I didn't trust anyone except my brothers. But she was the only girl I'd ever met that made me want to change that.

"You aren't wrong." I offered, sliding down to lean my back against the door.

"If it makes you feel any better," she added, "I don't trust you either."

I had to laugh at that admission. *Smart girl.*

"Why's that?" I grinned, closing my eyes to focus on the sound of her lyrical voice.

Because I rarely used my own, voices naturally stood out to me. As I grew older, voice analyzing was a natural progression that I sort of picked up along the way. You could tell a lot about a person by their voice. Stevie's voice was soft and sweet, but not in a weak way. There was power behind her words and it took strength to emanate that with such soft tonality.

"Because I don't know you. This is the first time you've talked to me without a threat in your tone."

She wasn't wrong. It was also the first time I didn't feel the need to fight whatever was happening between us. She offered a piece of her past; it was only fair that I offered her some of mine.

"Could I..." I winced, hating how weak it sounded. "I'm going to s... share something with you."

"Okay..." She trailed off, waiting for me to speak.

"Our parents died too." I blurted, then immediately knocked my head against the door. This sharing shit was so fucking stupid, but I couldn't stop now.

"Cy and I were s... six when it happened, Atlas was eleven, and Ezra was nine. We had no immediate family, s... so we went into the system."

I paused, debating if I should go further. Anyone armed with google and our last name could find the admission I gave her, but what I was about to share went much deeper. It was something we rarely spoke of, even to each other.

"We got s... separated when Cyrus and I got fostered. Ez got fostered a few years later while Atlas s... stayed in the group home until he was sixteen."

"At first our foster parents, Ryan and Joanne Kincaid, s... seemed like the blonde-haired, blue-eyed, all American couple. Cyrus and I, with our dark hair and perpetual frowns didn't really fit in with that image, but we agreed to try, anyway. We missed our b... brothers, b... but we thought The Kincaids were going to be the normal parents we'd always wished we had." I said, releasing a deep exhale and knowing just how wrong we were.

"It d... didn't take long for Ryan to discover my s... stutter. He was a very particular man, and he hated the attention and pity my s... stutter would draw when we were in public.

He genuinely believed he could beat the s… stutter out of me and when that didn't work, he started beating Cyrus and I for s… sport. Whenever I could, I'd force Cyrus to trade places with me s… so I could take the brunt of his abuse. I figured, my brain was fucked, anyways. What kind of damage could another couple of hits do?" I asked, laughing darkly at my ignorance.

"As it turns out, a lot. After Atlas got us the fuck out of there the minute he turned eighteen, all the doctors, therapists, and s… speech pathologists he forced me to see confirmed what we s… suspected. My s… stutter could've gone away on its own with time and therapy, b... but thanks to the s… severe brain trauma I endured at the hand of The Kincaids, all I could do now is try my best to not trigger it. Our childhoods weren't very different. Maybe our paths were d… destined to cross."

"Yeah. Maybe…" She trailed off, her voice thick with emotion. "Thank you for sharing that with me."

"Thank you for listening." I quipped, stretching as I rose to my feet.

I had enough kumbaya time to last me a lifetime. Stevie didn't sound like she hated me, and I could live with that. I turned to leave, then paused. Realizing I forgot to tell her the best part of the story.

"My s… story has a happy ending." I admitted, trying to choose my words carefully. I was going to reveal something to Stevie that no one but my brothers knew. It was pertinent information that could get us in a lot of trouble if it fell into the wrong hands, but I had an overwhelming urge to trust her. "Cyrus and I killed Ryan Kincaid the s… second we had a chance, and we've never regretted it."

"I hope you get yours one day too, Pet."

TWENTY-ONE

Ezra

3AM, THE DEVIL'S HOUR. AS I STARED AT THE CEILING FAN circling above my bed, I reflected on the night's events and smiled serenely at myself. Most of the time my brothers write off my decisions as crazy or impulsive, but everything I do has purpose. Bringing her to face the demons at Hell's Tavern was the only way to see if she really could survive in our world.

Tristan and Cyrus weren't ready to face it, but it was obvious she intrigues them. Even Atlas' behavior with her was out of character for him and he had just met her. She was affecting all of us, and I was the only one crazy enough to embrace the chaos she brought. But I needed to make sure she wasn't weak, because the last thing any of us needed was to get too attached to something that would break.

As my mind began thinking about what Stevie's presence in our lives would mean for all of us, a small sound from the room next door interrupted my thoughts.

I made my way to the wall and pressed my ear against it, hoping my thoughts and insomnia weren't fucking with me. *Nothing.*

After a few beats of silence I was on the brink of giving up, when a soft seductive moan sounded through the wall. It was a breathy sound that garnered my cock's full attention and suddenly; the night was still young. *What was my angel dreaming about?*

Each breathy moan that escaped her lips pulled my mind further away from my room and closer to hers. When just lavishing in her moans proved too much for my cock to handle, I finally gave in and let my fist slowly work out the built up tension that the naughty girl next door had caused.

Closing my eyes, I imagined her perfect lips wrapping around my rigid cock. Her soft velvety tongue flicking out to lap at the bead of pre-cum already forming. The feel of her long tresses grazing the skin of my thighs as she moved excruciatingly slowly. Drawing out my pleasure while simultaneously driving me towards insanity.

Nothing with her would come easy. I could see the fire burning in her eyes, even when she tried to snuff out the flames in front of us. She was anything but the docile creature her looks would lead one to believe.

Even if she let me fuck her, I know she'd make me work for every moan and shudder that left her body. She'd fight every single orgasm my cock would brutally pull out of her unyielding body. Gritting her teeth and digging her nails into my flesh to suppress her screams of pleasure because she didn't want to give me the satisfaction. But two could play that game, and I could be just as merciless.

Stroking my cock more feverishly, I imagined my tongue flicking and biting and lapping at her sensitive nipples until her pussy was practically pulsing for me. Her luscious body pressed against mine, pleading for the sweet release that only my cock could supply. But stopping would be too easy on her. *No.* I wouldn't stop licking and nibbling until her primal need took over and her delicate fingers began ripping strands of hair from my head. I wanted her so maddened with lust that all she could see was me, all she could feel was my cock, so close yet still so far out of reach.

I'd pull away and stare her down, admiring her hungry, desperate expression. She'd eye my painfully rigid cock, eager for it to fill her, but my teasing wouldn't stop. I'd grip her long silky locks in a firm hold and bend her naked body over. There was something thrilling about getting a firecracker like her into such a vulnerable position, and like the good girl she was, my Angel would bend for me.

I'd press against her from behind and fuck would my cock fit perfectly between her delicious ass cheeks. I'd continue to tease her, sliding my length back and forth, back and forth, but never allowing it to slip into where she so desperately wanted it. My head would rub against her sensitive little clit, sending fissures of pleasure across her body until she was practically vibrating with need, but I still wouldn't give her the release she wanted.

Not until she'd finally get fed up and turn around to look me deep in the eyes. I needed her to know that I was the one giving her the fucking pleasure. That I was the one making her feel so alive.

As soon as her sultry brown eyes locked onto mine, I'd lift her up in one swift motion and drop her, impaling her on my rigid cock and forcing her to take the full length in one powerful thrust. There would be no easing into it or starting out slow. She needed to see and feel the full effect she had on me. Then I'd give her the most unrelenting and brutal pounding of her life. We'd fuck until all the rage and combative energy dissipated, filling the room with sweat, anger, and unadulterated lust.

"Fuck, Angel." I groaned as my balls tightened and my cock pulsed at the vivid imagery playing in my mind. Streams of cum seeped over my hand and down my shaft, creating a sticky mess and leaving me feeling light-headed and spent.

Fuck. If just thinking about her could elicit this kind of reaction, this girl was going to be the death of us all.

After grabbing a towel to clean myself up, I laid back on my bed and stared at the ceiling fan circling above my bed. She gave me an extra reason to smile as I crossed my arms behind my head and finally closed my eyes to sleep.

I don't know how long I slept before a gut-curdling scream interrupted my rest. The voice was unmistakably female, and she was fucking terrified. I shot up from my bed and ran towards Stevie's room. *Someone was hurting my girl.*

TWENTY-TWO

Stevie

"No! Please! Get off of me!" My pleas fell on deaf ears as they continued to rip more fabric off of me.

"You wanted to act like a whore Steph, I'm just giving you exactly what you wanted." Spat Gavin, as his two masked friends continued to paw at my exposed flesh.

I stared into his eyes, silently pleading for him to stop this, but nothing but cold soulless orbs stared back at me. The Gavin I once knew wasn't there anymore.

It was only a few months ago that he was the guy invading

179

my dreams and here he was orchestrating my worst nightmare.

"Hurry the fuck up!" He barked, causing the foreign hands wrapped around my wrists to dig deeper into my flesh.

Surely someone would stop this. Someone would hear my screams and pull them off of me. But the more the crowd cheered, the more my hope dissipated. No one could hear us, and no one was coming to my rescue. It was the biggest football game of the year at CHU, and Gavin and his friends had somehow overpowered me and dragged me underneath the metal bleachers filled with drunk college football fans.

There once was a time when I thought that garnering Gavin's attention was the best thing that could ever happen to me. He was charming and sweet. Not the funniest or handsomest guy on campus, but he was from a good, reputable family. The fact that he even noticed me felt like a tremendous win. I wasn't even technically enrolled at CHU. I just helped in the library and in exchange, the school offered to let me sit in on classes during my free time. It was in one of those classes that Gavin noticed me, and for the first time, it felt like my bad luck was finally turning around.

Everything took a turn for the worse when his actual personality began to show. Slowly, Gavin's superiority complex seeped into our relationship. He didn't like the way I wore my hair, so I changed it. Then, he didn't like my clothes, so I changed those. It soon got to the point where I felt like being with him was changing who I really was. So, I ended things. Gavin couldn't stand the fact that I, the orphaned girl from the wrong side of town, rejected him.

From that moment forward, he made it his personal mission to make my life a living hell. The rumors he'd spread *around campus were vicious, but I always held my head high and came off unaffected. I didn't give a fuck what he or his douchebag friends thought of me, and I think that alone was what drove him to tonight. His ego needed him to affect me, to leave a permanent scar in his wake.*

"Don't do this." I begged, as salty tears rolled down my dirt covered cheeks.

"Shut up, bitch!" Gavin spat as his free hand pressed my face into the ground and his other hand worked to unfasten his belt.

Squeezing my eyes shut, I braced myself for the pain that I knew was coming. My watery eyes focused on the hazy crowd above me as he violated me. I refused to look at his friends as they watched. If I couldn't picture the looks on their faces, maybe tonight's events wouldn't haunt me. Maybe I'd be able to have a normal life after all of this.

After he finished, I laid there numb, staring off into the distance. Gavin's icy hand painfully squeezed my jaw, forcing me to look into his eyes.

"I don't know boys, she doesn't look broken enough yet." He hissed, pulling out his silver pocket knife.

"Gavin, come on, bro." The guy holding my wrists mumbled.

"Dude, Zeke is right, she's had enough. Look at her." Argued the guy holding my ankles.

"Fuck off, Derek!" Gavin spat, tilting his head to stare back at my lifeless eyes. "She's a whore and I need to make sure anyone who ever touches her knows it."

The swift flash of metal reflecting light caught my eye just before the pain smashed into me. I shrieked in agony as the jagged blade bit into my flesh. My screams were gut-wrench-

ing, and despite my attempts to quiet them, they were unstoppable.

Darkness surrounded me and my body became encapsulated in soothing warmth. I no longer felt the blade piercing my skin or the rough hands pinning my body to the ground.

Did I die?

This flashback came to me almost every night, and it always ended the same. With me cold, broken, bloody, and alone on the hard dirt underneath the bleachers. I'd envision the moment the poor janitor found me and threw his jacket on me to offer me some decency. And relive the painful realization that what Gavin did would scar me for life. I'd see the sad and remorseful looks each officer and medic gave me as they wheeled me into the ambulance. See those same looks on the doctors and medical teams that helped me in the hospital.

"Shh, everything's going to be okay." A familiar voice whispered into my ear.

My eyes flashed open, and I took in my strange surroundings. This wasn't my room. It looked similar to mine, but the color scheme was different. Instead of classic black and cream tones, the room was doused in icy blues and soft greys, almost as if I were in some alternate universe. *Maybe I was still dreaming?*

I shifted my position slightly, trying to get my bearings, and that's when I felt it. The warm body pressed firmly against my back.

Where the hell was I and who the fuck was that?

My breath hitched as a heavy arm wrapped itself across my stomach and pulled me closer, enveloping me in the distinct scent of lavender and smoke. *Ezra.*

"I know you're awake." Ezra whispered, snuggling his chin in the crook of my neck. "Go back to sleep, Angel."

"Wha- where am I?" I whispered, trying to hold back the terror inching up my spine.

"My room." He explained, in a sleepy voice. "I figured you'd rest easier here."

Either I was really going crazy or every answer he gave made sense. Still, that didn't explain why I was naked. I couldn't feel any barriers between his skin and mine. I had fallen asleep in my sweatshirt, but the only fabric attached to my body was my thong.

"Why are we naked?" I asked, my voice just above a whisper.

"You sweated through your sweatshirt and I'm wearing boxer briefs." He mumbled, matter-of-factly. "It's not like I'm seeing anything you didn't already show me."

"I-" I hesitated, at a loss for words.

He had a point, but still. He shouldn't have taken me without asking.

"I shouldn't be in here." I mumbled. "I should go."

I made a move to leave, but his arm gripped me tighter in response.

"Look Angel, if it makes you feel better, this means nothing. I still want to hurt you. In fact, I'll probably dream about hurting you in the most delicious ways possible, but tonight, you need me to be someone else. Someone safe. I'll be that man for you tonight."

I wanted to fight him on it. I wanted to scream bloody murder until one of the other guys came to pull him off of me. But something about what he was offering had me intrigued. His warmth chased away the nightmares that haunted me almost every night, and he hadn't tried to kill me. Yet. *Maybe it would be okay.*

I told myself that the only reason I didn't fight him on it was because he would kill me. But the truth was, there was something calming about his room and the feeling of his arms around me.

I barely slept the rest of the night, but it wasn't because of the nightmares. The comfort I felt in Ezra's arms terrified me more than any nightmare ever could.

TWENTY-THREE

Cyrus

"Morning." Atlas grumbled, sitting in his usual seat at the kitchen table. I gave Tristan a nod as I bit into my toast, and we both eyed our big brother with suspicion. Ever since his reappearance at the tavern last night, he's been on edge.

The shit with Melanie was the obvious reason. Though even she could never usually get him that riled up. That combined with his disappearance the other night seemed so out of character for the man who meticulously planned out nearly everything he did.

"Good morning." Ezra singsonged, strolling into the kitchen.

"You're in a s... surprisingly good mood." Tristan quipped, raising a brow as he watched Ez take his seat.

"You would be too," Ezra chirped, giving us a pointed look as he loaded up his plate with food the cooks had prepared for us, "if you had a night like mine."

Tristan and I exchanged skeptical looks. *Ezra was always a little off, but this chipper mood was strange, even for him.*

"Eat your fucking breakfast." Mumbled Atlas with his eyes latched onto his phone. "We've got a lot of shit to do today and we don't have time to deal with your antics."

"No problem, Dad." Ez retorted with a wink as he bit into his toast.

Atlas let out an exasperated breath as he laid his phone down and massaged his temples.

"Speaking of shit to do," Atlas continued, "one of us needs to stay and watch the girl. Apparently, she can't go out in public and stay unnoticed."

"I'll do it!" Tris and I offered at nearly the same time.

"Wonder twin powers, activate." Ezra mumbled with a chuckle, loading up his plate with another serving of potatoes and eggs.

Tris and I stared at each other before shaking our heads with annoyance and leaning back into our chairs. The twin thing could be really obnoxious sometimes.

"I should do it." I said, stating the obvious.

"Why's that?" Tris asked.

"Because, she's obviously more comfortable with me out of all of us."

"Bullshit." He retorted. "When s… she thought I was you, she nearly bit my head off for touching her."

"Wait a fucking minute," Atlas roared, tossing his phone on the table. "you two idiots have touched her?"

"Technically, three idiots." Ezra said, leaning back with a smug look on his face.

That statement caused all hell to break loose as our eyes zeroed in him. The room erupted in shouts and accusations as the four of us fought over who should stay with her and why we'd be the best fit. The conversation slowly morphed into cutting remarks and personal attacks, the four of us completely forgetting the real reason we were fighting to begin with.

Tristan claimed he should stay because out of the four of us, he was the least affected by her. I called bullshit on that right away. I saw the way she mounted him, and I saw the moment he debated letting it happen. The fact that he wanted to be around her at all was a sign of trouble. Tris was a recluse. He normally wanted nothing to do with anyone except for the three of us, yet here he was offering to babysit. Something didn't add up. She had to mean more to him than he was letting on.

Atlas took himself out of the equation almost immediately. I glanced at him and noticed that for the first time in a long time; he didn't look so well put together. His hair was disheveled and the circles underneath his eyes were prominent. His outfit was still polished and pressed, thanks to the maids, but he seemed off. There was something about Stevie's presence in our home that was causing him to lose the composure he spent years building. By the looks of it, he wanted to stay as far away from her as possible.

Ezra got voted out almost immediately by the three of us. Whatever happened with them last night had already done enough damage to Ez for the day. I don't think any of us wanted to see what more time with Stevie would do to him. Or to her, for that matter.

"Damn, I shouldn't have opened my big fucking mouth." Ez said, giving us all a sad smile as he slumped in his chair.

"Let's bring this to a vote." I said, counting on the fact that Atlas and Ezra both didn't like how interested Tristan seemed.

"Voting is bullshit." Tris seethed, crossing his arms over his chest. "Fuck it. I'm out too."

"Well, shit." I said, gleaming. "Looks like I'm stuck babysitting the little fireball."

"Keep your hands to yourself, asshole." Tris spat, brooding in his seat.

"Fuck, let's try to be adults about this." Atlas said, chastising us all. "There's no need to devolve into fucking animals. She's one girl, monitoring her should be easy and in the future you guys can rotate."

The sound of a feminine throat clearing had all of our heads turning simultaneously.

"Sorry to interrupt." Stevie offered, leaning against the doorway. "I smelled the food and I just really need something to eat."

When I thought about it, I realized we hadn't fed her at all since she'd been with us. She was probably starving. *We were fucking terrible babysitters.*

I needed to make amends for our neglect right away. Stevie was going to love being taken care of so much, she'd never want to leave us.

Wait, what the fuck am I thinking?

She'd leave our asses the minute she had a window of opportunity. I saw the look in her eyes when we told her what her role was here.

Malcolm had lied to her and us. We should've expected as much. But the situation felt less fucked-up when we thought she agreed to be ours.

Now that we knew her a little better, it was obvious she didn't agree to any of this.

We should let her go.

Better men would.

Unfortunately for Princess, none of us were planning on being the one to save her.

"Angel." Ezra called over, patting his thigh. "Sit."

I could see the reluctance in her movements as she headed towards Ezra. She was teetering. Caught between outright rejecting or fueling the affections of a psychopath. Both paths were dangerous, and as she looked at the rest of us, she could see that none of us were going to bail her out. The decision was hers to make.

The moment she caught Atlas staring daggers at the two of them, suddenly her steps seemed more sure and within seconds she was in front of Ezra. Ezra beamed at the three of us while Stevie sat on his lap as directed.

"Such a good girl." Ezra cooed, smoothing her hair. "You deserve a treat."

Ez fed her forkfuls of eggs and potatoes while kissing her lips between each bite. Stevie looked terrified, but made no move to stop him. She sat perfectly still and accepted everything Ezra offered her.

It was the most chaotic, forced intimacy I had ever seen.

Even Tris, who pretended not to give a fuck, and Atlas, who barely knew the girl, looked uncomfortable. I wanted to step in to stop it. But he wasn't technically hurting her. If anything, he was treating her more delicately than I had ever seen him treat anything in his life. Even as kids, Ez always had a fascination with destruction, but Stevie was bringing out a whole new side of him. He was almost... nice. Well, as nice as a man with a mind like his could be.

"We're late." Atlas growled, shooting up from the table. "Ez, come join Tris and I whenever you're done playing with your fucking food."

Atlas took one last look at Stevie before storming off, with Tristan following a few steps behind him.

"Sorry Angel," Ez said, standing up and placing her on his now empty chair, "Cyrus is on guard duty. Stay out of trouble, okay?" He asked, tilting her chin up to lock eyes with her.

"Okay." She whispered, offering him a small smile.

That seemed to satisfy Ez, and he gave her a quick kiss before jogging off.

Once everyone else had cleared the kitchen and it was just her and I, I spoke up.

"So... that was interesting." I remarked, taking a sip of my coffee.

"Yup." She answered shortly, focusing her attention on her plate.

Okay. Stevie obviously wasn't going to address what happened, so I changed the subject.

"How much of that little argument did you hear?"

"Enough." Stevie mumbled, looking down at her fork as she stabbed her potatoes.

"Listen Princess, it's not what you think-"

"Look, I get it." She said, cutting me off. "You guys didn't realize how much of a fucking burden keeping me around would be, and now you're fighting over who has to watch the pet."

"You are not a pet."

"Can I leave?"

"Of course not." I said, stating the obvious. "But you have freedoms, and there are perks to belonging to us."

"What, you mean besides being treated like Ezra's personal plaything?" She retorted with an eye roll.

"Has he hurt you?" I asked as my jaw clenched. I couldn't stomach the thought of anyone hurting her. Especially my own brother.

"Yes." She stammered, then paused. "Well, no. No, not really. He's possessive and doesn't understand boundaries, but he hasn't hurt me."

My jaw relaxed a fraction. I didn't know what I'd do if Ezra hurt her. His obsession with her was obvious, and I couldn't blame him. She was so much more than any of us ever expected her to be.

"If you'd give us a chance, you'd see that there are some benefits to living with us." I continued, running my fingers through my hair.

"Like what?" She asked, eyeing me with suspicion.

"Well, you're under our protection and we can give you anything you want."

"Anything?" She asked, cocking a brow.

"Yes, anything. Name it."

She laughed for a few beats until she realized I wasn't joking. I could see her mind working, trying to scour her thoughts for something that she truly wanted. I meant every word I said. One of the many perks of our business ventures was that we had a surplus of money and resources. She could have anything she wanted, all she had to do was ask.

Maybe my brothers weren't ready to acknowledge it, but she was creating a space for herself in our lives. Day by day, hour by hour, she was burrowing deeper and deeper under our skin. But we still didn't know what her motivation was for being here and more importantly, what was making her want to stay.

"Okay." She said, looking up at me. "You know what I really want?"

I nodded silently, readying myself for whatever answer she threw my way. Cars. Jewelry. Hell, even her own fucking place on our property. We could afford it all, but her answer would tell me everything I needed to know about her intentions.

"Could we go to Hell's Tavern again?" She asked, biting into her lower lip. "It was fun to get out of the house and I could really use another round of Jessie's Hellhounds."

That was it? That was her big ask? Damn, either this girl was perfect, or she was playing us, hard. I had just given her the golden opportunity of getting whatever she wanted, and all she wanted to do was go to a fucking bar for a drink. A fucking bar that we owned, no less.

"I'll see what I can do." I said, tilting my head to the side and staring at the strange girl sitting in front of me.

With that answer, she gave me the first huge smile I had seen from her. I hoped it wouldn't be the last time I saw it on her face.

TWENTY-FOUR

Stevie

AFTER BREAKFAST, I KEPT TO MYSELF FOR THE REST OF THE day. I knew Cyrus was lingering somewhere, but after the morning's events, I wasn't ready to face him or really any of them, if I was honest.

I was ashamed. Ashamed of what Ezra made me do at the kitchen table. Ashamed of how much I liked it. Ashamed of how disappointed I was when he had to leave. And I was even ashamed that thinking about it now made my heart beat faster. *What's wrong with me?*

I wasn't stupid. I knew that his fascination with me was fleeting. But I have never had someone treat me so tenderly, yet send my pulse skyrocketing at the same time. I was as enamored as I was terrified of Ezra. It was intoxicating. He made me feel alive, and that scared the hell out of me because I knew I was just a game to him. Nothing more than a toy to enjoy until he gets bored.

Even if Ezra's affections towards me were genuine, he had no idea who I really was beyond these walls, and neither did any of his brothers. Well, except for Atlas, but that didn't seem to matter to him anymore.

The really tragic thing about Atlas was that I would've accepted him for who he really was if he had just trusted me from the beginning. It might have taken some adjustments, but I would have accepted The Reaper side of him. Hell, my past wasn't perfect, but I did what I needed to survive and I could understand that for him and his brothers, this was their way of surviving in this world. I could accept that.

What I couldn't accept was the secret, bitchy girlfriend. I'm sorry, *fiancée*. The one he neglected to mention while he let me throw myself at him almost every single night. That betrayal stung. But I didn't know what was worse, that he didn't tell me about her or that Melanie was everything I could never be.

Since the messy scene at Hell's Tavern, Atlas' cold shoulder treatment of me had been consistent, and it was obvious his brothers knew nothing of our history. Apparently, we both thought better of telling our siblings about each other. *Maybe we were more alike than I thought.*

As volatile as I expected them all to be, they've all been consistent with their treatment of me. Cyrus looked at me like he wanted to fuck me. Tristan looked at me like wanted to kill me or save me. Ezra looked at me like he wanted to eat me. And Atlas refused to look at me at all. It was my own treacherous body that wanted to change things and blur the lines between captive and captor.

It had only been a few days and already I was losing sight of why I came here. I needed to protect Alex, and I sure as hell couldn't do that while being stuck here. I needed a solid plan of escape and unless I got my hands on one of their access cards; I was fucked.

***

"KNOCK, KNOCK." Cyrus said as he opened my bedroom door. His eyes searched around the room before settling on me. "Wear this," he said, tossing a garment bag on one of my armchairs, "and meet me downstairs in five."

His words sounded more like an order than a request. It was almost as if asking just wasn't in his vocabulary. I had complicated feelings towards Cyrus. I knew he had the power to end me at any moment, but I couldn't shake the feeling that he enjoyed having me around. We had this fiery banter between us and even though he could be an asshole, I liked fighting with him.

I slipped the zipper of the garment bag down and felt the buttery fabric graze against my knuckles. As the bag fell to the floor, it revealed a royal blue mini dress. It was that same form fitting buttery fabric as the dress from the other night, but this dress hit just above the knee and had a high slit. So apparently Cyrus was a fan of Jessie's dress on me.

As I slid on the dress, Jessie's words from that night replayed in my head. *"They're literally going to be eating out of the palm of your hand."* Maybe this was my chance to test that theory and who better than Cyrus to be my test subject.

"IT'LL JUST BE US TONIGHT." Cyrus called out, probably hearing the click of my heels descending the stairs.

I circled the staircase and froze when I saw the kitchen setup. Cyrus had pulled out all the stops. Standing in front of the kitchen island was a chef preparing dinner for us and as the aroma of his ingredients hit my nose, my mouth salivated.

"What is this?" I asked, my face a mixture of shock and confusion.

"Dinner." Cyrus said, as his eyes took in my outfit.

"Why are you being so nice to me?" I asked, eyeing him curiously.

"I wanted to show you what life with us could be like, if you embraced it." He said, running his hand through his silky dark hair.

"It's not like I have much of a choice, either way." I said, lowering my voice as I glanced at the chef.

I didn't know how freely I could speak in front of him. Sure, I was in my own shitty situation, but that didn't give me any right to put anyone else at risk.

"Don't worry about Alessandro." Cyrus said, seeing

where my mind was at. "He works for us and understands how much we value our privacy."

"Sit." He said, gesturing towards the dining room table that served as the front row to my humiliation only hours ago.

Alessandro laid out a feast for us. With each course of the meal, Alessandro would explain each dish and describe the ingredients and special preparations he took. I didn't know what half of the things he offered were, but every single bite was delicious.

Our appetizers were slices of ripe melon wrapped in prosciutto. I thought the combination would be awful, but the flavors pair well together and I had to stop myself from gorging on them.

The second course was the most delicious lobster bisque I had ever tasted. Truthfully, it was the only lobster bisque I had ever tasted, but everything Alessandro touched tasted like magic.

For the main course, he treated us to shrimp scampi pasta. I could taste the freshness in every ingredient, and the buttery sauce he made was to die for.

My tastebuds were overstimulated and my belly was full by the time he revealed dessert, but I couldn't turn away the decadent chocolate soufflé Alessandro had carefully prepared. The moment its creamy texture hit my tongue, my mind catapulted into pure bliss. *No wonder the rich seemed happier. If they could afford to eat like this every day, I would be too.*

As I eagerly dug into my soufflé for a second bite, I looked up to find Cyrus's eyes focused on me.

Fuck. I scarfed all that food down like a behemoth, and he was probably regretting treating me to this meal. I was mortified.

I had never learned proper etiquette, and The Reapers seemed like the type of people that would turn their nose up at that. My cheeks flamed as I slowly lowered my fork and folded my hands in my lap.

"Why did you stop?" Cyrus asked from across the table.

"I'm full." I chirped, looking everywhere but back at him.

"Bullshit." He countered, getting up from his seat and bringing his own soufflé.

As he made his way towards me, my heart pounded in my chest. *Had my rude behavior finally set Cyrus off?* He seemed the most even keeled out of all of his brothers, but maybe that was just because I hadn't done anything to trigger him yet.

"Eat." He ordered with his brows furrowed.

"I'm not hungry anymore." I said, shrugging my shoulders and praying like hell that he'd drop the subject.

"Lie." He spat as his nostrils flared.

"So, you're a human lie detector now?" I scoffed, piercing my eyes at him.

"No." He offered. "I just watched the way you reacted to that soufflé. You want it, so eat it."

I shook my head in response. I would not be bullied into putting on another show for him. I wasn't some fucking monkey that danced when he said dance. At least I could have some pride in the fact that I didn't know he was staring at me before. But doing it again while I knew he was watching felt dehumanizing.

Without another word, Cyrus dunked his finger into his own chocolate soufflé, crumbling its crisp cake-like surface and digging deep into the gooey fudgy parts. He held it up to my lips and nudged my mouth open, dipping his chocolaty coated finger deep into my mouth. I licked it off, running my tongue up and down his finger while keeping my eyes locked on his. He slowly withdrew his finger, and I watched with a mixture of shock and fascination as his soft tongue swiped out to lick up the remnants I left behind.

"Now fucking eat." He said, flashing me a toothy grin as he grabbed a spoon and dug into the rest of his dessert.

And with that, I grabbed my spoon and began eating again. After a few bites, Cyrus spoke up again.

"I used to eat like that too, you know." He said, peering up at me through his thick lashes.

"Like what?"

"Like I didn't know when my next meal was coming." He said, digging in for another bite. "It took years to shake it off, even when food was no longer a scarcity."

He said it so nonchalantly that I almost thought my ears were deceiving me. I said nothing in response. It was such a small admission, but it gave me a lot to think about. I had spent all this time thinking that they were cut from a different cloth than me. That I was beneath them and we would never have anything in common. But the more I got to know them, the more I was seeing just how alike we were.

TWENTY-FIVE

Cyrus

AFTER DINNER, I WALKED STEVIE BACK TO HER BEDROOM. Alessandro had set up a little surprise for her and the sappy fuck that I was, wanted to see her reaction. When Stevie was genuinely happy, her eyes turned into these glossy little almonds that I could've sworn fucking sparkled. It was stupid, but I couldn't get the goddamn thought of seeing the sparkle out of my head.

"What's all this?" She asked as she pushed through her bedroom door and spotted the bar cart.

"All the ingredients to make a Hellhound." I said, leaning up against the door frame.

"That… is surprisingly cool of you." She said as her hand reached out to palm one of the freshly cut grapefruits.

"Yup, I'm chock full of surprises." I said, backing away from her door. "Have a good night, Princess."

"Wait." She called out, halting my retreat. "You aren't going to drink with me?"

I spun around to face her.

"I wasn't planning on it." I answered honestly.

"Come on, you're going to make me drink alone?"

I could feel her chestnut eyes boring into me, willing me to stay. I knew that the moment I looked up again, my eyes would lock with hers and I would be done for.

Fuck it. If I was going to hell anyway, one drink with a beautiful girl wouldn't kill me.

"Fine." I conceded with a smirk. "One drink."

"YOU'RE LYING!" Stevie howled as she took another sip of her hellhound and flashed me an enormous smile.

"I swear to God." I said, shrugging my shoulders as I leaned back into the cream armchair. "If they had caught us, Tris and I would've been the only seven-year-olds in Caspian Valley to ever go to jail. We were some bad-ass little kids."

"God, I could totally picture you all as mini versions of yourself." She said, shaking her head with a smile before stepping towards the bar cart.

"Ready for another?" She asked as she swirled the half-empty bottle of vodka.

"Are you trying to get me drunk, Miss Alexander?" I joked, playfully scowling at her.

"Possibly…" she retorted with a grin, "is it working Mr. Cole?"

I shook my head and smiled.

She had me feeling like a drunken idiot alright. The strange thing was, it had nothing to do with the alcohol coursing through my system.

When we first met, I had the distinct impression that she was some spoiled princess. Rebelling against Daddy because he didn't give her everything she wanted. But after getting to know her over the last few days, I had the nagging feeling that my assumptions were way off.

People rarely surprised me, yet she was a walking contradiction. She never said or did anything I expected her to, and frankly, it was hard to keep up with her.

Stevie was an enigma. A force energy that crashes into your life and fucks everything up or unfucks everything up depending on how you perceived it. She was fascinating. A complex puzzle that the problem solver within me was dying to solve. I needed to know more about what made her tick.

"So, Stevie Alexander, what is it you want out of life?"

"Come on," she said, raising a brow as she shook her head at me, "you can't ask me that."

"Why not?" I responded, taking another sip of my drink.

"I don't know. Given my situation, can I even want things anymore?"

"Of course you can. Being here isn't a death sentence."

"So says one of the assholes holding me captive…" She

deadpanned, staring off into the night sky that encompassed her room's entire far wall.

The turn of the conversation instantly sobered me up. I stared at her disappointed expression and wanted to kick myself for even bringing it up. She was just telling the truth, so why did her words bother me so much?

Probably because I was the stupid fuck that decided to 'wine and dine' our fucking toy. What for? To win her over? I didn't need to win her over, she was stuck here whether she liked it or not.

Shooting up from my seat, I moved to gather my suit jacket and leave. I had overstayed my welcome as it was, and I didn't need to let this conversation get any more out of hand. She belonged to us, and listening to her complain about it would only result in me fucking everything up. Feeling sorry for her wasn't an option.

TWENTY-SIX

Stevie

THE ROOM'S TEMPERATURE DROPPED TEN DEGREES IN AN instant. *Nice one, Stevie. Per usual, you just had to open your big fucking mouth.*

It was as if for the last few hours Cyrus had slowly stripped away the wall between us; the one that separated us as captor and captive. He let me in. My big stupid mouth had just convinced him to work overtime to build that wall right back up.

"Let's just forget I said anything, okay?" I asked, standing up from my seat and walking towards his.

"It's fine," he said, reaching for the jacket he had slung over his armchair, "I really should go, anyway."

"No," I said, placing my palm against his chest, "you don't need to leave. Stay. Please."

He stared at me for a moment as he tried to decide what to do next. It was obvious I had struck a nerve and I could see the indecision all over his face. It was the first time I had a genuine conversation with someone in days, and the selfish part of me didn't want it to end.

I didn't understand it, but something about Cyrus made me feel at ease. Maybe it was because he was one of the few people who had seen my scars and didn't treat me like I was broken. He didn't know everything about my past, but by now he knew enough to make some judgments about who I was, yet it was as if my past didn't matter to him.

I needed to think of something, anything to keep him talking. After sleeping next to Alex for almost sixteen years of my life, the solitude I felt by staying alone in my room was maddening. I didn't know if I could survive more time alone.

"How about we play a game?" I blurted.

"A game?" He asked, a gleam of mischief in his eye.

"Yeah… truth or dare?"

Ugh, really Stevie? What is this, a fucking thirteen-year-old's sleepover?

"Alright, Princess. I'll play." Cyrus said with a gleam of mischief in his eye. "But let's add a twist. If you refuse any request, you drink." He said, flashing me a sinister smile.

Butterflies swirled within me. I told myself that it was just nerves about the questions he'd ask. If playing a stupid drinking game kept him hanging around a little longer, so be it. I desperately needed the company.

I retook my seat next to his and watched as he carefully took off his suit jacket and got comfortable again. As Cyrus moved to place his suit jacket on his chair, a sleek card slipped out of its pocket and tumbled towards the hardwood floor.

I knew exactly what it was before it had even hit the ground. I had seen that card countless times. Had obsessed over it ever since I saw Ezra use it on the back entrance of Hell's Tavern. I never thought I'd get a chance to be so close to one and there it was, out in the open and staring right back at me. An access card.

It was the key to getting back everything Malcolm and The Reapers had stolen from me.

My Freedom.

My life.

Alex.

By some miracle, Cyrus had yet to notice it in the front of his armchair. I knew I only had seconds to stop him before he took away my only chance at escaping.

"I'll go first!" I blurted, a little louder than I meant to.

"A little eager there, tiger?" He asked, shaking his head with a chuckle.

"Maybe a little," I smiled, trying to mask the panic I was feeling.

My cheeks flushed as his emerald eyes gave my body an appreciative glare as he sat back in his seat. Even though I was slightly mortified, my little embarrassing outburst gave me more time to think. Cyrus had missed the access card laying mere inches from his left foot. I needed to act quick if I was really going through with this.

"So," I began, as my heart pounded in my chest, "truth or dare?"

"I'm a risk taker," he said, rolling up his crisp white sleeves, "dare."

It took a few seconds for my stupid, thirsty eyes to stop staring at the thick, tattooed forearms he revealed. *Now is your chance dummy, don't blow it.* I racked my brain, trying to think of a dare that would distract him long enough for me to grab the card.

"I dare you to let me straddle you." I said, softly biting into my lower lip.

It was a low blow, and I felt like an asshole for using my body against him, but I needed to make sure he stayed seated.

If I were being honest, there was a small part of me that had been fantasizing about sitting on his lap ever since I saw the envious look he gave Ezra at the kitchen table. But this was about escaping. It didn't matter that my reckless pussy was already wet just thinking about rubbing against his lap. *She* didn't give a damn about keeping us alive, so she wasn't allowed to be in charge.

The hungry look he gave me in response told me everything I needed to know. I had played my cards right.

Kicking off my heels, I slowly strode towards him. Cyrus' face took on a primal look as his eyes devoured each languid movement. Once I approached him, I slowly leaned in and pressed my lips against his ear.

"Close your eyes…" I whispered.

Without hesitation, he obeyed. I only had a few seconds before he'd be expecting to feel the weight of my body on top of him, so I pressed my right foot against the access card and carefully slid it underneath his seat.

Gathering up the silky blue fabric of my dress, I planted each of my knees on either side of his hips and let the full weight of my body crush against him.

"You can open your eyes now." I said, wrapping my arms around his neck.

"Fucking hell, Princess. Never what I expect." He murmured, sinking his teeth in his lower lip. "So, does that make it my turn?"

"Oh, right," I said, shifting to get off of him. "Here, let me just-"

"Not so fast." He said wrapping his arms around my waist and holding me in place. "I dare you to keep this spectacular ass on my lap for the rest of this game."

"Hmm…" I joked playfully, "that's a shame because I'm picking truth this round."

"Who knew you could be so cruel?" He joked, pressing his forehead against my chin after flashing me a devious smile.

I wanted to laugh with him and relish in the playful banter, but in the back of my mind; I knew I was a liar. The irony of his words was unsettling. He had no idea how cruel I could be to protect those that I love, but he would soon find out.

"Alright, so truth it is," he continued, not missing a beat and refusing to let me move an inch, "who gave you the scars?"

It was probably the last time I was going to see him, and I no longer saw the point in lying.

"A guy I thought I knew." I said, looking down at my hands folded between us.

He gently grasped my chin and tilted it up.

"Did he pay for his crimes?" He asked, his voice eerily calm as his captivating eyes searched mine.

"Yeah." I answered with a frown. "With a slap on the wrist and six months of community service."

"Explain." He spat through gritted teeth.

I didn't even know where to start. Even with it being four years ago, it was hard for me to talk about what happened, let alone speak of the fucked-up fallout.

"I guess that's what happens when you have friends in high places. Or in his case, a daddy in high places." I said with a shrug. "It doesn't matter anyway, it was years ago."

I could feel his entire body stiffen at my words, and I knew he didn't like my answer. The past was the past and there was nothing he or I could do to change it. No matter how badly we wanted to.

"Your turn." He said, after a few beats of silence. His hands were still firmly planted on my hips, but I could feel the change in the way he held me. Almost as if I were this fragile thing that would crumble if he applied too much pressure.

Fuck. Why was he doing everything so right? He held me like how I wish someone would've held me the night Gavin attacked me. In his arms, I felt safe and important and worthy of love.

Fuck. Fuck. Fuck.

"Truth or dare?" I blurted after realizing I took way too long to respond.

"Truth." He said, looking deeply into my eyes.

"What are you thinking right now?" I asked, my voice just above a whisper.

"You really want to know?" He asked, a clear warning in his tone.

I nodded. *I wanted to know.* This game had gone way further than I planned, and after everything I told him, his answer meant something to me.

"I'm thinking that I want to kill the asshole that hurt you." He hissed, clenching his jaw. "I'm thinking that you're the strongest woman I've ever met. I'm thinking that your body..." he paused, grabbing my waist and pushing me down harder against him for emphasis, "this fucking body, feels perfect against mine and maybe I'm a real asshole for this, but all I can think about now is how warm and perfect your pussy feels against my cock."

I was at a loss for words. The few times I shared what happened, the immediate reaction was always pity. *'I'm so sorry that happened to you, Stevie'* or *'Stevie, you poor thing'* were usually the go-to phrases, but his response was so unexpected. The truth of the matter was, what I went through was ugly and hearing about it made people uncomfortable.

But Cyrus wasn't uncomfortable with what happened to me, and he didn't look at me with pity in his eyes. Even as I spoke about it, the primal hunger in them never left, if anything, it intensified and I was caught off guard by the depth of the man I had so quickly labeled as one dimensional.

It was then that I understood why Cyrus was so dangerous. He may have looked normal, may have acted and sounded like your typical hot himbo, but he was a wolf in sheep's clothing. He was the handsome, smooth talking villain that you'd never see coming. The smart, intense, and beautiful man that took advantage of people's lowered expectations of him so he could catch them off guard when they least expected it.

"My turn." He said, grazing his index finger underneath one of the thin straps on my shoulder. "Truth or dare."

I bit into my lower lip, contemplating what to do. If I said 'truth', I'd end up revealing more details about a life he wasn't supposed to know about. Choosing dare was its own can of worms, but I didn't want to risk getting more attached to the man that could see beyond my scars.

"Dare." I said, looking up into his eyes.

"Terrible answer." He growled, gripping my hips and pulling my body closer to his. "Hmm," he said, rubbing the soft stubble on his sharp jaw, "I dare you... to let me taste that pretty little pussy of yours."

I should've been pissed. His words were filthy and what he wanted to do to me was even filthier. But the way he slowly enunciated each word had my pulse skyrocketing and my thighs straining. I didn't want to acknowledge the effect his words had on me. Let alone what the sensation of feeling his cock hardening below me was doing to my body.

But I couldn't deny the truth. I wanted him. *Badly.*

I had spent my entire life walking on eggshells, always trying to make the most practical and smartest decisions. *But what has being good ever really done for me?* Aside from a few minor crimes as a kid, I had done everything right, and I still ended up here. Still ended up having a shitty mother who left me with an even shittier stepfather. Still ended up being owned by The Reapers.

For once in my life, I didn't want to be good or smart.

I wanted to be bad, and Cyrus was the perfect man to guide me into the dark side.

"You aren't just going to taste me," I said, leaning in to press my lips to his ear, "you are going to devour me."

"Are you sure you want to do this, Princess?" He asked, pulling back to look me in my eyes. "Because once I have a taste, I don't think I'll have the strength to stop myself from gorging on you."

Was I sure? Cyrus was right. The sexual tension was too strong for either of us to ignore, and I knew that once we started, neither of us would want it to stop. But when I looked at him and I thought about how he made me feel, there was no question in my mind. No nagging feeling of uncertainty. I wanted Cyrus, and he needed to know that I was ready to take on everything he offered.

"Cyrus, I want you to eat my pussy until you're satiated and spent." I said, brazened from the hungry look in his eyes. "Is that clear enough for you?"

Cyrus ran his fingers through his dark hair, before flashing me a wicked grin as he gripped my chin.

"How the fuck can a mouth so beautiful spew such filthy words?" He asked, rubbing his thumb across my lips.

I parted my lips and sucked, slowly sliding my tongue up and down the pad of his thumb. His eyelashes fluttered as his head lolled back and I watched, fascinated, as the last bit of restraint left his body.

In an instant, he gripped my chin and captured my mouth in a ravenous kiss. I expected to taste urgency on his lips, but his tongue and lips were slow and languid as they moved with mine, almost as if time were inconsequential to him. We tasted each other, our tongues moving and exploring as our bodies created delicious friction against each other. He kissed me like he was savoring it, drawing out each tantalizing stroke of my tongue and tug of my lip.

"You taste like sin, Princess." He said, pulling back with a smirk. I nipped it at his lips in response.

"Shut up and kiss me." I taunted, running my fingers through his thick hair as our mouths collided again.

His tongue massaged mine as my body rolled and grinded against his unabashedly, feeling more and more uninhibited by the second. The need to feel him everywhere was overwhelming. I wanted his spicy scent all over me and for him to consume my every thought.

His hands slowly slid down the sides of my body, leaving a scorching trail of heat in their wake. Every single part of my body felt like it was on fire, yet all I wanted to do was burn in the inferno he created.

Feeling restrained by our clothes, I undid Cyrus' black silk tie, while his hands massaged my ass. I tossed his tie to the side and began unbuttoning his crisp white shirt while my hips swirled and grinded on his lap. An appreciative groan escaped his lips and the next thing I knew, I was being lifted into the air, as his powerful legs carried us towards the bed.

Cyrus' hands latched onto my waist as he pried me off of him, tossing my body on the bed with a devilish smirk. I landed on the silk black sheets in a heap of crazed lust and frazzled nerves.

"Eager girl," he tsked, looking at me with hooded eyes, "I think I need to remind you who is in control here. What do you think, Princess, should I put you in your place?"

My heart thundered in my chest. I didn't know what he had in mind, but I knew I could handle whatever he threw my way.

"Y-yes." I stammered, staring at his chiseled torso peeking through his shirt.

"Good girl," he cooed, "take off your dress and lay flat on your stomach."

The authoritative tone of his voice had me jumping at his words. I scrambled to my knees, grabbed the silky fabric of my dress and tossed it over my head in one swift motion. I slid my fingers under the sides of my black thong, preparing to slide it off too when a loud tsk stopped me. I froze and looked up to find Cyrus staring at me. His eyes were as hungry as ever, but he had an almost amused look on his face.

"Did I tell you to take that off?" He asked.

I winced, pulling my hands away as I shook my head in response.

"That was your one warning," he said, licking his lips, "next time you disobey, there will be consequences. Continue."

This dominating side of Cyrus was sexy as hell. I almost wanted to disobey him again just to see what consequences he had in mind. But as I heard him loosening his belt, I thought better of it, and laid down instead. If I was going to make it out of there in one piece, it was better to be on my best behavior.

The second I laid flat, I felt the bed dip. There was something so thrilling about not being able to see what was going to happen, but feeling the anticipation of knowing something was coming. I felt Cyrus' powerful thighs straddle my legs and in a split second, both of his hands had gathered my wrists above my head and restrained them with his black silk tie.

Before I could even register what was happening, the loud

crack of his palm against my bare ass rang out across the room. The hit stung, and I could already feel the heat emanating from where his hand landed. No one had ever spanked me before. It was equally horrifying, as it was a turn on. Cyrus was serious about punishing me, and the masochist in me was dying to know what other kinds of torment tonight would bring me.

Cyrus gave me another two hard slaps to my ass, and then his lips were on me. Starting from the nape of my neck, he kissed and licked a delicious trail down spine while his hands rubbed and touched and squeezed my body. With every inch he moved, my body pulsed, like all of my nerve endings were seconds from imploding. When his tongue reached my ass and began licking and sucking on my sore skin, my eyes rolled into the back of my head as I relished in the feel of him. His mouth was so soothing and his touch was so gentle, I had almost forgotten that he was the one to bring me the pain to begin with. Then, without warning, his mouth vanished.

My body mourned the loss of his touch and I tried to shift around to see what happened.

"Don't fucking move." He hissed, and I froze, feeling his fingers slide up and down my folds. I was soaking wet as it was and his mouth hadn't even touched my pussy.

Like a flash of lightning, he flipped me over onto my back. Even with the bind, my hands scrambled to cover the scars that marred my stomach. It was a reflex I hated. Most men that I'd been with since the incident averted their gaze completely or pretended like they didn't notice. But not Cyrus. He took hold of my wrists with one powerful hand and raised them high above my head, exposing my body to him completely.

"Don't hide from me." He said, gently tracing my scars with his other hand. "These scars are marks of a fucking warrior, wear them with pride, Princess."

And then my world shifted. Flinging my legs over his muscular shoulders, Cyrus got to work. His expert tongue dove deeply between my legs, sending delicious pleasure to every inch of my body. Even with my thong still in the way, I could feel the glorious stroke of his tongue as he licked my pussy with the perfect amount of pressure and at just the right angle. Cyrus was oral god and I would worship at his fucking alter every night, if he let me.

"Cyrus..." I begged, as my entire body shuddered from his touch, "p-please."

"Please, what, Princess?" He mumbled, now moving his lips to suck and lick at my sensitive bud.

"The thong..." I cried with a shaky breath. "Get rid of the fucking thong."

His fingers ripped my thong off of my body with one firm tug and now that I could finally feel all of him, the delicious sensation of it all was too much to handle. My hips bucked and my back arched as he continued his assault on my pussy. I wanted to take his cock in my mouth and return the favor, but Cyrus' hands were firmly planted on my hips and he refused to let me budge.

He lapped and licked and stroked and sucked my pussy until an intense orgasm rocked through my entire body and I screamed his name like it was a prayer.

"Wow." I murmured, staring up at the ceiling, with him still lapping lazy circles on my clit as his hands worked to untie my wrists. "That was... amazing."

He laughed to himself as he lifted my body and tucked me into bed.

"What about you?" I asked, looking pointedly at the large imprint of his hard cock still in his boxer briefs.

"We'll have plenty of time for that later, Princess." He said, crawling in bed next to me. "Tonight was about you. Now let's get some sleep."

He wrapped his arm around me and I snuggled into his warm embrace, almost forgetting that there wouldn't be a 'later' for us. Or any of The Reapers, for that matter. I didn't want to feel, and yet each of them were evoking emotions no one else could. I had only been here a few days and already my priorities were skewed. I could no longer deny what was happening. I was falling for my captors. But I couldn't let that happen. I *wouldn't* let that happen. I knew what needed to be done.

TWENTY-SEVEN

Stevie

I waited for what felt like an eternity for Cyrus' breathing to become rhythmic. Only then was I able to relax a fraction. But the question in the back of my mind remained, *could I actually do this?*

I needed to take the opportunity while I had it. He was my captor, and that access card was my way out. The longer I stayed, the less I'd mourn everything I lost. My freedom. My future. Alex. Alex *needed* me.

Inching out from underneath his heavy arm, I carefully

slipped out from under the silk sheets. The moment my bare skin left his warm embrace, goosebumps littered across my skin. The chill seeped deep into my bones, but I refused to back down from the plan. It was now or never.

Wrapping my arms across my chest with a shiver, my eyes tried to peer across the dark room and assess the distance to the card hidden just underneath the arm chair. It looked to be about seven steps there and another four steps to the door. Eleven steps. *Just eleven steps, Stevie, you can do this.*

Tiptoeing as lightly as I could, I made my way towards my freedom.

On step one, my knee cracked, and I winced.

On step two, I picked up my dress and slipped it back on, thankful that he didn't rip it off.

On step three, the hardwood creaked and my entire body froze. I glanced back at Cyrus and prayed like hell that he hadn't heard it. The room was silent and the soft snore that he'd had moments ago vanished. *Had he woken up? Had he seen me?* I was on the verge of panic when his soft snoring picked up again, making the tightness in my chest ease.

Releasing a shaky breath, I carefully took steps four, five, and six as fast as I could. It was like ripping off a bandaid. The quicker I moved, the quicker I could get the hell out of there.

On step seven, I bent over to grab the access card from underneath the chair when the soft scent of citrus hit my nose. My eyes locked on the obvious culprit, Cyrus' jacket. The scent was nothing compared to what Cyrus smelled like up close, but that didn't stop my body from reacting to it.

My already pounding heart began thundering in my chest as panic poured into my bloodstream. *"We can't leave him,"* my stupid body seemed to scream, *"he keeps us safe."* My treacherous body wasn't thinking clearly. All she wanted to do was crawl back under his arms and bask in Cyrus' comforting scent.

God, why did he have to smell so good?

And say all the right things.

And make me feel less alone.

Tears welled in my eyes as I gnawed on my bottom lip. I knew there would be no going back after this. If I walked out of there, Cyrus would never forgive me. He had let me in. He had told me about his life and I had a feeling that wasn't something he talked about with just anyone.

Could I betray him like this?

Could I betray all of them?

I was still upset at Atlas, but aside from hurting my ego, he hadn't intentionally hurt me, *had he?* He was a good friend to me before all of this. Was it his fault that I interpreted what we had as something more? He hadn't told me about his life, but it wasn't like I had been very forthcoming with mine either. And Ezra. Maybe he didn't understand boundaries, but when he held me the other night, he chased away my nightmares. Even Tristan seemed to warm up to me. When he thought I was in trouble, he stood up for me. They've all been really good to me… *haven't they?*

"Stevie?" A voice laden with sleep called out in the darkness.

Fuck. Fuck. Fuck. Cyrus was awake.

"Just going to the restroom," I whispered, trying to breathe through the heart attack he had nearly given me, "be back in a sec."

No, you won't, you fucking liar.

229

"Okay, beautiful." He mumbled, crashing his mussed-up head back against the silk pillowcase.

After closing the door behind me, I took a deep breath and tip-toed down the hall. I made a quick pit-stop at the bathroom, making sure to keep the faucet running and to lock the bathroom from the inside. I figured that could distract Cyrus for at least a few minutes, and I needed all the help I could get.

Once I cleared the second floor and descended the stairs, I stopped caring about being quiet and focused all of my attention on getting out of there. But there was one fatal flaw in my plan for escape, the entire first floor was shrouded in darkness. It was a moonless night and even with the floor to ceiling windows, my eyes couldn't make out a thing in the darkness. There was no way in hell I could chance switching on the light, who knew if Cyrus was even still in my room and the light would be a blaring sign that something was up.

I stumbled through the foyer, trying to feel my way along the walls. If I could just find the front door, I'd make it out without no one none the wiser.

"Princess, you okay in there?" Cyrus called out, knocking on the bathroom door.

Fuck. I couldn't answer him, and it wouldn't be long before he'd be trying to rip the door off its hinges.

My movements became more frantic as I struggled to orientate myself in the darkness. I tried to listen for what Cyrus was doing, but all I could hear was the sound of my heart thundering in my chest as my hands roamed the walls.

"Stevie," his thunderous voice called out, "trust me, you don't want to fucking do this."

That was the problem. These men kept asking me to trust

them and my idiotic-self actually wanted to. *But why should I trust them?* What did they do to earn my trust? Not a damn thing. I may have fucked myself by coming here, but I wasn't about to fuck myself even more by staying.

The moment my hands grazed the innocuous black access panel, my heart leaped in my chest. *Freedom.* I slapped Cyrus' access card against the panel and closed my eyes, waiting for the beep to signify I had made it.

When I scanned the card, something happened that I didn't expect. Just as the sound went off and the access light turned green, the lights turned on and I froze at the site of Cyrus flicking the light switch.

He was on the top of the stairs, too far for him to reach me in time. He and I both knew that the moment he tried to run for me, I'd bolt out of the front door and lock him in behind me. I had his access card, and I'd bet my life savings he didn't have a spare hiding in his black boxer briefs.

Cyrus said nothing as we stared each other down, but I knew exactly what his eyes were saying. I could feel them piercing into me, begging me not to take that last step. And a big part of me wanted to listen. I could live this life with them. I could forget about my old life and enjoy all the things that they were offering, but the one thing I could never leave behind was Alex. She needed me, and it didn't matter what my body wanted. Family was more important than anything.

I closed my eyes as I opened the door. I felt like a coward, but I just couldn't face seeing the disappointment in his eyes.

After slipping out of the front door, I slammed it shut and stuffed all thoughts of Cyrus and my unexpected feelings for him into a tiny box deep in the back of my consciousness. I still hadn't made it out, but I knew there was no going back after this. Cyrus would have to scramble to find a spare access card, so that would at least buy me a few minutes. But time was precious, and I had to get a move on if I wanted to get back to Alex.

Stepping out into their front entryway, I bolted towards the familiar pathway I took when I arrived. I stopped just before the water, the sensor triggered, and I waited as long as I could for the slate slabs to rise above the surface. Time wasn't on my side. If I waited too long, I knew Cyrus would catch me.

As soon as I could make out the dark grey shapes of the steps just under the surface of the water, I ran for it. Feeling the water icy splash up my legs and the slippery slabs glide against my bare feet, I bolted, knowing I was so close to freedom I could almost taste it. Then the unthinkable happened.

I slipped.

WATER RUSHED into my mouth as the icy water shocked my body into action. My hands flailed and thrashed underwater, trying to grasp for the help that wasn't there. I could feel myself sinking, but no matter how hard I kicked or wiggled, my body would only sink deeper.

After a few moments of struggling under its bottomless depths, my vision blacked out. I couldn't tell if it was because of the lack of light below the surface or if my eyes were too weak to stay open. My lungs burned and as my last spurts of energy dissipated, I gave up the fight.

I couldn't believe I was going to die this way. I'd always assumed it would be at the hands of someone else, but never by my own stupid decisions and never like this...

Water exploded around me as millions of air bubbles rocked my body back and forth. I felt the water rush by me as powerful arms latched around my lifeless body and began pulling me upwards. The moment we broke the surface, my soaked body was pushed towards the edge of the concrete and I clawed out of the water with everything I had.

I laid out on the concrete and searched for my savior as I pulled in deep, ragged breaths. Cyrus broke the surface and I watched as he pulled himself out of the water and stared at me from the other side of their moat.

"Thank you." I rasped, still trying to catch my breath.

He said nothing in response, just stared at me with his penetrating emerald eyes. Cyrus had purposely given me an out. He and I both knew that if I made a run for it now, there would be no way he could catch up.

Indecision weighed on me. I wanted to be with Alex, I needed to keep her safe. But Cyrus had just saved my life. Could I just leave him again and pretend that what he did meant nothing when in reality it meant everything?

"Just go." Cyrus spat, deciding for me. "If you don't want to be here, leave."

I felt my heart fracture as I laid there and watched him leave. Once the front door shut and the lights downstairs turned off, I knew that the damage I caused would leave lasting marks on the both of us.

I couldn't bear to face the mess I made any longer, so I picked myself up off the floor and I ran. I ran as fast as my body would allow me. I ran towards my freedom. I ran away from my fears. I ran until the strange pain in my chest became too much to bear and my lungs screamed for a reprieve.

Stopping to catch my breath, I peered into the distance and saw the colossal iron gate a few yards away. The dark moonless night was a blessing. It meant that while I couldn't see very much in the darkness, neither could the guards that surrounded the property. Cyrus stopped chasing me. But that didn't mean he'd call off the guards if they found me.

My first instinct was to gun it for the gate. It seemed as if my body was in flight or fight mode and she desperately wanted to get the hell out of there. But I knew the only way I'd ever get out is if the guards didn't suspect there was a problem.

I crept towards the gate on silent feet. Every creak or shuffle in the night had my heart threatening to explode in my chest, but I was too close to stop now. Once I reached the giant metal structure, I climbed up with ease. The detailed ironwork of the main gate gave my hands and feet ample places to latch on to and the adrenaline coursing through my veins gave me the strength I needed. Every step I took was a step closer to what I wanted, yet the dull ache in my chest persisted.

On the descent, thoughts of Cyrus crept into my mind.

He caught me. He had me in his arms. Why did he let me go?

Too distracted for my own good, my foot slipped on one of the slick iron bars and I fell, crashing to the ground and landing hard on my hands and knees. I stood up with a wince and accessed my injuries. The gravel had dug into my knees and palms, and I could see the blood already forming.

As I readjusted my still drenched dress and got my bearings, two bright lights shone out of the darkness and focused themselves directly on my back. *Fuck.* I thought, cursing my arrogance. The guards must have been watching my pathetic attempt at escaping the entire time.

"Can you cut the lights?" I yelled, trying to shield my eyes from the blinding light as I turned to face them.

Within seconds, they cut lights, and darkness surrounded me again. As my eyes struggled to adjust, I peered into the darkness and could just make out the silhouette of a man approaching.

Squeezing my palms at my sides, I paced back and forth and tried to rack my brain for what to do next. I never planned on getting caught by the guards, then again, I never planned on making it as far as I did.

His silent approach was my first sign that something was wrong. He should have been scrambling to come grab me and doing a lot of screaming at me, but the only sound I heard was the quiet thud of his boots crunching against the asphalt.

He carried a flashlight and aimed it directly at my face. I squinted into the light, trying my best to shield my eyes from the obnoxious rent-a-cop fucking up my retinas.

"Jesus. You caught me okay?" I called out, rolling my eyes. "Enough with the fucking light."

As soon as the light cut out, my vision obscured, and a heavy hand squeezed my throat, instantly cutting off my airflow. Everything happened so fast, I had no time to react. One minute I was complaining about the fucking flashlight and the next, my lungs were burning and my vision was waning.

TWENTY-EIGHT

Stevie

WHEN I CAME TO, THE FIRST SOUND I HEARD WAS THE PURR of an engine. I could feel the gentle vibration of the wheels beneath me and knew that wherever I was, I was in motion.

"How much did you give her?" Asked a voice that sounded light years away.

"Enough." Said another, sounding just as muddled.

My head felt as if it were caving in on itself. Fear trickled up my spine. Something was wrong. The tiredness I felt went beyond any normal grogginess I'd ever experienced before.

When I finally mustered enough strength to peel my eyes open, darkness overtook my vision. Panicking, I violently twisted my head from side to side, terrified I had somehow gone blind. That's when I felt blindfold tightly bound around my eyes and the restraints around my wrists and ankles. I tried to lift my hands to my face, but they fell weakly back into my lap.

"Don't fucking move." A man's voice hissed into my right ear.

His voice felt much closer than the other two, and as I felt out my surroundings, I realized I was in the backseat of a car.

"She's awake." A man to my left called out.

Multiple voices started speaking up, and I had a hard time deciphering what they were saying. Every word they said seemed distorted, almost as if a thick haze was jumbling the translation.

"Whereyam I?" I stammered, the words strangely slurred together.

They had given me something. They had to have. This wasn't normal. None of this was normal. When none of them answered, I tried again.

"Whadoyou want?" I cried out, no longer caring how pathetic I sounded.

"Nothing. Everything." The man to my right mused. "You're the one with a decision to make."

"Fuckoff, withee riiiiddles." I growled.

The words came out slower than I intended and lost a bit of their edge on their way out.

"My, my, you've got an awfully filthy mouth for such a good girl, Stephanie." The man to my right retorted.

My movements faltered. Stephanie? Nobody had called me Stephanie in years. How did he know who I was?

"You have two choices." He went on. "Tell us everything you know about The Reapers or die a very slow and very painful death."

"I-I donknow anything." I mumbled, trying to yank at the bindings on my wrists but barely making a dent. Every single muscle in my body felt like it was treading through mud.

"Liar." A different man's cold voice interjected, turning my blood to ice. Based on the trajectory, he had to have been sitting in the driver's seat.

"Maybe she needs more... motivation?" A different man taunted from behind me.

Who the hell were these men, and what did they want with The Reapers?

I felt the sting of a sharp tug on my scalp and my head reared back instinctually. Tears pricked my eyes, but I refused to let them fall. I would not cry over these assholes.

"Mmm." The man grasping my hair groaned, running his nose against my exposed throat. "I think we need to fuck the answers out of her."

No.

"You'd like that wouldn't you?" The man to my right murmured, rubbing his calloused knuckle against my jaw. "The Reapers may take pity on you if you tell them we fucked the truth out of you."

I feverishly shook my head.

I would never agree to that. I wasn't stupid enough to think they'd go through all this trouble of drugging me and kidnapping me to just let me go if I played nice. No matter what I did, I was going to die.

"Don't worry." The man behind me murmured, sinking his teeth into my earlobe. "I'll try to be gentle."

"Enough with the games." The man to my left boomed across the car, causing the hand grasping my hair to retreat. "Talk or die. Those are your fucking options."

"I knoownothing." I hissed, the words flowing from my mouth like thick putty. "I'm jussa toy. Their p- property."

"You sure about that?" The man driving asked.

"Yesss." I spat through gritted teeth.

If I was going to die, I wanted it to be on my terms. I'd want to go out knowing that I wasn't a coward and that I looked death square in the eyes and told him to go fuck himself.

My body flung forward as the car came to a screeching halt. The only thing that stopped me from flying through the window was the two enormous arms that lashed out to keep me in my seat. My relief was short-lived. In an instant, they opened the car doors and proceeded to yank me out of the back seat.

"Are you sure those assholes are worth dying for?" One of the men asked, as he pressed a cool blade to my throat.

I said nothing and swallowed, feeling my throat bob against his sharp blade.

Tears stung my eyes as warm blood trickled down my neck. I wasn't ready to die, but I also wasn't ready to sacrifice Atlas, Ezra, Tristan, and Cyrus to live. I had no idea what information they could use against them, but I refused to give them anything.

"Enough." One of the men said, causing the blade against my throat to disappear.

A rogue tear trickled down my cheek as a storm of relief

and panic swirled within my chest. I was happy I wasn't dying, but also terrified of finding out why he kept me alive.

Fast hands worked to untie my ankles before moving on to my wrists. Were they letting me go? I carefully stood up. What was this? Some kind of sick game?

"Canneye leave?" I asked, too scared and disoriented to rip off the blindfold myself.

"Not until you're punished." He mused, positioning my body to stand in front of him. "Bend over." He growled.

Was this man out of his fucking mind?

Feeling the heat rush to my cheeks, I weighed my options. I could refuse, fight, struggle, and most likely still end up bent over his knee with an even angrier man or I could agree, deal with the embarrassment, and still be able to sit for the next few days. The best choice was obvious, albeit mortifying.

Swallowing the lump in my throat, I felt for his lap and crawled over it. Holding my breath, I prayed that this was the only thing they'd make me do.

Cool air brushed against my bare flesh as he lifted my dress, exposing my ass for the others to see. I could feel their eyes boring into my skin, but I couldn't bear to remove the blindfold and witness their reaction.

"What were you thinking?" The man hissed as the crack of his palm against my flesh echoed into the air.

My eyes welled with tears, but I wouldn't cry in front of them. I refused to.

"If anyone out there saw you leaving our home, they would not be as kind. There wouldn't be an option. They would fucking kill you." He spat.

Our home.

"A-Atlas?" I asked, swinging my arm to try to pull down my blindfold.

He answered me with another punishing smack to my ass. It *was* him. I had never been around Atlas when he was this out of control. The hits to my ass were wild and erratic, like he himself had no control over what his body was doing.

My pussy pooled with wetness and I had to stop the moans from clawing their way out. His anger. His volatile rage shouldn't turn me on, but it did. I liked this side of Atlas. The one who didn't treat me like I was off limits. I wanted him to break me. Wanted him to shatter me into a million fucking pieces because at least then, I'd have proof that he actually gave a fuck about me.

"Being important to us will get you killed." He boomed, following up with another slap.

My pulse accelerated wildly. I was important to them. I thought about the other men watching. Ezra, Cyrus, and Tristan. None of them made a move to leave, but the tension in the air was palpable. They all watched Atlas smack my flesh repeatedly without so much as a word of protest. I could tell that what he was doing bothered them. I just didn't know if it was because they wanted him to stop or because they wanted to do it themselves.

Embarrassment flamed my cheeks as I felt the evidence of my enjoyment sliding down my thigh. I was sure with their view of the action, they could see my wetness' unmistakable gleam.

"How could you be so fucking reckless?" Atlas hissed, giving me another ruthless slap that jolted my body forward.

I whimpered, doing everything I could to stop myself from begging for more. I enjoyed the power behind each blow. Enjoyed that I had the power to make such a ruthless and stoic man turn so crazed and primal.

"That's enough." Cyrus said, whipping my blindfold off and tossing it to the ground.

Atlas' smacks waned as he focused his eyes on his brother. My traitorous body writhed against him, already missing his touch.

"Oh, and I'm supposed to trust your judgement?" Atlas asked as he grabbed me by my hair and forced me to my feet.

Cyrus' jaw clenched but said nothing in response.

"Exactly," Atlas said, inching towards Cyrus' face, "we wouldn't be in this mess if it wasn't for you. You're an idiot for letting her trick you."

The way he emphasised the word 'her' had shame licking across my skin. I had done this. I had been the one to push Atlas over the edge. I had never seen him so angry before, and the man I had known the longest was unrecognizable with the murderous look in gaze.

Now, when I looked at him, I no longer saw DC, the mysterious businessman that came to visit me every night. I only saw Atlas, the cold and ruthless leader of The Reapers. The man responsible for instilling fear in the heart of an entire town. DC was an illusion I had tricked myself into believing, but Atlas was the real fucking deal.

"Does Mel know about your twisted little fascination with our pet?" Cyrus spat, staring daggers at his brother.

"What the fuck are you talking about?" Atlas retorted with a scowl.

"Come on, you enjoyed punishing her almost as much as she enjoyed being punished by you." He spat, giving me a once over.

My cheeks flamed.

"Bullshit." Atlas hissed, shaking his head in denial. "This was a punishment, nothing more."

"Look at her." Cyrus taunted, nodding his head towards me. "I know what she looks like when she's turned on." He smirked, eyeing my body up and down. "I've seen that shit, firsthand."

The crunch of knuckles against flesh echoed in my ears.

I moved to stop them, but a muscular arm wrapped around me, stilling my movements. *Tristan.*

"This isn't your fight." Ezra whispered, moving to stand on my other side before pressing his lips to my ear. "They need to figure this out, otherwise we'll always be fighting over you."

I didn't know what to say, but he mentioned the future and it gave me hope that they weren't going to kill me for trying to escape.

"Oh, and Angel?" Ez hissed, licking the blood from my throat with a lavish stroke of his tongue. "If you ever try to leave us again, I will kill you."

He said it so matter-of-factly; I had no doubt in my mind that he meant every single word.

***

AFTER THE FIGHT WAS OVER, Ezra pulled Atlas away and they loaded up into the front seat of Ezra's car without another word. Cyrus turned to follow them, but I reached out and grabbed his arm.

"Cyrus," I spoke up, finally mustering the courage and gaining enough of my feeling back to do so, "I'm sorry."

"No, you're not." He said smiling, causing the split in his lip to spread even further. "You aren't sorry for what you did. You're sorry you got caught."

"That's not true. I-"

His hand struck out, closing my throat with a tight grip.

"Let me make one thing perfectly clear." He hissed, tightening his grip. "The Cyrus you saw at the house is dead. I may be an idiot, but I'll never make the mistake of trusting you again." He growled, crashing his lips into mine.

The kiss was bitter, painful, and angry. It stole the last bits of oxygen I had in my lungs and had spots clouding my vision. I knew I could die if he didn't relinquish his hold on my throat, yet I wanted the pain. I craved it. The pain distracted me from the ache betraying them all had created in my chest.

After he broke off our kiss, he released me. My chest filled with oxygen and sorrow as I crumpled to the ground. Tears stung my eyes, but I batted them away. I knew I deserved to feel every ounce of the hate he had towards me, but that didn't stop it from hurting like hell.

It was why I never let people in to begin with. I knew that when the dust settled, the only thing I'd ever get out of letting people in was pain. And even though it wasn't what I intended, for those few hours, I had let Cyrus in.

"Tris, tie her up and throw her in the trunk." He ordered, not even bothering to look at me. "I don't think any of us can stand to look at her right now."

TWENTY-NINE

Stevie

THE DAYS AFTER MY ESCAPE ATTEMPT BLURRED INTO EACH other. The semblance of freedom I had before was gone, and in its place were the very real guards posted outside of my bedroom door.

They only allowed me trips to the restroom and only when Tristan, Cyrus, Atlas, and Ezra were nowhere in sight. Other than that, all of my privileges vanished.

The guys were smart. They changed the guards every day, so I never saw the same guard twice. Not that I would even try anything with them anyway, but they had themselves convinced that the only reason I had messed with Cyrus was to escape. I couldn't even stomach the idea of them knowing the truth.

None of them would even as much as check in on me. It was like I no longer existed in their world. My room sat between Ezra's and Tristan's so I knew they hadn't completely left. But the feeling of solitude was still very real and was slowly driving me insane.

Every time I'd hear a creak from the hardwood or a little cough from one of their rooms, my heart would pound in my chest and I'd feel the familiar rush of excitement each one of them elicited within me. I became obsessed with hearing those sounds. I knew I needed to change what was happening to me, before I succumbed entirely to the madness.

Day nine of total isolation is when it hit me, I needed to stop eating. I could survive days without eating, but they had no way of knowing that. I needed to get my point across to them somehow. If I could just talk to one of them, maybe I could get them to change their minds and allow me the freedoms I had before.

Three times each day the guards would knock on my door and leave a tray of food outside, and every single time I'd ignore their knocks and refuse to even look at it. I wasn't completely destructive. I still took the water they brought me, but my hunger for freedom was stronger than any hunger pains I had to endure.

On day eight of my hunger strike, I laid myself out on the cool hardwood floor and tried to meditate the nausea away. The dizziness was hitting me in waves, but I knew I was close to making them crack. So close to having my freedom.

The night before, I'd heard Atlas scream at the guards when he noticed that my food hadn't been touched again. It was the first reaction I'd gotten from any of them in almost two weeks, and with it, hope bloomed in my gut. They needed to think that I'd rather die than live like this because, the truth of it was, being alone was killing me.

I closed my eyes as another pang of hunger hit my stomach. I could get through this, I just needed to be strong and distract myself. The first thought that came to my mind was to tell myself a story. It was what I did as a child, to help find peace at night after a tumultuous day with my mother.

I let out a deep breath and let my mind flow, searching for one of the many fairy tales I memorized as a child. The tale of Beauty and the Beast was the only story my mind could come up with, and I cursed at the irony.

Out of all the fairy tales, Beauty and the Beast was my least favorite as a child. I never understood what possessed Belle to love someone who was so undeniably awful to her.

She was beautiful and kind, and The Beast was bitter and cold. Her father being there was a complete misunderstanding, but the asshole of a beast didn't care. He used her father's mistake to his advantage, and he stole a girl he had no business taking.

After some time together, Belle began sympathizing with The Beast and before she knew it, he became the center of her universe. Someone she couldn't fathom living without. She fell in love with a monster.

The similarities to my situation weren't lost on me. Here I was obsessing over my own monsters. Falling so easily into my own distorted fantasy that I blatantly ignored the cold, hard facts.

The Reapers were bad people. Deranged killers who accepted a girl as payment for a fucking debt. Lying, cheating, and stealing were regular business practices for them. They didn't understand the concept of boundaries and they saw me as nothing more than an object, something to play with whenever and wherever they wanted.

Yet for all their faults, deep down, I knew I was just as bad as they were. I didn't care about the blood on their hands. I had no qualms about the punishments they dealt, and if I'd done my fair share of lying, cheating, and stealing in my own life to survive. In the grand scheme of things, that was what they were doing too. A sick part of me even enjoyed being owned by them, they felt like the family I never got to have.

But this wasn't a fairy tale. The Reapers weren't my knights in shining armor who were going to magically turn into princes if I just loved them enough. They were unapologetically themselves, and nothing I did was going to change that. The question was, was I willing to accept them for all that they were?

The question lingered in my mind even after the darkness started to cloud my vision. It didn't feel like I was being pulled into a normal slumber, but I was tired of the pain and I knew if I gave in, the familiar nothingness that had always made me feel invincible would welcome me with open arms. So I went willingly into the darkness and avoided answering the question I already knew the answer to.

THIRTY

Tristan

I SHOULDN'T HAVE BEEN WATCHING, BUT I JUST COULDN'T help myself. She needed to be punished. Needed to know there were consequences for her actions, but that didn't mean I couldn't check in on her.

When we bought the house, we outfitted every room with hidden security cameras. I monitored the cameras in both our businesses and our home, but I made it a point to never check the footage in our house unless it was absolutely necessary. Monitoring Stevie felt like a necessity.

As I sat at my desk and turned on the live feed to her room, she was nowhere in sight. I switched screens to the hallway camera and found her guard, Tony, posted in his usual spot.

It was just after 8pm and her dinner still sat untouched outside of her bedroom door. I had to give it to her. The girl was as stubborn as a fucking mule.

After watching her for the last couple of weeks, I knew her daily patterns like the back of my hand. She wasn't in bed, not sitting in front of the fireplace, nor staring out of her window. The only other place left was her closet and it was the one space in her room the cameras couldn't pick up on. I scrolled through my phone and tried not to stare at the empty screen. She'd show up, eventually. It wasn't like she could go anywhere else.

Ten minutes had gone by and I glanced at the monitor again. It wasn't like her to be out of view for that long. I searched the screen, trying to pick up on any clue that some-thing was wrong, but nothing seemed amiss. She just vanished.

Barrelling out of my room, I threw my door open and barked at Tony for the key to her door. Tony fumbled, caught off by my sudden appearance. He was taking too long to find the fucking key on his key ring and I was growing impatient. Stevie would've heard the commotion and come to the door by now. Something wasn't right.

After jamming my shoulder into the door with full force a few times, I ripped the door off of its hinges. As soon as I entered the room and spotted Stevie, my stomach dropped. I found her laid on the floor looking like she was on her fucking death bed. Her frail body looked so tiny in the white nightgown she wore. Her skin was paler than before and gone was the rosy flush of her lips and cheeks that brought her expressive face to life.

Fuck.

I pulled her into my arms as Tony's dumbass stumbled in after me.

"Call a fucking ambulance and tell my brothers to get their asses in here, now!"

Tony frantically nodded his head and raced for the door as I checked her vitals. Her breathing was shallow, and she felt cool to the touch, but she had a steady pulse.

"Fuck." I cursed, pressing my lips to her cold forehead. "Hold on, baby. Help is coming."

"What did Dr. Roswell s... say?" I asked, eyeing Atlas as he reentered the room.

After getting her stabilized, the doctor pulled Atlas aside to discuss Stevie's condition in private. He was probably trying to pinpoint how her health had deteriorated so much under our care.

"She's stable." Atlas grunted, looking out her window at the dark sky. "She needs to rest."

Ezra gave Atlas a somber look as he brushed Stevie's hair out of her face. As soon as the medics laid her on her bed, Ezra curled up next to her and since then, had refused to leave.

"She needs to fucking eat." Cyrus retorted, pacing at the

foot of her bed. "This shit," he said, gesturing to Stevie's sullen body, "has gone on long enough."

He was right. We set out to teach her a lesson, but we were going about it all wrong. She ran because she didn't trust us, but keeping her locked up would only strengthen that distrust. Besides, she wasn't the only one that created this mess.

She may have walked into our world willingly, but we were the sick fucks that welcomed her with open arms. We were the ones who thought her presence wouldn't affect us. That all she'd be was a token of our power.

But Stevie was so much more than that. She didn't seem fazed by the blood on our hands. She had seen the damage we could cause, had been exposed to the lifestyle and attention we garnered, and she still wasn't intimidated. She was one of us. Even if we didn't want to admit it. Even if she couldn't admit it to herself.

"Just be grateful Dr. Roswell let us keep her here for now." Atlas said, turning to face us. "He wants us to bring her by his office next week for a follow up."

Dr. Roswell was on our payroll. The old man knew what kind of businesses we ran and had stitched us up in a flash more times than I could remember. His discretion was something we could rely on. But above anything else, Dr. Roswell was a good man who took his code of ethics seriously. If he found out we were holding Stevie against her will, he would flip his fucking lid.

"So, things have to change." I said, holding her frail hand in mine.

"Indeed, they do." Atlas sighed, running his hand through his hair. "Indeed, they do."

THIRTY-ONE

Stevie

I AWOKE TO FOUR SETS OF EYES FOCUSED ON ME AND NO recollection of what had happened. Stoic expressions painted each of their faces as they watched my eyes slowly flutter open and I could tell that whatever happened, wasn't good. I glanced around, trying to get my bearings. We were in my room and aside from the four massive men and the shattered door, everything was as I left it.

"What happened?" I asked, wincing at the dryness in my throat.

"Your reluctance to eat is what happened." Atlas chastised, handing me a glass of water.

I took a small sip and averted my eyes, feeling the weight of each of their gazes. I felt guilty, but I couldn't understand why. So I went a little too far with the hunger strike, but it wasn't entirely my fault. They were the ones who drove me into madness. If anyone should feel bad, it's them.

"How long have I been out?" I asked, watching as my hand swirled the water in my glass.

Ezra sighed, brushing his tattooed fingers against mine.

"A few days, Angel." He said, pressing his lips to my knuckles.

My eyes flashed up at that news. *Days.* That combined with the time I'd spent locked away meant that it had been over three weeks since I last spoke with Alex. Three weeks since I knew she was safe.

"When did you guys find me?"

They forbid the guards from ever entering my room. The only interaction I had with the guards was when they knocked on my door to offer me food and when I'd knock back whenever I needed a restroom trip. As part of my protest, I limited my trips to the restroom to twice a day, which meant that the guards wouldn't have thought anything was amiss until at least the next afternoon. *How long had I been laying there alone?*

"Luckily, Tris spotted you." Cyrus said, clapping Tristan on his back.

"What do you mean, he spotted me?" I asked, piercing my eyes at Tristan.

"We have surveillance cameras." Tristan mumbled as he crossed his powerful arms with a grimace.

"Cameras." I scoffed, shaking my head with disdain.

Of course they had fucking cameras. So Tristan's been watching me. While I've been literally dying for some form of human interaction, Tris had been getting his fucking kicks from spying on me.

"Well, I hope you got your fucking money's worth." I hissed.

"Relax, Princess." Cyrus insisted, moving to stand next to his twin. "We outfitted the entire house with a security system before we knew you existed. It was an omission. Not a lie."

The anger brewing underneath my skin dissipated. Cyrus was right. It wasn't as if he installed the camera specifically for me, and I'd be lying if I said it didn't make me a little happy to know that Tristan missed me as much as I missed all of them. It made the feelings I had developed for them in such a short amount of time seem a little less crazy.

"Anyway," Atlas spoke up, taking a seat at the foot of my bed, "it seems we're at an impasse. The four of us would like to keep you alive, but you seem hell bent on doing everything you can to get yourself killed."

I wanted to smile at his admission. They still wanted me alive. Despite all the trouble I had caused and all the bullshit I pulled, they still wanted me in their lives.

"Well, what do you suggest?" I asked, fighting the smile that threatened to surface.

"Behave like the good little angel you are," Ezra asserted, flashing me a sinister grin. "and we'll give you your house privileges back."

"No deal." I said, crossing my arms over my chest. "For whatever reason, the four of you want me around. Which means I'm the one with the bargaining power. If I'm going to stay here and I mean really stay and do this, there needs to be some changes. I need to come and go as I please and I want my old job back."

"No." Tristan said, shaking his head. "We've already told you, you're not s... safe out there alone."

"Then I'll work at Hell's Tavern." I offered, grasping at straws as I sat up in my seat.

"Jessie can train me. I'll only work when you guys are there and you can keep an eye on me the entire time."

"Clever girl." Ezra cooed, patting me on the head.

"She has a point." Cyrus chimed in, reluctantly. "Besides, we already know she'll just try to run again if we keep her locked up. "

"Fine." Atlas groaned with flared nostrils. "You start next week."

THIRTY-TWO

Atlas

"Fuck!" I cursed as the scorching liquid spilled onto my skin. I shook my hand, trying to shake away the sting, but the bright red welts formed, anyway. Everything that could go wrong had been going wrong lately, spilling my fresh cup of coffee was merely the icing on the cake.

For the past couple of nights I've been out, trying to smooth things over with Melanie to no avail. It had been a couple of weeks since Stevie and Mel's fight, and I wanted to assure myself that all loose ends had been thoroughly tied. I needed to be sure the fight had blown over before we gave Stevie the freedoms we agreed to.

When I arrived at Melanie's penthouse, the polite conversation over dinner quickly turned into a drawn out interaction that lasted several days. Everything was political in our world and when Melanie insisted I stay in the guest room her staff had prepared, I knew if I refused, she and her family would take it as a personal dig. I didn't give a fuck about the ramifications for myself, but my goal was to keep Stevie safe, which meant that I needed to play nice with Mel, so I kept her company and bided my time.

During the day, I'd accompany her to mind-numbing social events. Listening to her drone on and on about the latest gossip with some of the most pivotal figures in Caspian Hills. I never cared to rub elbows with the societal snobs of our city. But after spending so much of her life trying to prove herself to these people, kissing ass was Mel's full-time job.

Melanie assumed that showing up with me on her arm would give her the respect she craved, but nothing would change the way people viewed her family. Sure, The Diaz Cartel had money and power, but no amount of wealth could make people forget that a good chunk of their profits came from human trafficking. The Reapers weren't saints by any means, but the one thing we never dabbled in was flesh.

The days with Melanie were painless compared to the nights. Each night, I'd sling back shot after shot of Jack Daniels while she got more and more bold with her advancements. I wasn't normally much of a drinker, but I needed a buffer to stop myself from wanting to strangle her. Besides, I knew I could chalk up my perpetual softness around her to whiskey dick and avoid the fury that would come whenever I refused to fuck her. It was a pain in the ass, but I did it all hoping to make nice with the woman that was out for Stevie's blood.

Stevie was reckless and impulsive, but she didn't deserve to have to deal with Melanie's wrath. Mel had only fucked with her because of her ties with me, and she wouldn't even be in this mess at all if it wasn't for the stupid decisions I made.

During our last dinner together, I finally brought up the real reason for my visit.

"Thank you again for being so hospitable, Mel." I said, looking up at her from across the ostentatious dining room table.

"Of course, darling." She crooned, tapping her napkin against her wine-stained lips. "You know I'm always happy to take care of my fiancé."

I gave her a smile I didn't feel and continued.

"There is one other thing I wanted to run by you." I paused, circling the whisky in my glass. "I'm hoping that you'll find it in your heart to forgive my guest for being so disrespectful. Rest assured, my brothers and I have already put her in her place. She should have never laid a finger on you. I don't think this needs to escalate any further. Don't you agree?"

"No." She hissed, tossing her napkin to the floor. "I do not agree. You must think I'm some kind of idiot. You haven't given me the time of day in the five years we've known each other. You didn't think it would strike me as odd that you were suddenly so willing to stick around? I figured you had an ulterior motive for coming here, and I should've fucking known it was her."

"Melanie," I scolded through gritted teeth, "be rational. She didn't know how important you were to us. She does now."

"You aren't fooling anyone, Atlas." She hissed, sipping her red wine. "She's a complication that needs to be eliminated. When I get my hands on her, and I will fucking get my hands on her, you and your men won't do anything to stop me. Not unless you want our little agreement to end."

"Thanks again for the hospitality." I spat, rising from my chair. "Sorry I can't stay for dinner, I've suddenly lost my appetite."

Shoving the chair out of my way, I grabbed my coat and left the room. This entire visit was a complete waste of fucking time. Melanie's resentment hadn't faded since their fight. It had only festered. She wasn't over what happened and she wouldn't be until she got her revenge.

"You can't keep her hidden forever, Atlas!" She yelled, watching me as I reached for the handle of the front door. "She's going to get what's coming to her one way or another."

Melanie was a crazy bitch, but she was right. We couldn't keep Stevie hidden forever, and the longer she stayed in our world, the more in danger she'd be.

I stared at spilled coffee and let out a deep sigh. *Fuck it.* The coffee was supposed to help me clear my head, but liquor was a much better remedy for the shit I had going on.

I opened our liquor cabinet, reached for the bottle of Macallan scotch and took a swig, relishing in it's familiar burn.

Cyrus padded into the kitchen, stopping by the fridge to pull a water bottle out. He cocked a brow when he noticed the bottle of scotch in my hand. But said nothing as he took a seat on a barstool and pulled out his phone.

"Where is everyone?" I asked, wiping my mouth with the back of my hand.

It was around 9PM and the house was abnormally quiet.

"Ez and Tris are in the dungeon." Cyrus quipped, looking bored as he swiped through his phone.

"And Stevie?" I asked, trying and failing to sound nonchalant.

"She's in her room." Cyrus said, looking up at me. "How'd it go with Mel?"

"Not good." I said, loosening my tie as I leaned over the kitchen island. "We can't keep Stevie, it's not safe for her. I'll have the maids pack up her things in the morning. She's going home."

"This is her home," Cyrus asserted, pressing his lips firmly together, "don't you think she deserves some kind of say in this?"

"No. I don't. I'm doing what's best for all of us. Keeping her here will just complicate things."

And remind me every day that I can't have her.

"Bullshit." He spat. "Stevie is staying. We aren't your fucking foot soldiers. You can't just snap your fingers and expect us to follow blindly. Tris talks to her. Even Ez has some sick fascination with her. She's good for them and you know it."

"Yeah." I retorted with a scowl, "and what about you?"

"What about me?"

"Baby brother, spare me the act, alright? Let's not pretend that your cock doesn't have a dog in the race. It was obvious what happened the night she tried to run away. Her scent was all over you."

"Is that the real problem, At? Is it that she's sleeping alone in her room right now and it drives you insane knowing you can't do anything about it?"

"I'm engaged."

"Yeah, and why is that?" He asked, with a sarcastic smirk. "Money? Power? Because there's no way in hell it's love."

"You have no idea what you're talking about or what kind of sacrifices I've made for you assholes." I hissed, giving him a sideways glance as I took another swig of scotch.

Everything I did was for them. They were just too fucking blind to see it.

"That's the problem," he said, narrowing his eyes at me, "you never tell us shit. How are we supposed to help you if you never clue us in?"

I had no response. I was done discussing my personal life and ready to forget this conversation ever happened.

"We aren't kids anymore." He said, giving up as he stood to leave. "Let us help you carry the fucking load every once in a while."

Stevie hadn't told my brothers about our past, and part of me was grateful for her discretion. My brothers already had their suspicions about Mel and if the truth came out, no way in hell would they ever let me go through with the arrangement. The other part of me. The bitter, angry asshole part wished she'd at least acknowledge that I wasn't the only one who felt something. That it killed her as much as it killed me to keep my distance. That I wasn't the only one fighting my insane jealousy.

I took another swig from my scotch bottle, savoring the burn in my chest.

I always thought I could never stomach the idea of seeing Stevie with someone else. That no one else would ever be good enough for her. Then I saw her with them. Ezra, Tristan, and Cyrus were the only fuckers on this planet who meant something to me. And seeing the effect she had on them was a humbling experience. I tried to fight it. Tried to push her the fuck out of our lives as soon as I saw the signs. But how could I want them to stay away from a girl that has enough room in her heart for all of them?

I was happy for my brothers. She was good for them. But Stevie Alexander was poisonous to me. Every time I thought of Stevie, I'd get these crazy ideas in my head. Crazy ideas that I had no business fucking thinking about. In fact, I shouldn't be thinking at all. What I really needed was to forget. Forget Melanie and her stupid fucking vendetta. Forget my brothers and their need to butt into my personal life. And as I took another swig of my 18 year single malt scotch, I vowed to forget the girl that I loved first, but could never love again.

THIRTY-THREE

Stevie

A LOUD CRASH BOOMED OUTSIDE OF MY BEDROOM, SHOCKING my body awake. I scrambled out of bed and rushed towards the freshly installed door, trying to see what all the commotion was about.

I spotted Atlas a few feet down the hallway, seated with his head between his knees and with what looked like the remnants of a glass frame scattered all around him. The normally polished and put-together man looked completely out of sorts. His grey suit was wrinkled, his hair was disheveled, and there was a half empty bottle of scotch grasped in his right hand. He took a swig and smiled bitterly to himself, unaware that I was watching him.

"Atlas?" I hesitated, approaching him with caution. "Is everything okay?"

"Well, look who it is." He sneered, taking another swig. "The girl of the fucking hour."

The sarcasm on his tongue stung. His anger combined with the alcohol on his breath was a volatile combination, reminding me so much of Malcolm during his benders. This wasn't the man I knew. Not in the slightest.

"You know what? I'll leave you to it." I said, retreating to my room. "I just wanted to make sure you were okay, but you obviously aren't in the mood for company."

"Oh, don't you worry your pretty little head." He sneered, tipping his head back with a smug smirk. "I'm fine. Besides, I don't need *your* kind of help right now."

I couldn't ignore the blatant jab. I should have. In his condition he was liable to say anything to get a rise out of me, but I was tired of standing by while the strings that once tied us together slowly frayed. It was only a matter of time before everything imploded on us.

"What the hell is that supposed to mean?" I challenged, staring him up and down.

"It means that unfortunately for you, my cock is off limits. I'm engaged and the type of healing you've used on my brothers won't work for me."

I suspected my relationships with his brothers bothered him, especially after the fight with Cyrus, but it hurt to hear the words come from his lips.

"That's a fucking low blow and you know it." I said, swallowing hard as our eyes locked.

"It's the truth." He hissed, getting up to his feet. "I'm sorry if you can't fucking handle it."

I couldn't deny that there was a spark with each of his brothers. I tried to fight it. Hell, I even physically ran from it. But the connections proved too strong to deny. I could tell it upset Atlas, but what he was saying was bullshit. His words made my feelings sound cheap and wrong. Like I was toying with each of them just for my own sick amusement. There was nothing amusing about falling for four men that you know you should hate.

"Don't talk to me about the truth okay?" I said, shaking my head with a sneer. "Let's talk about the fact that you fucking lied to me for over two years!"

He squeezed his eyes shut, saying nothing in response, so I continued.

"Gee, I wonder why that was? Could it be because you had a fucking fiancée you wanted to keep hidden?"

It was something I wanted to ask him since the day I saw them together. I knew it wasn't my place to be jealous. He and I had only ever been friends, but I hoped for more, and it pissed me off to know that he had kept me straggling on like some idiot while he went home to his fiancée every night. Confronting him felt cathartic and once I started releasing all of my pent-up frustrations, the questions wouldn't stop coming.

"Why the secrecy? That's where you've been the last couple of nights, right? Why hide the only fucking thing you seem to care about from someone you considered a *friend*?"

His movements were swift, like a bolt of lightning striking

through the sky. One minute he was on the floor and the next, he was hovering over me and pinning my body to the wall. The sweet smell of scotch mixed with his heady scent of amber and sandalwood had mouth watering and I hated myself for wanting him, even while I hated him.

"We," he hissed as he caged me in with his arms. "were never friends. What I divulged to a fucking stranger is entirely up to me."

"You're an asshole," I said, biting my lip to hold back my tears, "And a fucking liar."

"Yeah," he said, with a half-hearted smile, "well that makes two of us."

"What are you talking about?" I asked, narrowing my eyes. "I never lied."

"The shiner you rocked at the shop." He replied with a rigid expression. "You didn't honestly expect me to fall for the whole 'I fell into a door' thing, did you?"

"I..."

He wasn't wrong. I was mad at him for lying, but only because his truths had come out sooner than mine did. And I still had secrets he knew nothing about.

"You had your secrets and so did I." He hissed, baring his teeth. "Let's not pretend you're holier than thou just because my shit came out before yours did."

I blinked at him, not knowing what to say.

"Who hit you that night, Stevie?" He challenged, looking into my eyes.

His nostrils flared as he waited for an answer. I had nothing to say. He was right. I was as much of a liar as he was.

"Who the fuck hit you?" He snarled, slapping the wall next to my head.

I bit into my lower lip and flinched, still used to anticipating the pain when someone would yell at me like that. His eyes flashed to my mouth, and I held my breath, too terrified to move. Fiery heat radiated between us as I stared into his unsettling deep brown eyes. If nothing else, he deserved one truth.

"Malcolm," I breathed, averting my eyes, "okay? It was my fucking step father. Is that what you wanted to hear? The fucked up girl got beat by her parents so now she fucks anyone that will give her attention."

The pain on his face sliced through my chest. I never wanted to see that look on his face. Pity. Tears welled in my eyes and this time I let them fall freely. Even if I wanted to, I was too far gone to stop them now.

"Fuck, Stevie." He said, trying to wipe away the tears that kept coming. "I'm sorry, okay? I'm so fucking sorry."

He pressed his lips against my cheeks repeatedly, desperately trying to catch the salty tears as they fell, and for a moment, I let him. Basking in the embrace of the first man who made me feel and the only man that had ever broken my heart.

His chaste kisses grew more intense as he held my trembling body in his arms. I warred with myself. Too selfish to stop it, yet also too scared to let it go any further. Atlas was off limits, despite what my greedy heart wanted. I knew that once he was sober, he'd regret it and end up hating me even more if I let it go any further.

"No." I said, pushing him away after finally talking some sense into myself. "Atlas, we can't do this."

He immediately let go, and I fought the urge to cry out at the emptiness I felt without his arms around me.

"This isn't right," I said, trying to reason with him. "you're drunk and you have a fiancée. I don't want to be something you'll regret in the morning."

A bitter smile formed across his lips as he grabbed his bottle of Macallan and took another swig.

"If only things were that simple. Keep running from the truth, little girl." He warned as he walked towards his room. "It's safer for everyone involved if you do."

THIRTY-FOUR

Stevie

DESPITE MY ATTEMPTS TO GET SOME REST, EVERY TIME I closed my eyes, the nightmare would come. It was the same one that visited me nearly every night. Only this time, when I felt the jacket get thrown on my body, I'd look up and see Atlas looking at me with pity in his eyes.

I needed to clear my head and there was only one space in this house that had become my home away from home. *Ezra's room.*

I slipped out of my room and into Ezra's on silent feet. He

and Tristan were gone for the night, but Ezra had told me to come to his room whenever I didn't feel like facing my demons and tonight, had definitely become one of those nights.

Ezra's room was the complete antithesis of where you'd expect a man like him to live. Unlike the unhinged and unpredictable man, his room was the picture of calm and serenity. Ice blue walls, lavender diffusers and soft, luxurious throws and linens accented the space. Taking a deep breath in, I soaked up his comforting scent of lavender tinged smoke and felt the pressure in my chest ease. His scent worked like magic for my anxiety.

Ezra set the far corner of his room up as a makeshift art studio. Large canvases laid scattered across his tarp-covered floor. Some blank, some partially finished, and some nearly completed. I knew some of them had blood on them, but I tried my best not to think about that.

As I snaked through the canvases, checking out his work, I paused, spotting a blank canvas with a full acrylic paint setup already laid out next to it. I wasn't tired and Ezra had told me that painting was cathartic for him. Maybe getting some of my frustration out on canvas wasn't such a bad idea.

Seconds turned to minutes and minutes turned to hours as I poured my heart out onto the canvas. I didn't have a clear picture in my mind, only that I needed to get whatever was in my chest, out.

It wasn't until the sun's first rays of light rose in the sky that I realized how long I'd been working on the canvas. Up close, the canvas looked like a chaotic symphony of colors that had no real purpose or design. But when I pulled back to look at the full 3' x 3' canvas, I could see exactly what it was supposed to be as clear as day. Four figures held one smaller one. A woman. At first I thought they were restraining her, but if you look at her feet, you can see that they weren't touching the ground. They're holding her up.

"It's beautiful, Angel." Ezra murmured, moving to stand beside me.

I didn't hear him come home and yet somehow; his appearance didn't surprise me. Ezra had a knack for showing up precisely when I needed him to.

"I know which is which." He murmured, pulling me in to press a kiss to my neck.

"How can you tell?" I asked, melting into his powerful hold. "I can't even tell what I created."

"Sure you can, it's an interpretation of the way you see each of us."

"That one." He said, pointing to the one whispering into the smaller one's ear, "is me. I'm the devil on your shoulder, baby."

"That one." He said, pointing to the brighter one laughing, with his hand running through his hair. "Is Cyrus. You see him as your light, the one that brings you joy."

"That one." He said, pointing to the blurry darker one with his hands around the small one's waist. "Is Tristan. You see him as your stability, but there's also some mystery around him."

"And what about that one?" I asked about the last one, that seemed a step back behind the rest.

"That one may be the most interesting of all." He said with a cocked brow.

"Why do you say that?"

"You're holding hands, but it's out of the view of the rest

of us. Almost like the connection is a secret." He mused, giving me a pointed look. "Anything you want to share?"

"Yes. No." I said with a grimace as I shook my head. "When did everything get so fucked?"

"Long before you ever came into our lives." He mused, taking a seat on his ice blue couch. "Sit with me, Angel. I think it's time you learned about who my brothers and I were before we became The Reapers. "

I trekked towards the couch and sat next to him, eager to learn more about the men of this house.

"One thing you should know," he said, shifting his body towards me, "is that Atlas lives up to his namesake. He carries the weight of the world on his shoulders and does what he can to protect us. But when he feels like he's failed, he refuses to forgive himself."

I gave him a small nod. It was always clear to me that Atlas was their leader, but I had this idea in my head that he was making decisions and bossing everyone around simply to coax his own ego. I missed the glaringly obvious truth behind his actions. Trying to control everything was his way of protecting them. And me.

"He's not a bad guy. He just does whatever it takes to-"

"Keep you guys alive?" I finished for him as I smiled to myself.

"Something like that." Ezra replied as a soft smile formed on his lips.

"That seems to be a running theme these days." I mumbled, leaning on his shoulder.

"Hmm?" He asked, pressing his lips against my forehead.

"It's nothing." I said, shaking my head and looking up at him.

The familiarity and intimacy between us should have been scary. It had become almost second nature for me to crawl into Ezra's arms and be soothed by his presence. It was to the point where sometimes I didn't even realize my body was moving towards him until my skin pressed against his.

It was the same for Ezra, too. Sometimes, when we were just sitting on the couch, his hand would mindlessly reach out and start twirling my hair. The connection between us was more than just friendship and more than just sex. It was a deeper, soul connection. Almost as if our bodies had practiced this dance their entire lives, and they knew each other's movements by heart.

"You were about to tell me about your guys' past."

"Right." He said with a firm nod as he shifted in his seat and faced straight ahead.

His tattooed fingers tapped on his knees as he searched for his next words. I reached for his left hand and laced my fingers between his. Whatever he was preparing to share seemed big, and he needed to know that I was right there with him.

"My brothers and I were all born in Caspian Valley, and for the first few years of our life, we had a decent upbringing. We weren't the richest family by any means, but our parents did what they needed to get by and for a while our lives were good."

I scooted my body closer to his, sensing he needed the comfort.

"When I was seven, The Diaz Cartel killed our parents right in front of us. They weren't the target. Just innocent bystanders in a drive-by shooting that got out of hand." He grimaced as he nervously rubbed his fingertips against my knuckles and searched for my eyes. "Kind of comes with the territory when you live in a shit neighborhood."

I squeezed his hand, silently urging him to continue.

"After they died, we had no family to turn to. Our parents had no siblings, and their parents had died long before any of us were born. With nowhere to go, our only option was the system."

My heart broke for all of them. I knew what it was like to lose a parent at a young age, and I couldn't imagine losing two loving parents so young. It must have been terrifying.

"Tris and Cy were fostered almost immediately. They were only five at the time and still had that cute innocent thing going on, so it made sense." He chuckled and I smiled, picturing the two of them as broody little kids.

Tristan told me about his foster father and the abuse he had to endure as a kid. If Tristan and Cyrus didn't kill the bastard, I would've killed him myself.

"Atlas and I weren't so lucky. Years ticked by while we lived in the group home, waiting for someone to give a fuck about the damaged kids the world forgot."

He winced as he said the words and I immediately shifted closer, resting my head against his neck. It was difficult for him to share this story, but I was grateful that he was sharing it with me.

"When we got word of a woman wanting an older kid, Atlas and I didn't know how to feel. We wanted to be excited, but we'd seen too many couples blatantly ignore us once they learned what we'd witnessed. They worried our parent's brutal murder made us predisposed to violence. Go figure."

"Then it happened." He said, with a bitter smile on his lips. "She selected me. I was the fucking chosen one. Laura seemed nice enough, but even back then, I wasn't one to trust right away. I needed my brother, but she insisted on only having room for one of us."

"Atlas saw my hesitation, and he pulled me aside, insisting that it was a golden opportunity I shouldn't pass up for him. And deep down, I wanted it. I just needed to know At would be okay without me."

"So I agreed to go. And it's a choice that's haunted both Atlas and I ever since."

I released his hand and wrapped my arms around his waist, bracing for the impact of what was going to happen next.

"Laura wasn't what she seemed, and I found that out almost immediately after my arrival."

I bit into my lip and hung on every word as he continued.

"Laura liked pain, both eliciting it and feeling it. When she selected me, it had nothing to do with her wanting to be a mother figure and everything to do with me being strong enough to both handle the pain she wanted to give and being able to give it back to her just as hard. She just wanted someone naïve and helpless to force into her sick sexual game." He paused as his jaw clenched.

I'd never met this woman, but I hated her more than I had ever hated anyone in my life. I couldn't stop picturing Ezra as a child, so excited for this new mother to replace the one he lost far too soon. How innocent, kind, and good he was before she marred his soul with her twisted desires that a child should've never been a part of. I mourned the innocence he lost at the hands of someone who was supposed to take care of him. Supposed to love him.

"The scars she left, both physically and mentally, have

fucked me. I know I'm not normal. I know I should feel remorse for the misdeeds I've done, but I don't. And I don't think I ever will." He confessed, giving me a pained expression.

I was at a loss for words. I could see now that Ezra wasn't crazy, he was just a man who found a way to survive in a fucked up world. He was right. He would never be "normal"; but who the fuck wanted normal, anyway? I know I didn't. I tried the normal, safe route, and I still got burned.

"That's okay."

"You don't get it," He cut me off, flashing me a bitter smile. "I'm addicted to you and I don't have a conscience that warns me to stay away. Every single part of me wants to devour you. To take everything you have to give and maybe more than you're willing to spare. If you let me, I'll rip off your wings and pull you straight into hell, Angel."

I swallowed, contemplating my next words. Ezra needed to know that I wanted everything he had to give. Every single fucking thing. He wasn't a part of some bad girl streak or a fun lay that I'd regret in the morning. He was Ezra. The man that still terrified me even while he soothed me. The man that held me like I was precious to him yet would just as easily snap my neck if I ever betrayed him. Nothing was normal about any of us anyway, and I was in far too deep to care. He and his brothers were already all over my skin, like a pungent perfume I couldn't wash off.

I placed my palms on the edges of his sharp jaw and gently turned his head to face me.

"I'm already ruined." I said, flashing him a sad smile. "You just have to decide if you want to join in on the debauchery."

Ezra lunged for me. His lips crashed into mine with a ravenous kiss as the weight of his body crushed me into the couch. My heart hammered in my chest as I felt his powerful hand slide up my throat and I felt his fingers grip it in a tight vise.

"Ready to play, Angel." He growled,

"Yes." I croaked, flashing him a smile.

And all at once, Ezra was everywhere. Stealing my breath and simultaneously breathing life into me. Ezra had the strength to crush my windpipe. And as he squeezed my throat a fraction tighter, I knew that if he wanted to kill me, he could. But that was the most addictive part about it. The control, the submission, the trust. To the outside world it may have seemed flawed, but for us it was perfect.

Pulling his mouth away from mine and his hand away from my throat, he traveled down my chest and latched his mouth onto one of my already perked nipples. He licked and sucked and bit and lapped each overstimulated little bud as his hands roamed my body, touching and exploring every inch of my skin.

Moving his hands down further, his fingers explored my pussy, sliding up and down my already slick folds with torturously slow strokes. I threw my head back and moaned, relishing in the feel of his fingers as they brushed against my sensitive clit.

Ezra flashed me a wicked smile as he pulled his fingers away from my center and rubbed the sticky gleam onto my lips.

"How do you taste, Angel?" He mused with a grin as he watched me lick my lips clean.

"Taste for yourself." I purred.

Grabbing hold of my knees and slamming them to my chest in one swift motion, Ezra wasted no time as he dove headfirst into my pussy and began lapping and flicking my sensitive little bud to the point of cruelty. Every time I'd inch closer to release, my body would tense up, and Ezra would stop what he was doing to pop back up and flash me a wicked smile before diving in again. It was the sweetest form of cruelty I've ever experienced.

The bastard knew what he was doing, and after the fifth round of his little game; I had reached the point of insanity. My nails dug into his hair and back as I pushed his mouth against my clit fervently, but he easily overpowered me and popped back up again.

"Ready for my cock?" He noted, biting into his lower lip with a sexy smirk. "You've been such a patient girl."

"You are a cruel bastard." I growled. His relentless torture fractured the little composure I had left.

He chuckled and flipped my body over on all fours. I arched my back instinctively, preparing for the gift of sweet release. Using his knee to spread my legs wider, Ezra slipped down his pants and hissed when his thick cock touched the wetness seeping out from me. I smiled at that, it served him fucking right for being so cruel.

"Angel," Ezra warned as he slipped on a condom and moved his fingers inside of me, "you're too tight. I'm going to need you to take a deep breath for me."

I did as I was told and was rewarded with his thick, velvety shaft, stuffing me to the hilt in one powerful thrust. On shaky knees, I leaned into each deep thrust he gave, lavishing in the feel of his cock and the way his powerful legs slapped against my ass.

"Good girl." Ezra groaned, squeezing my ass with his large palm. "Such a fucking good girl."

Ezra's hand reached around my body to find my clit with expert precision and started to rub it in rhythm with his powerful thrusts. Stroke, rub. Stroke, rub. I leaned into each delicious thrust and rolled my hips with each tantalizing rub until all of the sensations became too much for my oversensitized body to handle. An intense orgasm ricocheted through me, splintering my mind and catapulting to the heavens.

I wanted to implode from the sheer bliss of what he was doing to my body, but Ezra was still there, holding my body up as he continued his delicious assault. My pussy squeezed his cock until his own orgasm took hold of his convulsing body and he released a deep throaty groan that rumbled in my chest. Our bodies crumpled into a sweaty, lust-soaked pile of limbs as we both came down from our temporary high.

As we laid there spent, with our bodies tangled together, I knew that there was no point in fighting the pull I had towards Ezra. We were co-dependent, toxic, and crazy as hell, but the connection we had was visceral and no amount of denial was going to change that.

He had shared a sliver of his past with me and after all the nightmares he helped me through, the least I could do was share some of mine. As our fingers interlocked and we nestled into the couch, I was ready to bare my soul to Ezra.

"Can I tell you how my nightmares started?"

THIRTY-FIVE

Ezra

THE SOUNDS WERE MADDENING. MUFFLED BY THE BAGS OVER their heads and the tape across their mouths, it was anyone's guess what they were saying. Narcissistic men who turned into blubbering cowards the moment they faced a true predator.

"You don't have to do this!" The blonde one wailed, wincing as our eyes landed on him, "We- we have m-money. A shit ton of it. Name your price. I'll transfer the funds right now if you-"

His words died off as I slowly shook my head, pressing my finger to my lip for emphasis. This wasn't about money or power. This was about revenge. This was about justice. This was about *her*.

Gavin Anderson, Zeke Davis, and Derek Holmes. It didn't take long for us to find the fucks who hurt our girl. After Stevie laid out all the sordid details of their crimes, all it took was eighteen hours for Atlas and Tristan to connect with their contacts upstate and another twenty-eight hours for Cyrus and I to track the fuckers down and bring them here.

Cyrus sucked his teeth with a loud tsk as he glared at the three men hoisted up in the center of the room.

"Stupid bastards." Cy remarked with a smug smirk, "Why the fuck do they always assume money can save them?"

I could see the rage building within him. Like ticking time bombs, each of us had been on edge ever since we convened to discuss the girl who pervaded our home and our minds. Turns out, Stevie had been through enough bullshit to last her a lifetime, and getting thrown into our world was merely the icing on the cake. It was no wonder she survived us. After the shit she'd been through, Angel could survive anything.

Even the bastard who bartered her life had a full list of transgressions against our girl. Tristan put out an APB for Malcolm Warner the minute he learned who she really was to him, but the asshole had made good on his word and vanished. He would get what was coming to him, eventually. Our connections were on the lookout and with his addiction, it was just a matter of time before he showed up on one of our dealer's doorsteps. There was a special place in hell for men who harmed the girls they were supposed to protect.

The demons that normally laid dormant in all of my

brothers were surfacing tonight. I could feel the anticipation in the air and the adrenaline already coursing through my veins. My demon was hungry, and I was ready to satiate it.

"I'm afraid daddy's money won't help this time." I taunted, running the tip of my sharp blade along each of their exposed throats as I strolled by them.

They each jolted and squeezed their eyes shut as the icy metal grazed their skin. As if they expected their deaths to be that quick. That would be far too merciful. What we had planned would be exactly what the sick fucks deserved; slow and excruciating punishment.

"What do you want from us?" The balding one asked, his body trembling as he looked into my soulless eyes.

"Think back to your most heinous crime, gentlemen. It is time to reap what you sowed."

"You know Amber. Is that it?" The blonde one spoke up again. "Look man, the party got a little carried away but I swear to god she never told us to stop."

"Jesus," Cyrus spat, looking at the three of them with disgust, "can we kill them now?"

"Unfortunately," I hissed, glaring pointedly at the pathetic bastards, "that isn't our decision to make."

There was only one person who deserved to have the first cut, and she hadn't arrived yet. If we killed them now, we'd be deciding for her and there was nothing Stevie hated more than having things decided for her. She would be the one to decide their fates. No one else.

THIRTY-SIX

Stevie

DO YOU EVER FEEL LIKE YOUR PAST JUST WON'T FUCKING DIE? Like, no matter how many times you bury that bitch, she just keeps resurrecting itself. The minute Atlas, Tristan and I stepped into the basement of Hell's Tavern, my past reared its ugly head again. Only this time, the bitch was way more ugly than I remembered.

Strung up and hanging from the center of the room were the monsters that haunted my dreams. Fear froze my body as I stood in the darkness and watched them sway. My mind had replayed that nightmare so many times that even four years couldn't dilute the effect they had on me.

They were still alive. Bruised and battered, but cognizant enough to avert their eyes when they heard people entering the room.

Gavin, the boy I thought I could love, hung limply in the middle, while his two asshole friends flanked his sides. Time had not been good to Gavin. His once lean, tan, and athletic body was now bloated and pale. Probably the result of years of excessive drinking combined with the haughty desk job his daddy probably secured for him.

Time hadn't been good to his friends either, but I didn't give a shit about his friends. They were just the pathetic boys who hung on Gavin's every word and helped him orchestrate my worst nightmare.

"Why?" I breathed, flashing my eyes to the four men I knew orchestrated the whole thing.

It was a loaded question, if there ever was one. I knew why The Reapers brought Gavin, Zeke, and Derek here. They were the men who had hurt and defiled me in the worst ways imaginable. If there was one thing I knew about The Reapers, it was that they didn't take kindly to people touching what was theirs. What I couldn't understand was why they brought me into it.

"They are your d... demons, baby," Tristan said, touching the small of my back, "it's time you faced them."

I stepped forward into the light on shaky knees. *I could do this*. I could confront the demons that haunted my nights.

"You?" Gavin asked incredulously as soon as I stumbled

into the light. "You are what this is all about? Jesus fucking Christ." He spat, shaking his head with disbelief. "Look, gentlemen, the pussy was good. But it was never *that* good."

Shame flamed my cheeks as I turned my head away from them. Before he raped me, I had willingly had sex with him. I had chosen him because he was the safe, smart choice. I wanted a normal life, and he seemed to fit the mold. I was so distracted by his image that I missed all the glaring warning signs. Gavin Anderson was a monster.

"Shut the fuck up." Atlas hissed, crushing his knuckles against Gavin's nose with a swift punch.

Gavin's head jerked back violently, and within seconds blood was trickling down his face. Stunned into silence, he blinked back tears as his eyes shifted between the five of us.

"What am I supposed to do with them?" I asked, chewing on my lower lip.

"Whatever you want, Angel." Ezra said, moving to stand beside me. "You're the one in control here."

"She's fucking all of you. Isn't she?" Gavin declared with a harsh laugh. "Damn Steph, I didn't think you had it in you. Babe, if you wanted a foursome, you should've just said so. Derek and Zeke would've been down."

I flinched at the sound of bones cracking as Cyrus kicked in Gavin's knee cap. The scream that escaped Gavin's lips was guttural, but the idiot continued mocking me even as he teared-up in pain.

"You're as pathetic as ever, Steph." He winced, putting weight on his other leg as he spit out the blood still dripping into his mouth. "Letting them fight your fucking battles. Still the weak little bitch that you always were."

"Gavin, shut the fuck up, idiot." One of his friends hissed. "You are going to get us all killed."

Gavin may have been a stupid asshole, but he was right. The Reapers were fighting my battle for me. If I wanted to prove that I could survive in their world, I needed to step up and show it.

My eyes darted around the room, looking for something I could use to show I meant business. In the far left corner of the room, I could see what looked to be a table, topped with a variety of tools.

"Can I?" I asked the guys, gesturing towards the corner.

Surprise briefly flashed across all of their faces before returning to their usual stoic expressions.

"You have free rein, Princess." Cyrus offered, eyeing my every move.

I floated towards the tools, fascinated by the sheer amount of choices I had. There were no guns or large knives, nothing that would make death come quickly. Each tool would make the pain as excruciatingly slow as possible, and I was having a hard time deciding.

The Reapers probably assumed I was only trying to scare Gavin and his friends. But in the pit of my soul, I knew that I didn't want to just scare them, I wanted to fucking hurt them. I wanted to make them pay for their crimes in blood.

Then I spotted it. A pocket knife. It was almost an exact replica of the knife Gavin used on me that night. This one's blade was a little sharper, but the size and shape of it was uncanny. Talk about poetic justice.

I stalked towards the three of them, forming a sinister smile on my face. I wanted to elicit the same fear their violence had given me night after night.

"She's not going to do anything." Gavin snarled, glancing at both of his friends. "She doesn't have the fucking balls."

"It's funny you should say that," I said with a smirk as I slid the blade down his bare fleshy gut. "I think I'll start with removing yours."

Tiny beads of sweat dripped down his brow as he watched my blade glide lower and lower. Just as the tip of the blade reached his waistband, I paused, wanting to relish in the fear in his eyes. His eyes were frozen, locked on the blade that was mere inches away from cutting off his most vile weapon.

I slashed the blade up his stomach and laughed, feeling the blood splatter hit my face.

"Like I'd ever choose to go near that tragic excuse for a cock again." I sneered, smiling as he shrieked in agony.

After the first cut, Gavin's body tried to curl in on itself, but the ropes biting into his wrists wouldn't allow it. I smiled to myself at that. His pain, his pure agony would be on display for us the entire time.

The sweet smell of violence engulfed the room as I continued my assault on Gavin's body. Slashing and slicing wherever the blade would land. My movements were frantic and deranged as sticky sweat coated my skin, but I couldn't stop myself.

I wanted him to suffer. I wanted him to feel every slice in his bones. I didn't want to just scar his skin; I wanted to leave a permanent mark on his soul. I wanted to hurt him as badly and as deeply as he hurt me. I wanted to make him pay.

It wasn't until Tristan was pulling me away and Ezra was wrapping my wounded hand, that I realized Gavin was dead. He had always seemed like this immovable force. Like this persistent ghost that would always haunt me. But as I looked at the blood on my hands and the cold bloody body hanging from the castors on the ceiling, I realized Gavin was human. He felt pain like a human, bled like a human, and ultimately, he died like a human.

"Are you okay?" Atlas asked, tilting my blood-stained chin up to face him.

"Yeah. I'm fine." I said, nodding my head as Ezra dressed my wounds, "it's mostly his blood."

"Not what he meant, baby." Tristan mumbled, throwing his black jacket on me as Atlas began wiping the blood off of my face.

"You guys came prepared." I noted, seeing their full medical supply kit. "Cool."

The three of them stared at me like I had sprouted another head.

"Are you sure you're okay?" Atlas asked, pulling his brows together with a scowl.

Why the hell did no one believe me? I was totally fine. Relieved, even.

"She's fine." Cyrus quipped, walking over to us. "Maybe if you guys weren't surrounding her like a bunch of mother hens, she'd give you a normal response. Stevie, let's go get some air."

Fresh air wasn't a bad idea. Atlas had cleaned most of the blood off my face, but I could still taste Gavin's death in the air. I couldn't believe I had ended a life only a few minutes ago. I expected to feel guilty. To have this monumental conflicting moment, where I struggled with my moral compass. But that didn't happen. He committed his crimes, and I dealt out the punishment he deserved. I had no second thoughts about what I did. It wasn't normal, or expected, it just was.

"What about them?" I asked, eyeing the two men still hanging from the center of the room.

"We'll take care of it, Angel." Ez said, giving me a wink. "Go with Cyrus."

Cyrus led me up the stairs and out the back entrance of the building. Once we stepped outside, he leaned against the wall, pulled out a pack of Camel Crushes, and held the pack out to me, offering me one. I wasn't normally a smoker. But hell, I just killed a man. A little poison wouldn't hurt me.

I took a cigarette from the pack and fidgeted with my hands, not knowing what to do. I had no problem murdering someone, but being alone with Cyrus had me turning into a nervous wreck.

"Here, let me." He said, grabbing the cigarette and placing it between my lips.

Our eyes locked as he flicked his Zippo, and the flame flickered to life. I took a deep inhale and averted my eyes as he stepped away, trying to stop the emotions from bubbling up.

"Thank you." I hesitated, trying to find the right words, "For this. For being here. I know I fucked things up between us and I just... thank you."

Cyrus stalked towards me, his emerald eyes a storm of emotions I couldn't decipher. His large hand gripped tightly around my jaw as fear and excitement rushed through me, sending my pulse skyrocketing.

"Let's get one thing straight." He spat, as our eyes locked, "You are ours and I take care of what's ours. Don't thank me for something that's a given. Alright?"

I visibly swallowed and gave him a nod, doing everything in my power to avoid thinking about the last time we were this close.

"I have to help clean up," he said, releasing my jaw, "come inside when you're ready."

"You aren't going to stay to keep an eye on me?"

"There's no need." He drawled, reaching for the door. "You're a smart girl, by now you know what will happen if you run."

I smiled to myself like a fucking idiot, then immediately cursed. My idiotic pussy would be charmed by a back-handed compliment laced with threats.

I leaned against the wall and closed my eyes. Savoring each drag of my cigarette as the warm sunshine kissed my face. It was hard to believe that so much had happened, and it wasn't even noon yet.

I flinched as I felt a strong hand wrap around my bicep. *What the fuck was with people grabbing my arms?*

"Jacob?" I asked, peering up at the man holding me in place. "What the fuck are you doing here?"

It *was* him. Last I heard, they fired him shortly after my first visit to the bar. If the guys knew he showed up out of nowhere and grabbed me like this, they would annihilate him.

"You shouldn't be here." I said, pulling my arm out of his grasp. "Get out of here. Now."

"Listen, I know. Jessie mentioned you might be by today." He said as his eyes shifted around us. "I've been waiting for you for the last couple of weeks and this may be my only chance. I kept ignoring the calls and deleting the voicemails because I didn't know who it was. I don't know how she got my number, but there's something you need to hear."

For a moment I stared at him like he was a lunatic. I had barely spoken to the guy a few weeks ago, and we were acquaintances at best. I didn't give a fuck about what was on his voicemail. It had nothing to do wi-

Fuck. *Alex.*

As soon as I realized, I snatched the phone out of his hand and looked at the text messages. Fifteen unanswered and all from Alex.

"I deleted a few, before I knew what it was..." Jacob admitted, scratching his head as he averted his eyes.

"You could've at least responded and told her she had the wrong number."

I was taking my anger out on him and it wasn't fair, but I was pissed.

"I know alright, I'm sorry. Just listen to the voicemails and you'll see why I had to find you."

"Stevie, that girl called again. I know you said to stay away, but she's saying that The Reapers have you chained up in their basement and that she's a friend. I don't trust her, but I don't know what to believe. I need you to call and tell me it's not true. Fuck, please tell me it's not true."

Numbly, I pulled the phone away from my head and tapped the next voicemail. This wasn't happening, this could not be happening. There was only one person who would have it out for me. *Melanie.*

"Stevie, I don't give a fuck what you say and you can beat my ass later, but it's been two weeks and I still haven't heard from you. She wants me to meet her at Maria's Cantina and I'm going. I need to know what happened to you."

Alex sounded so upset in her last voicemail that it nearly choked me up. I knew how hard it was for me to live without her, but I never stopped to think about how she would feel, living without me. Melanie took advantage of her biggest fear and was using it against her to get to me. I was the one she really wanted.

"When did you get the last one?" I hissed, piercing my eyes at Jacob as I deleted the evidence from his phone.

Jacob shook out his stupor and looked up at me.

"Huh?"

"When. *The fuck.* Did you get the last one!" I screamed, tossing his phone back at him in a blind rage.

"Two days ago." He winced, rubbing the spot where his phone hit. "Jesus. Anger problems much?"

I wanted to murder him, but then I'd have two dead bodies on my hands and would be no closer to saving Alex.

"Jacob, I need a ride. Can you grab your car and meet me behind the fire escape in one minute?"

"I don't know if I should..." He trailed off. "You seem pretty angry and I don't want to get involved."

I let out an exasperated breath and pulled him towards his car.

"You can and you will. My friends, The Reapers, you've met them, right? They're in there right now. If they find out you refused to help me, I don't know what they'd do. But if you help me, I can guarantee they'll never know you were here. It's up to you."

"You're a crazy bitch." He mumbled with a scowl as he stepped into his car.

"I'm aware." I said, heading towards the backdoor. "Fire escape. One minute."

Shutting the door behind me, I paced towards the women's

restroom. I couldn't let them see that anything was wrong. I tried to keep my movements relaxed and my expression blank despite the storm brewing inside of me.

"Stevie. Is everything okay?" Atlas asked, stopping me just before I entered the restroom.

"Yeah, fine." I said, giving him a tight smile. "You've asked me three times already. I'm beginning to think this is some kind of prank."

"You seem a little... on edge." He responded, looking at me suspiciously.

"Was it too much for you?" Tristan added, moving to stand next to Atlas.

They were asking about the murder of the man that had done the most heinous things imaginable to me. In all honesty, it wasn't. It was cathartic. The rush I got from exacting my revenge gave me a high unlike any other, but the news about Alex had sent me crashing back down.

"I'm fine. I just really need to use the ladies' room." I said, faking a little potty dance.

"You s... sure?" Tris asked, with a penetrating stare that went straight to my gut.

"Yes." I said, giving them a smile I didn't feel, "I'll be right back."

And just like that, I lied to them. *Again.*

Guilt gnawed at my gut as I walked through the restroom, and I felt it even more as I climbed through the fire escape. By the time I hopped into Jacob's red Camaro the tears had completely blurred my vision.

"Where to?" Jacob asked, anxiety warbling his voice.

"Maria's Cantina on second street." I said, turning away

so he couldn't see my face. "If anyone asks, tell them I ran away."

I expected the feeling of guilt to lessen the further we got away from them, but it only kept ripping me further apart. I was doing this for Alex, for the only family I had left, so why did I feel like such a traitor?

THIRTY-SEVEN

Stevie

AFTER FIFTEEN MINUTES OF UNCOMFORTABLE SILENCE, WE finally pulled up to the front of Maria's Cantina. With its Spanish-styled architecture and stunning floral landscaping, the building itself was breath-taking. But that wasn't the reason I was having trouble breathing.

This part of the city was like a ghost town, especially this early in the day. And apart from the few stranglers of people walking down the street, there was no one around. Not only was I about to go into this place blind, but if something were to go down, no one would be coming to my rescue.

I didn't have time to linger on the 'what-ifs'. It had been two days. Forty-eight entire fucking hours since she last called. Who knew if Alex would even still be there, let alone if she was still alive. But on the drive over, she didn't answer any of my calls, and this place was the only genuine lead I had. I couldn't afford to leave a single stone unturned.

After thanking Jacob for the ride and for letting me use his phone, I stepped out of the car on shaky knees and made my way inside. Passing through the bougainvillea wrapped arch-way, I followed the cobblestone path through the eerily quiet courtyard as my heart thundered in my chest.

Alex had to be here. She just fucking had to be.

Approaching the door with caution, I reached for the sleek metal handle and pulled, finding the door bolted shut. I peered into the tinted glass and saw nothing but empty tables shrouded in a dark room.

I tried knocking, seeing if that would help, but when no one answered the door, I knew something was wrong. I ran towards the side of the building, seeing if I could find another way in, but the back entrance was just as empty, with not a soul in sight.

Melanie had my sister and was doing god-knows-what to her, just to get to me. Alex was paying for my stupid mistakes and as I thought about what that could mean, tears came rushing to the surface. But I would not just wait here and let myself cry. I needed to take action. I needed to get Alex back, even if it was the last thing I ever did.

I stormed back to the front courtyard, refusing to take the silence for an answer. Melanie was in there and she was going to give Alex back right fucking now. I stomped up to the door and pounded on the glass as hard as I could.

"Where the fuck is she!" I screamed, slamming myself into the glass door. "Alex, if you're in there, I'm going to get you out. I swear to god, she will rue the fucking day she stole you!"

I heard the loud crack before I felt it, and then the ringing in my ears started. As my body crumpled to the ground and my face smacked against the cobblestone walkway, my vision blurred and a bitter taste filled my mouth. My breathing became labored, and I blinked back tears as I tried to see my assailant. Blue patent-leather stilettos stepped into my line of sight just before my lids became too heavy and everything faded to darkness.

THIRTY-EIGHT

Atlas

I SHOULD'VE BEEN WORRIED ABOUT THE MESS IN THE basement, but all I could think about was her. I wanted to taint Stevie from the moment I laid eyes on her. With her hair that smelled like honey and her perpetual scowl, the first night we met, all I could think about was throwing her against the counter and bringing her into hell with me. She was too innocent and way too good, but I wanted her anyway. And maybe that's where I fucked up.

Slowly pacing the perimeter of our usual VIP lounge, I couldn't shake the feeling that something was wrong.

"This isn't like her." I said, looking down at Tristan and Cyrus. "Something's wrong."

"S... she said she's fine, bro." Tris noted, trying to pull me out of my head. "Just s... sit down and take it easy."

"I can't take it easy." I roared, darting my eyes between the both of them. "I know Stevie. Probably better than all of you do. The girl that just stalked into that restroom, wasn't fucking her."

"What are you talking about?" Cyrus snarled, sitting up in his seat. "You avoid her. You treat her like she's fucking a nuisance. Now you think that you somehow know her better than us?"

I slipped up. My concern over Stevie's behavior muddled up my thoughts, and I said something I shouldn't have. I kept the truth from them for a reason and while my brain floundered, trying to remember exactly what that reason was; I clenched my jaw and turned away, not ready to explain myself.

"Seriously," Cyrus challenged, not willing to let it go, "how is it you know her better than us?"

"We knew each other before this whole fucking thing started." I spat, baring my teeth. "Before she ever walked through our fucking door, Stevie was mine. She was one thing I selfishly hid from our world, but somehow, she still ended up being tossed into it. It wasn't supposed to be like this." I sighed, running my hands through my hair. "Everything got so fucked and I honestly don't know how to un-fuck it."

"Why d... didn't you tell us?" Tristan asked, shaking his head in confusion.

"Because I was trying to protect her." I confessed, squeezing my eyes shut. "And all of you. Because I thought if I could just get her out before anyone noticed her, our secret would be safe. I should've known it was a dumb plan. How could I possibly think no one would notice her? That's like asking someone not to see a blinding fucking light."

"Look," Cyrus said, lightening his tone, "I know you're concerned, but Stevie is a part of our world now and with that, comes the occasional violence and murder. We'll keep a close eye on her and if she isn't herself in a few hours, we'll figure it out."

"There's one flaw in your plan." Ezra boomed as he walked in the room to join the three of us. "Stevie's gone."

***

AFTER TRIS PLAYED BACK the security footage, it was easy to figure out how Stevie escaped. Within seconds of entering the bathroom, she climbed out of the emergency escape and into a fiery-red Camaro. There was only one stupid fuck we knew that would drive such a monstrosity. Jacob fucking Daniels. The asshole Jessie fired a month ago. Jessie should've passed on hiring him from his fucking name alone. Jacob Daniels? He should've just committed to the douchebaggery and went by Jack.

Jacob, the bright bulb that he was, had a big presence on social media. Not only did that help coax his ego, but it helped us pinpoint his exact location. Two minutes ago, he had tagged himself at Second Street Cafe and captioned his post, 'In desperate need of bottomless mimosas, who's down?' By the looks of the photo he shared, Stevie wasn't with him. Which meant that wherever he left her couldn't have been far.

It took us ten minutes to get to Second Street Cafe and another five to park our fucking cars. It was a Sunday afternoon, and the place was already bustling with the brunch crowd. Trying not to draw any unwanted attention, I left the others outside in the back alley, while I searched for the man of the hour.

As soon as I spotted the pretty-boy sitting by the bar, I hooked my arm around his neck like he was an old college buddy and yanked him out the back door. To the tipsy bystanders, it just looked like a friendly drunken frat boy greeting, and Jacob stood no chance of fighting me off. Jacob was a big guy, but I was bigger.

"Where the fuck is she?" Cyrus growled, grabbing Jacobs shoulders and shoving him against the building brick wall.

"Where is who?" Jacob asked, as his eyes darted around the four of us.

"You know exactly who he's talking about." Ezra hissed, fixing his gaze on him. "You can either tell us what we want to know, or waste more of our time and still end up telling us what we want to know. One way is much more *messy*, but it's your funeral."

Ezra flipped out his pocket knife and advanced on the man with lightning speed. This wasn't a game for him. Like us, Ezra wanted answers, and he wanted them now.

"Okay! Okay!" Jacob cursed, jerking his body as he tried and failed to get out of Cyrus' hold. "I'll tell you everything, just don't fucking cut me. Blood makes me queasy, man."

If I had any lingering doubt about Jacob's involvement in

Stevie's disappearing act, it vanished. Jacob may have been a bumbling idiot, but there was no way he could've masterminded her disappearance. The man clearly got goaded into taking what was ours. The question was, by who?

"Talk." Ezra hissed, pressing the knife against his Adam's apple. "How did you know she would be there?"

"I- I asked Jessie to text me. There... there was this girl." He stammered, pulling out his phone. "She kept texting and c... calling, looking for Stevie a... and I didn't know what to do. There were messages and voicemails, b... but Stevie deleted them all."

Tristan snatched the phone out of his hand and got to work. Aside from being our eye in the sky, Tristan had a knack for hacking. He'd be able to access the deleted files and restore the supposed voicemails Stevie had deleted.

"What girl?" I asked, pulling out my Colt Python revolver and pressing it against his temple.

It may have been overkill given the blade against his throat, but my anger needed a target. Jessie wasn't innocent in all of this either, we kept her in the loop with the club, simply because we didn't want her to witness any of our business and she was the only other person with an access card to the club. We would deal with her when she got back into town. No matter how pure her intentions were, she should have never shared Stevie's location with him.

"It's Alex." Tristan murmured, flashing us one of the text messages on Jacob's phone. "I'd seen the name in S... Stevie's phone b... before, but assumed it was an ex."

"Who the hell is Alex?" Cyrus asked, looking at Jacob and Tristan.

"Stevie's little sister," Tristan said, sliding through the

restored text messages, "and apparently the girl Malcolm had meant to give us."

The news of a sister was new information, but the fact that Stevie had taken her place didn't surprise me. I knew there was something else that made her want to come to us. Something besides saving her piece of shit stepfather's life.

"Where the fuck did you take her?" Cyrus asked, slamming Jacob's body against the wall again.

"Maria's Cantina," Jacob stammered with a wince, "a couple blocks down the street. You can't miss it. Big fucking sign. I swear to god that's all I know."

The four of us released Jacob and made our way back to our cars. We knew Maria's Cantina, and we knew it well. Not only was it the best Mexican place in town, it also housed the worst criminals this city has ever seen. Maria's Cantina was one of The Diaz Cartel's favorite hangouts, which could only mean one thing.

Melanie Diaz took our girl and in doing so, incited a fucking war.

THIRTY-NINE

Stevie

I AWOKE TO THE DISTINCT SMELL OF DECAY SURROUNDING ME. My head throbbed as my eyes peeled open and my blurry surroundings came into view. A lone lightbulb swung above me, creating a halo of light in what looked to be the center of a dark and empty room.

I didn't know how long I was out or who attacked me. Whoever brought me here had left me with my wrists bound above my head and my feet just barely touching the floor. I wiggled my fingers, trying to bring them back to life as I yanked the ropes biting into my wrists.

"Don't bother." A feminine voice hissed. "There's no way in hell you're getting out of those."

Like a caged animal, I whipped my body around in a circle, trying to see where the voice was coming from. Still disoriented from the blow to my head, I recognized the voice, but I just couldn't place it.

A slight figure stepped into the light and I had to do a double-take, just to make sure my eyes weren't deceiving me..

"Jessie?" I asked, narrowing my eyes. "What is all of this?"

"Sorry, Love." She smirked, circling around my body. "It's really nothing personal."

How the fuck was bashing me in the head and chaining me up not 'personal'? We hadn't known each other long, but I considered her someone I could trust. Someone that I could've one day called a friend. *What the fuck was this?*

"Where the fuck is my sister?" I hissed, swinging my body to follow hers, "What did you do to Alex?"

"Alex? Hmm... The name rings a bell..." She said, flashing me a sinister grin. "Relax. When sissy came by, all my men did was snatch her phone and kick her to the curb. She's probably still alive out there looking for you. Such a shame that she'll never know what happened to her big sister."

My chin quivered as rebellious tears raced down my cheeks. Alex was alive, and for that I was grateful, but it hurt to know that I was abandoning her. That I was leaving her out in the world alone with no answers and no clue as to what happened to me. I failed her; I failed everyone.

"Why are you doing this?" I screamed, baring my teeth. "Why me?"

"It's simple, really." She stated matter-of-factly. "I told you to stay away from The Reapers, warned you they wouldn't want to be with someone like you, and you didn't fucking listen to me." She hissed. "Here's a little clue, Stevie. I don't like being ignored!"

"But why would that matter?" I asked, still not understanding her logic. "Why did you want me to stay awa-"

"Did they tell you we grew up together?" She asked, cutting me off as she dreamily stared out into space. "Oh, who am I kidding?" She asked, shaking her head with a smile. "Of course they didn't. They never like to talk about the past. But our history together goes way back."

The shift in her demeanor was jarring, but I nodded along anyway. She was obviously unhinged, and I knew that the longer I could keep her talking, the more time I'd have to figure out a plan. *I needed a fucking plan.*

"I only saw his brothers a few times before they were fostered, but Atlas and I were as thick as thieves growing up." She beamed, circling around me. "Like two peas in a pod."

"Atlas was a few years older than me, and at first, he hated it when I'd follow him around. But after a while he understood my need for him. He was the only one who could stop my monster from visiting me each night."

"David, my monster, was terrified of Atlas. I quickly learned that as long as Atlas stayed close by, David wouldn't go near me. Eventually, though, we grew up and went our separate ways. Atlas had his brothers to take care of and I went out to live on my own, but we still kept in touch here and there."

"I didn't know it at the time, but my monster had gotten meaner and angrier after he left the group home. He hated that he couldn't have me and was simply biding his time until the opportunity struck."

"David nearly killed me the night he found me alone outside of a nightclub. He and his friends beat me and raped me so brutally, that by the time they finished, I was barely recognizable. When I showed up on Atlas' doorstep, he and his brothers took one look at me and went out looking for blood. They killed David and his friends for what they did to me and from that day forward, The Reapers promised they'd *always* protect me. *Always.*"

"Even after the engagement news, I never worried that they wouldn't be able to keep their promise. Anyone with eyes could see that Atlas couldn't stand Melanie. But then you showed up and everything fucking changed."

"It doesn't have to change." I said, trying to appeal to her. "Nothing has to cha-"

"I've never been to their house, you know." She said, cutting me off. "After everything we've been through, they still keep me at a distance. But not you. No, you get the VIP fucking treatment. You get the rags to riches makeover. And you get to be in their hearts and under their fucking sheets." She spat, cutting her eyes at me.

"The Reapers are the only family I know." She hissed, vibrating with rage. "I will not stand by and have you rip that away from me."

Not only was Jessie delusional, her attachment to The Reapers was borderline psychotic. I had enough of hearing her sob story, and no amount of past trauma she had would make me forgive her for tearing me away from my sister and my men.

"If you're going to kill me," I hissed through clenched teeth, "just fucking do it already."

"Oh, Love," she laughed, "I'm not just going to kill you. I'm going to fucking destroy you. Well, technically they are." She said, casting her eyes at the group of men who stepped out of the shadows.

"It's the price I had to pay to get them to break in for me." She offered, wrinkling her nose. "You understand, right?"

And with that, she stepped away, allowing the group of nearly a dozen men with their faces shrouded in ski masks to step forward and surround me.

"They're going to find out!" I called out in a last ditch effort to talk some sense into her. "Once they find me, it won't take long for them to figure out who did it. And when they do, they'll never forgive you. You'll lose them forever."

"You don't think I've thought of that?" She screamed, rushing back towards me as she shoved the men out of her way. "As far as they're concerned," she hissed, inching close to my face, "I'm three states away, visiting a friend. If they somehow find out you came here, they'll never trace it back to me. This whole building belongs to The Diaz Cartel and after your fight with Mel, they'll assume it was her."

She was right about one thing, The Reapers would never suspect her. Hell, even I had a hard time associating the girl I met at Hell's Tavern with the crazy bitch in front of me. Her obsession with them was strictly one-sided, and she would be the curveball they never saw coming.

"Boys, do your worst." Jessie ordered, turning on her

heels. "Just be sure to call me back in before you kill her, I want to watch the life drain from her eyes."

The masked men surrounded me, trapping me in with their bodies. A set of rough hands reached for my dress and ripped the thin fabric off with one swift tug, and cool air hit my skin all at once. I knew that there was no point in struggling. Trying to fight them off would only end up making it worse.

The sound of a pant zipper sliding down made my skin crawl, and as much as I wanted to pretend I was unaffected by it, I couldn't stomach the idea of a strange man's hands on me. A body pressed against mine and I shuddered, repulsed by the contact.

The Reapers were going to come for me, I could feel it in my bones. But I needed to bide my time and keep myself alive for as long as I could. I needed to survive this, by any means necessary.

Closing my eyes, I allowed myself to fall deep into the recesses of my mind. I pushed myself deeper and deeper until I wasn't in this dark room at all. I was in the safest place I could think of. At home, with The Reapers.

The thought surprised me. When I first arrived, everything about their home terrified me. It housed the most cruel, dangerous, and murderous men I had ever met, and I never expected the ostentatious and cold space to feel homey. Yet in my mind, there I was, standing in my bedroom and smiling as I felt Atlas, Ezra, Cyrus, and Tristan surround me.

The Reapers were the reason I was in this mess to begin with and yet; I knew in my heart that there was no place I'd rather be right now than with them.

A set of hands gripped my bare hips, but I no longer felt the surrounding strangers, I felt my men. Cyrus stepped up behind me, capturing me in his embrace and as I inhaled, I could almost taste his delicious citrusy-spicy scent in the air. Tristan pressed close to my left, and I smiled, relishing in the masculine scent of freshly cut grass and leather that almost felt real. Ever the wild card, I didn't even have to try in order to feel Ezra's presence on my right. I breathed in his lavender and smoke scent like he was the oxygen I needed to survive. Then there was Atlas, the man that I loved first. His rich scent of sandalwood and amber brought me back to the time before any of this existed. When it was just me, him, and a cute little coffee shop. I was sad that our first time together had to be like this; I had always envisioned it differently. But I guess nothing in life goes exactly as planned.

I wouldn't take back the events that lead to this moment, because without them, I wouldn't have met The Reapers. They were my home. They were my safety net. And they were exactly where I wanted to be right now.

"I fucking love you," I proclaimed, with a trembling chin as the tears rolled down my cheeks, "each and every one of you."

I felt the bodies around me stiffen, swiftly ripping me away from my fantasy.

"What the fuck did you just say?" The man behind me boomed, turning me around to face him.

I laughed as I spat in his fucking masked face.

"Those words weren't for you, asshole!" I hissed, baring my teeth. "They weren't for any of you and when my Reapers find out what you've done to me, they will bathe in your fucking blood!"

The man smirked, pulling a knife from his back pocket and swiftly pressing the blade to my throat. The other men backed away, as I felt his blade pressing into my skin, almost as if the man holding me was the one really running the show.

"No one is coming for you, little girl." He hissed, licking my face with his slimy tongue. "And the only blood that will be spilled tonight, is yours."

My mouth had always gotten me into trouble, but this time, I had no doubt in my mind that it was going to get me killed.

There was a quiet certainty that hit me the moment I knew I was going to die. It wasn't a brief flashing of all of my wonderful memories, like I had always expected. It was long and excruciating. All I could envision were the people I was leaving behind. Alex. Ezra. Atlas. Tristan. Cyrus. Their smiling faces kept flashing in my mind, making me smile while simultaneously breaking my fucking heart.

At least I knew what true love was now, and it didn't scare me to feel it. I loved them. All of them and I didn't care if that seemed selfish or wrong. There was room in my heart for all four of The Reapers and what we had was beautiful, intense and ultimately tragic, but it was fucking ours.

FORTY

Cyrus

BEFORE WE COULD EVEN THINK OF STORMING INTO MARIA'S Cantina, we needed to come up with a plan. Who knew how many men they had inside, and while we had our own crews, it could take hours if not days to assemble them and we were quickly running out of time.

As Ezra drove his G-Wagon down the streets of downtown Caspian, Atlas gave Melanie a call, trying to see if Tristan could hack into her device and pinpoint her location.

We didn't think she would give herself away, but we figured the longer he could keep her talking, the more time Tris would have.

Atlas had been on the phone Mel for a couple of minutes, when out of nowhere, he broke off the call.

"What the fuck, man?" Tristan snapped, shutting his laptop. "I d… didn't fucking get it."

"There's no need." Atlas said, stiffly putting his phone away. "I know exactly where she is. Mel wants me to meet her for lunch."

"That makes no sense." I said with a scowl. "Why would she agree to meet you if she has Stevie being tortured somewhere?"

"Maybe it's to cover her ass." Ezra quipped, following the navigation to the new address Atlas entered.

"Yeah," Atlas said, running his hands through his hair, "maybe…"

WE ARRIVED at Bastian's Bistro a few minutes later and found Melanie outside in their patio section, enjoying the sunshine.

"Atlas," Melanie crooned, pressing her lips to each of his cheeks. "It's so good to see you. I didn't realize you were going to be bringing guests." She said pointedly as she stared at the rest of us. "I would've asked for a bigger table."

"Unfortunately, this is not a friendly visit." Ezra growled, bending down to get in her face. "We know you've taken

Stevie. Now tell us where the fuck she is and we may let you live long enough to finish that fucking spritzer."

"I don't know what you're talking about." She said, shaking her head as her eyes darted to Atlas. "Sure, she pissed me off and I may have made some threats out of anger, but I'd never do anything to incite a war between our families. You aren't the only ones who've lost people they loved to violence."

Mel was talking about Sebastian. Her high school sweetheart and the man everyone knew would've been her first choice for a husband. He came from The Distefano crime family and when news spread around town about him and Mel; it was his own family that killed him off. At least, that was the rumor. One day he simply vanished. Melanie mourned his loss for years. She even had this place built in remembrance of him.

"The voicemail mentioned Maria's Cantina." Atlas spat through gritted teeth. "That's one of your family's places."

"Maria's is getting a total renovation right now." She said, grimacing as she took a sip of her spritzer. "None of my family's men have been there in weeks."

"Take us then." Tristan demanded, pulling her chair out. "S… so we can see the truth for ourselves."

<hr>

AS WE STEPPED through the doors of Maria's Cantina, we could see that at least part of what she was saying was true.

The entire place was empty, with a bunch of construction supplies and white tarps hanging throughout it.

"I told you no one was here." She huffed, crossing her arms over her chest. "Now will you please let me move on with my day? I don't know where your girl went, but she didn't come here."

A flash of blue out of the corner of my eye caught my attention and on a hunch, I ran after it. If the place was empty, there shouldn't have been any movement. Maybe Mel was lying, maybe I was just imagining things, but I followed the path I saw it take and ran.

"Cyrus, where are you going?" Atlas called out, as the four of them chased after me. "She isn't here, we have to keep moving."

I turned a blind corner and froze, paralyzed at the sight in front of me.

"Jessie," I hesitated, feeling the others run off behind me. "what the fuck are you doing here?"

"I didn't mean to." She cried, throwing herself to her knees. "Well, I mean, I meant to, but it wasn't my fault. You guys were changing. Forgetting about the promise you made to me. I had to stop her. I had to destroy her before she destroyed everything."

"Where is she?" Atlas hissed, clenching his jaw as rage vibrated beneath his skin

"There." She said, as she pointed to an innocuous door down the hall. "She's probably dead by now. And if she isn't, you'll wish she were."

Atlas bolted, with Ezra and Tristan running a split second behind him.

"Mel," I asked, fighting my instinct to run after them, "can you hold her here while we-"

"Are you kidding?" She said cutting me off, slipping the small gun from the holster on her thigh and leveling on Jessie. "Go! This bitch almost caused a fucking war. I'm not letting her get away."

FORTY-ONE

Stevie

A SINGLE LOUD BANG RANG OUT AND THE GROUP OF MEN surrounding me froze.

"What the fuck was that?" the man holding me asked as a man to his right fell to the floor.

Something was happening in the dark. *Something big.* Shots rang out as body after body crumpled to the floor. I couldn't see anything, but I could feel the man holding me tremble in fear.

"What the fuck," he boomed, yelling at his men, "don't just stand there, do something!"

"I told you they would come." I hissed, not giving a fuck about the blade against my throat or the men dropping around us like flies. "If you'd like to keep your fucking limbs, I suggest you stop touching me."

The man's eyes flashed to mine, and I recognized the fear behind them. In an instant, he dropped the knife and bolted, leaving me alone in the middle of the chaos.

The bloodbath that unfolded around me was unlike anything I'd ever seen before. The smell of blood and violence permeated in the air as my men exacted their revenge with lethal precision. Once the guns stopped firing, the sounds of knuckles against flesh and gut-curdling screams filled the room.

The men Jessie hired didn't stand a chance against The Reapers, even with there being three times as many of them. I watched, entranced, as my four men made their way towards me, slicing and stabbing and brutalizing anyone that stood in their way. Even as blood splattered over their faces and numerous men tried and failed to disarm them, they never took their attention away from me. It was the most beautiful sight I've ever seen.

Atlas was the first one to reach me. And as his blood-soaked fingers reached for my binds and his knife sliced through the rope, the overwhelming need to cry barreled through me. They saved me, they actually fucking saved me.

He held me close as the chaos continued to unfold around us, but in that moment it felt like we were the only ones in the room.

Our eyes locked as Atlas unbuttoned his shirt and threw it over my naked body.

"Did they hurt you?" He asked, tilting my chin up to face him.

"No." I mumbled, shaking my head. "Not yet, anyway."

He released a heavy sigh as he pulled me in for a tight embrace.

"No one will ever try to hurt you again, Stevie. " He breathed, kissing my forehead. "Never fucking again."

I wanted to melt in his embrace, but I was equally as pissed at him. If they had shown up a split second later, it would've been too late.

"Fucking asshole." I growled, punching him in the chest. "What took you so long? I could've died before I had a chance to tell you that I... " I trailed off, too scared to say it out loud.

"That you what?" He asked, pulling away from our embrace to search my eyes.

"That I fucking love you, you dickface. I've loved you from the moment we met and I'm really tired of pretending like I don't."

"I love you too." He grinned, pulling me in for a punishing kiss. "I'm madly and stupidly in love with your infuriating, stubborn, and obviously suicidal ass."

"About fucking time you admitted it." Cyrus called out, as he, Tristan, and Ezra laughed at his expense. Atlas picked me up and threw me over his shoulder, ignoring the heckles and taunts.

As we made our way through the bodies they slaughtered, I couldn't help but smile. This was my family and no matter how fucked up and crazy they were, they were mine.

———————

I WASN'T SURPRISED to find Jessie held up in the corner as soon as we exited the room. I knew there was no way The Reapers would've let her escape. What I did find surprising, was the person holding her there. *What the hell was Melanie doing here?*

Atlas glanced at me as he set me down and I nodded, understanding what he needed to do.

"Mel," Atlas said, running his hands through his hair. "I don't know what to say-"

"I get it." Melanie said, cutting him off as her eyes focused on me, "When you find your person, you know."

"Thank you," I said, stepping closer and offering her a hesitant smile, "for bringing them here and helping them save me. You didn't have to stay and help, but you did."

"Yeah, well," she mumbled, averting her eyes, "maybe you aren't as weak as I thought."

"What do you want to do with her?" She asked, nodding her head towards the girl cowering beneath her.

All five sets of their eyes settled on me and I knew it was my decision to make. We could take her life. She had almost taken mine, and it seemed like the obvious choice. But after everything she lost, ending her life would almost be too kind. I wanted her decision to haunt her for the rest of her life. To know, every single day, that The Reapers were mine and she would never get her hands on them again.

"We won't kill her." I said, looking at Jessie with disdain.

"Are you sure?" Atlas asked, pulling me closer to his side. "The crime she committed is unforgivable. We have our history, but none of us would judge you for wanting her dead."

"I'm sure." I said, giving him a firm nod. "I want her to rot in jail and think about everything she lost for the rest of her life. Death would be too easy."

"I t... texted my connection at the D.A. office." Tristan mumbled, sliding his phone to Atlas.

"What is it?" I asked, seeing the surprised expressions written on their faces as the notification dings kept coming.

"Apparently," Atlas said, narrowing his eyes, "Jessie has a long list of transgressions they've been dying to pin on her. They did nothing about it before because she was under our protection, but now that she's not, she's fair game. They want her at the station as soon as possible."

"So what does that mean?" I asked, looking towards the four of them.

"It means," Ezra murmured, "that she is going away for a long, long time and it's time for us to get the hell out of here."

"But what about Jessie?" I asked. "And all the bodies?"

"Shit, she's right." Atlas cursed. "One of us needs to stay to clean up."

"Not fucking it." The twins said in unison, making the rest of us laugh.

"You guys get her out of here." Mel offered. "I'll bring Jessie down to the station as soon as my clean-up crew shows up. I texted them earlier. I figured it was going to get *messy*."

"Hey Stevie," Mel hesitated, "when you're feeling up to

it, would you maybe want to grab brunch or something?" She asked with a wince. "You know, let bygones be bygones or whatever."

"I'd like that, Mel," I said, softly nudging her shoulder, "or whatever."

FORTY-TWO

Stevie

As WE DROVE BACK TO OUR HOME IN COMFORTABLE SILENCE
and trekked up the familiar winding road, I couldn't help but
think about the first time I ever made the journey.

I couldn't believe that our paths had crossed only a month
ago, when it felt like so many things had changed. I experienced more sadness, lust, fear, hope, and anger in my time
with them, than I ever had in my entire life. The emotions
were always there, hiding in the depths of my mind. But I had

been an expert at concealing them, at building these intricate walls to stop them from revealing themselves.

Somehow, in the short time I'd been with The Reapers, those walls had come crashing down, leaving me open and exposed like never before. I expected the process to be painful, to feel rushed or overwhelming, but that wasn't the case in the slightest. It felt as if I'd always been theirs. As if my life had always been on this trajectory to find them, and even though it wasn't what I expected, what we had somehow made sense.

The Reapers were the knights in shining armor I never saw coming. The cold, vicious, and dangerous men who I thought would end me, but ended up being the ones to save me. It was clear to me now that they belonged to me, just as much as I belonged to them.

As I looked at the five of us, with our blood-soaked bodies and the buzz of adrenaline coursing through our veins, I knew I could no longer deny the truth. I was a fucking Reaper, through and through. I was terrified of bringing Alex into our world, but I knew with The Reapers by our side, it was the safest place she could be.

Being a Reaper wasn't about the blood on our hands or the ruthless reputation. It was about family and protecting what was ours. Alex, Atlas, Ezra, Tristan, and Cyrus were my family, and my family was perfect just the way it was. If anyone ever tried to fuck with any of them again, I would end them.

We would end them...

QUEEN OF THE REAPERS
EXCERPT

Stevie

THE TIRES SCREECH IN PROTEST AS EZRA SLAMS HIS FOOT ON the brake and pulls us to the side of the road. A brown cloud of dirt and debris settles around us as we come to a stop next to a long line of giant redwoods. I look at Atlas, Tristan, and Cyrus, but they don't seem phased by the unplanned pit-stop. Then again, they too probably need a moment to digest my request.

"No." Tristan says with a dismissive shake of his head. "It's a s... stupid idea."

Instead of letting myself react to his harsh refusal, I focus on the hem of the onyx suit jacket, barely grazing my thighs. The luxurious wool fabric is soft to the touch and as the other voices in the car chime in to the debate, I mindlessly run my thumbs along its pristine seams. It's a pointless distraction, but I'm desperate to focus on anything other than the chaos erupting around me, even if I am the catalyst.

It's been over an hour since we left Maria's Cantina, but there's still a hint of violence in the air. Almost as if it's haunting us. Refusing to let us forget the massacre we left behind.

"In all fairness," Cyrus drawls, casting a pointed look at his twin, "when have *you* ever thought any risk was worth taking?"

The icy glare Tristan shoots at Cyrus is enough to knock the wind out of me, but Cyrus just cocks a brow and chuckles. "What's the matter?" He asks. "Hit a little too close to home?"

The tension crackling between the two of them is thick enough to cut with a knife, and of course, I'm the one seated in the middle of their battlefield.

Aesthetically, the twins are nearly identical. The same piercing emerald eyes, the same dark disheveled hair you can't help but want to run your fingers through, and the same disarming good looks that should be illegal in such dangerous men. The similarities between the two stop there.

Cyrus is like fire. Explosive. Dynamic. And consuming. He could easily light you up and make you come alive, but on that same note, if you do him dirty, he'll engulf you in his inferno and burn your ass beyond recognition.

Tristan is like ice. Cold. Impenetrable. And unpredictable.

Getting through to him is like trying to chisel your way through thick walls of ice. Once you get there, the payoff will be worth it. But that's if and only if you can survive his frigid bite.

"Tris has a point." Atlas says, raking his fingers through his hair as he leans back into the passenger seat. "We have enough on our plate."

It doesn't take a genius to figure out I'm the 'enough' he's referring to. And as they each subconsciously glance my way, my suspicions are all but confirmed.

The weight of their stares burn into my skin, and the icy blast from the air conditioner does nothing to soothe the heat. Sweat coats the small of my back as little beads of moisture trickle down my spine. I'm in over my head, but letting them see my discomfort isn't an option. This conversation is too damn important.

Gnawing on my nails, I glance at the clock on the dashboard and grimace. It's only been a few minutes since Ezra pulled over, but the ensuing argument feels like it's been going on for hours. I know they care about me. Probably now, more than ever. But the problem is, this isn't about me, it's about her. And she isn't something they ever planned on.

"She's a liability." Ezra says, cutting into the conversation. He flicks the ash of his cigarette out the window and pulls another long drag before continuing. "Jessie used her as bait. It's only a matter of time before someone else does the same."

She's not a liability, she's family.

I feel my composure slipping and I know it's only a matter of time before my anger finds its way out. They're treating my sister like she's an inconvenience. Like she's some fucking business decision they need to weigh out. Like she isn't even a fucking person at all.

"We could s… send her away." Tristan says, looking down at me. "Keep her safe from this s… shit."

I almost scoff at his offer, but I stop myself short and maintain my cool composure. If the roles were reversed, I doubt he'd be so eager to send any of his brothers away. I'm sure they'd all fight with everything they had to stay together. I'm doing exactly what any of them would.

Tristan hooks his finger under my chin and tilts my head up. "S… Stevie, look at me." He says, locking his dark emerald eyes with mine. "We can keep her s… safe. Don't you want that?"

Goddamnit. He's putting me in an impossible situation. Deep down, I know he's right. My priority has always been to keep her safe. The only way to guarantee her safety is to keep her as far away from The Reapers as possible. They would never hurt her, but their enemies might. Sending her away *is* the smart choice, but he of all people should know, the smartest choice isn't always the right one.

"No." I sigh, avoiding his eyes as I jerk my chin out of his grip. "I know my sister. If I try to push her away, she'll just fight her way back to me. It won't work."

I don't need to look into his eyes to feel his disappointment.

"Fine." He spits, looking out into the dense forest surrounding the G-Wagon. "Don't come crying to us when she ends up f… fucking dead." He says the last sentence under his breath, but with the deafening silence filling the SUV, he may as well have screamed it.

"Look." Atlas says, pulling everyone's attention on him.

"It's been a long day and emotions are high. Priority right now is going home and getting cleaned up. We can discuss all of this shit later. "

Fuck. Fuck. Fuck.

When Atlas gives an order, they all follow his command like gospel. We're going home and no amount of pleading will get them to change their minds.

I want to trust that we'll continue this conversation when we get home, but after watching this discussion go up in flames, it's clear none of them want to bring Alex in. To them, she's a risk not worth taking.

"I'm not going home." I say, doing my best to keep my voice from wavering. "I'll walk if I have to, but I'm going back for her."

This could be my last shot at retrieving Alex. I have to fight them on this, even if they end up hating me for it.

I shift my gaze to the left and look at Tristan expectantly. The icy glare he shoots back at me stings, but I keep my face even.. There's a challenge in his emerald eyes, and I know there's no way I'm getting past him without a fight, so I shift my focus to the lesser of the two evils, his twin, Cyrus.

"Cy, can you let me out?" I ask, keeping my voice soft to disguise the frustration brewing within me.

Cyrus doesn't bother to look at me as he shoots out his clipped response. "Not happening, Princess."

What the hell.

"Cyrus." I say, gritting my teeth to keep my anger under control. "I don't have time for your little mind games. I need you to let me out. Now."

"No." His response is short, but the venom behind the word stings.

"Cyrus." I whisper, moistening my lips. "You can't be serious right now."

He clenches his jaw and lets out an exaggerated sigh.

"What makes you think I'm joking?" He snaps, narrowing his eyes at me. "What? Are we supposed to be your little fucking lapdogs now because we saved you?"

"That's not—"

"No, it is." He says, cutting me off as he inches towards my face. "We aren't those men, Princess."

"I just thought—"

"You thought what? That things changed? That the men who own you suddenly transformed from monsters into princes? I hate to be the bearer of bad news, P, but we're still The Reapers. The dangerous men you offered yourself up to on a silver fucking platter. You are ours. To own. To fuck. And to do whatever the hell else we want with. That hasn't changed, P, and it never will."

The cool veneer I was trying to cling on to immediately shatters. Fuck this and fuck all of them. If that's how they see me, then why am I even trying to get them to understand? If all I am to them is a piece of property, they'll never care about how I feel. Why would they? They have the power to do as they please and use my body any way they see fit.

No. The only way I'm getting back to my sister is if I fight for her. And if it's a fight they want, it's a fight they'll fucking get.

Like a flash of lightning, I lunge out of my seat and shove my way towards the door. In the back of my mind, I know it's pointless. Cyrus and Tristan can easily overpower me, but I refuse to back down. I have to fight for Alex, even if it is futile.

Constricting arms tangle around my body, but I don't stop fighting. For their parts, Cyrus and Tristan try to stop me without injuring me, but my kicks and shoves are getting more violent by the second. I hate them for what they're doing to me, and I hate myself for how far this is going.

"Stop!" The twins bark in unison, but I'm too far gone to listen to their orders. I've been constrained and restricted my entire fucking life and their blatant disregard for my needs just a lit a twenty-year-old fuse.

I scratch and I claw and I push and I shove until I can barely tell where my feet and hands are landing. Other voices start mixing with their protests and more hands are on me, but I block them out. I'm getting out of this fucking car now.

"GODDAMNIT STEVIE, THAT'S ENOUGH!" Atlas booms, pounding his heavy hand against the dash.

The anger and violence in his voice snaps me back to reality. I jerk my head in his direction and freeze. Fiery rage fills his eyes, and I can't help but cower under his narrowed gaze.

"Stop acting like a petulant fucking child." He spits, his breathing labored from trying to pry me off of his brothers. "We're going home. Now. End of discussion."

My bottom lip quivers and before I can block it out, an all too familiar emotion grabs a hold of me and pulls me under. Fear. Only this time the person terrifying me isn't my mother, it's Atlas.

I feel his anger and disappointment all around me, coating my skin and engulfing me. I'm drowning in it. I'm ashamed and, as much as I hate looking weak, I can't stop the tears from welling in my eyes.

"That's not my fucking home." I sputter, choking on my

words as my vision blurs with unshed tears. "That mansion is just a gilded fucking cage and you know it."

I'm screaming now and my emotions are swirling through me like a tornado of rage, shame, guilt, and sorrow. I can't hold it in any longer and the words are spewing out of me uncontrollably.

"You guys think you're so strong. The fucking Reapers. The men who elicit fear in everyone they meet. But you know what I think? I think you're four scared little boys trapped in the bodies of full-grown men. You control and manipulate and torture and trick your way into power because that's the closest thing to love and acceptance you'll ever feel. You think I'm some weak little girl that needs a prince to save her, but newsflash, I don't need your kindness, I don't need your love, and I especially don't need you. The only fucking thing I need right now is—"

My words die off the second I take in each of their pained expressions. Regret sinks into my stomach and festers, making me relive all the bitter words I threw at them. I want to apologize. To tell them I didn't mean any of it, but I can't even stomach the idea of facing them. I can barely breathe, let alone speak.

My eyes flicker to each of them and I study their hard features. Cyrus' brows are pulled together in a scowl and his fists are tightly clenched as he stares daggers at me. Tristan's eyes are low and he presses his lips in a hard line as he avoids looking at me altogether. Atlas' head is cocked and his mouth is slightly ajar, almost as if he can't believe I'm the one who spewed such venomous words. And Ezra is looking at me with a question in his eyes. Like he no longer knows what to think about me.

Hurting them feels like I'm ripping a piece of my own heart out, but my concern for my sister outweighs any feelings I have for them. It has to. I'm all she has left.

I glance at Ezra and catch his reflection in the mirror. He's looking out his window now, but as he pulls his cigarette up to his lips and takes a slow drag, his stormy grey eyes land on mine. *God, he is going to kill me. What the hell was I thinking?*

"Finish." Ezra orders, studying my expression from his rear-view mirror. "Might as well get it all out now."

He's right. My feeble attempt to put out the fire my words ignited was pointless. I've already said the worst of it and it's only fair that they hear my full thoughts before they decide what happens next. "The only thing I need right now is my sister." I breathe, pulling in a shaky breath. "She's the only family I have left. I'm ready to move forward, but she's the one part of my past I can't leave behind."

The second I release the words, it feels like a heavy weight has been lifted from my chest. Atlas, Ezra, Cyrus, & Tristan sit silent for a moment and stare off into the forest, taking a few minutes to mull over everything I said. I keep my eyes low and wait for a response. I think about elaborating further, but I already said more than enough as it is.

After several minutes of uncomfortable silence, Atlas is the first to speak up.

"Call her." He says, spitting the words out as if they taste rancid in his mouth. "Have her head to Alessandro's. Our men will take it from there."

"I can't." I say, my voice sounding smaller than it ever has. "I have no way of reaching her."

"Here." Tristan barks, carelessly tossing the familiar rose gold iPhone on my thigh. "Have at it."

Seeing my confiscated phone only fortifies the wall my outburst built between us. I avoid thinking about our past, but seeing my cell phone serves as a healthy reminder of how this started. Of how we started.

A few weeks ago, I was just their stubborn toy, and they were the men determined to put me in my place. Feelings have changed between us, sure, but the power balance needs to change if this is ever going to work. I'm not their toy anymore and it's about damn time they started treating me like it.

"You've had this on you this whole time..."

It's more of a statement than a question, but Tristan's casual shrug gives me all the answers I need. I'm not sure why it bothers me. It's typical controlling Reaper behavior. They want to keep me alive. That much is obvious. But The Reapers won't suddenly change who they are just because they want me around. Sadistic tigers don't change their stripes.

"Thanks, but I meant what I said." I say, slipping my phone into the jacket's pocket. "I can't call her. Jessie destroyed her phone. The only way I can reach her is if I go to her."

"Let me guess." Ezra scoffs, flashing me a deadly smile as he crushes his cigarette against the side mirror and flicks the butt to the ground. "You want this little reunion of yours to happen now."

Every fiber of my being is on edge as I try to predict what he'll do next. I know Ez, in a lot of ways, better than his brothers do, but that doesn't mean he's predictable. Ezra may care about me in his own twisted way, but the monster within him will always dictate what he does. It's as much a part of him as the tattoos coating his body.

Before Ezra can speak again, Atlas cuts in. "Okay." He says, rubbing his temple as he pulls a cigar from the glove box. "We'll bring Alex in." He offers, lighting it up and puffing out a thick cloud of smoke. "But if something happens to her from here on out, it's on you. Not us."

"That's fair." I reply, looking into each of their hard faces. "I'm the one that's bringing her in. So whatever happens to Al is on me."

Before I can even finish my thoughts, Ezra whips the G-Wagon around in a sharp u-turn and smashes his foot against the accelerator. The tires screech in response, kicking up a storm of dust as he jerks the car back onto the narrow road. His white knuckles angrily grip the steering wheel and it takes everything in me not to panic as he guns it down the hill.

We're going too fast and his brothers aren't even reacting to his antics, seemingly in their own worlds. I latch onto my seatbelt for dear life as he swerves dangerously down the winding cliff-side road. He's always threatened to hurt me, but I never imagined he'd try to kill us all like this.

I catch Ezra's stormy eyes in the rear-view mirror and hold his gaze, silently willing him to slow the hell down. I search for the Ezra I know, the one I sacrificed my mind, body, and soul to over the last few weeks, but I don't find him. The monster is the only one staring back and, as luck would have it, the fucker is pissed.

"Something wrong, Angel?" Ezra asks, his silky voice like a siren song for my stupid heart. The voice that chases my demons away and has the innate ability to soothe my nerves.

It's hard to believe it belongs to the same monster sitting behind the wheel.

Ezra thrives on the fear of others and no matter how much he scares me, fear is the one thing I can never afford to show him. Not if I want him to treat me as his equal and not if I want to be his.

Bringing my eyes back to his nearly black ones, I face him with my head held high and give him my full attention. He stares back at me unflinchingly as the car continues to swerve in and out of the opposing lane. Oncoming cars swerve around us with their horns blaring, but I don't even flinch. It's reckless, but I refuse to break his gaze, even at the expense of our safety. We're in a war of wills and I need to show him that not only am I unafraid of the beast, but that I fully embrace its chaos.

Bring it on, monster.

After a few minutes of heart-stopping close calls, Ezra is the first to break our stare-off, and as he does, a slow smirk spreads across his face.

"Clever girl." He remarks, locking his eyes back on the road. "Angel, don't mistake this kindness as a sign of weakness. Leaving us was never one of your options."

He doesn't need to elaborate any further for me to understand the threat behind his words. There will be no leaving The Reapers. Not now and not ever.

STAY IN TOUCH

To stay to up to date with my latest releases, announcements, and book recommendations, don't forget to subscribe to my newsletter at www.jessahalliwell.com

BOOKS BY JESSA

Fear The Reapers
Book One of The Reapers of Caspian Hills

Queen of The Reapers
Book Two of The Reapers of Caspian Hills

Wrath of The Reapers
Book Three of The Reapers of Caspian Hills

Brutal Enemies
A Dark Mafia Reverse Harem Romance
Release Date: TBD

Chronicles of The Damned
A Vampire Romance Charity Anthology
Releasing October 1, 2022

A NOTE FROM JESSA

Yesss! You did it! How are you holding up?

I know there's probably still a ton of questions running through your mind and you may despise me a little for holding out. But trust me, you'll get your answers soon and you'll see why it made sense to put them in Queen of The Reapers.

When I started writing Fear The Reapers, I initially set out to write a love story that I would want to read. One that explored the complexities of falling for the bad boys and what the fallout of that love could look like in the real world.

My characters are imperfect. Stevie makes impulsive mistakes. She lies and fucks up more times than anyone should. Atlas wants to control everything and has a hard time just letting himself be. Tristan is closed off and refuses to trust in others after being let down so many times. Cyrus is never taken seriously so he doesn't know how to express himself in a healthy way. Ezra craves violence and is terrified he'll hurt the people he cares about.

Their relationship evolves naturally. They come together

chaotically and they pull apart as intensely, just like in the real world.

I'm excited for you to see the next phase in their lives and I hope you've fallen in love with Stevie and The Reapers as much as I have.

Jessa

ABOUT JESSA

Jessa Halliwell is a Reverse Harem Romance Author who writes about angsty, torturous love mixed with a dash of danger. She loves writing romance only slightly more than she loves reading it. She's been known to binge read novels then spend the rest of the day sulking over the massive book hangover.

Jessa resides in Northern California with her boyfriend and her feisty Chihuahua named Juice. When she isn't writing, you can find her obsessing over her skincare routine, drinking an unhealthy amount of hibiscus tea, or probably crying over a really good book.

Follow me on tiktok: @jessahalliwellauthor

Join my Facebook Readers Groups: **Halliwell's Harem** *and* **Dark & Dangerous Reverse Harem Readers**

Made in the USA
Columbia, SC
10 July 2022

63125575R00209